The Black Sun Codex
Michael Maximillian

Dedication

To my father, whose love of history and storytelling sparked my own, and to all those who dare to chase shadows and unravel the secrets of the past. This book is a testament to the enduring power of human curiosity and the courage it takes to confront the unknown, even in the face of unimaginable peril. It is also dedicated to the intrepid spirit of researchers and scholars who dedicate their lives to illuminating the darkest corners of our history, often at great personal risk. Their relentless pursuit of knowledge, mirroring the dedication of Ana and Gábor, serves as a constant inspiration to us all. Their meticulous work provides the foundation upon which our understanding of the past is built, allowing us to confront the mistakes of yesterday and strive for a better future. This dedication is an acknowledgement of their silent heroism and a promise to continue the quest for understanding, even when the path is treacherous and fraught with danger, much like the journey undertaken by the characters within these pages. The sacrifices made in the name of knowledge, both fictional and real, must never be forgotten, and the pursuit of truth must always remain a beacon of hope in a world often shrouded in mystery.

Preface

The genesis of this novel lies not only in a fascination with historical mysteries and ancient conspiracies, but also in a deep-seated belief in the power of storytelling to illuminate the human condition. The fictional world of "The Black Sun Codex" is populated by characters grappling with themes of loss, betrayal, sacrifice, and the enduring strength of the human spirit. Yet, woven intricately into the thrilling narrative is a tapestry of meticulously researched historical facts and cultural details. From the imposing architecture of Transylvanian monasteries to the labyrinthine corridors of the Vatican archives, each location serves not just as a setting but as a crucial component in the unfolding mystery. The ancient languages, cryptic symbols, and the very act of deciphering the Black Sun Codex itself are intended to be as intellectually engaging as the plot itself. The research undertaken for this book encompassed linguistics, archaeology, and the rich history of Romania and surrounding regions. It's my hope that this immersion in historical detail will not only enhance the reading experience but also inspire readers to delve deeper into the fascinating past that continues to shape our present. The story of Ana and Gábor is more than just a thrilling adventure; it's a journey of discovery, self-discovery, and a testament to the resilience of the human spirit in the face of extraordinary challenges. I trust that the reader will be captivated not only by the unfolding mystery but also by the exploration of the human condition that lies at the heart of this narrative. The journey has been as enriching for the writer as I hope it will be for the reader.

Introduction

The whispers of ancient prophecies, the cryptic etchings on a dead scholar's body, and the relentless pursuit of a shadowy organization known as The Sentinel – these are the threads that weave together the complex tapestry of "The Black Sun Codex." This novel plunges the reader into a world where history and myth collide, where the seemingly disparate fields of linguistics and archaeology converge in a desperate race against time. The story unfolds against the dramatic backdrop of Transylvania, with its haunting landscapes and lingering echoes of ancient beliefs. Dr. Petru Lupu's death is not merely a murder; it is a catalyst, setting in motion a chain of events that will lead our protagonists, the resourceful linguist Ana Dragan and the disgraced archaeologist Gábor Varga, on a perilous journey across Europe. The Black Sun Codex, the ancient manuscript at the heart of the mystery, is not just a collection of enigmatic symbols but a key to understanding a catastrophic event predicted in a forgotten prophecy. As Ana and Gábor decipher the Codex, they unravel a conspiracy that stretches back centuries, revealing a hidden network of seismic triggers capable of unleashing global devastation. Their investigation takes them from the bustling streets of Bucharest to the remote peaks of the Carpathian Mountains, and finally to the hallowed halls of the Vatican archives. Along the way, they will face betrayal, capture, and the ultimate sacrifice, testing the limits of their courage, intellect, and loyalty. But within the danger, amidst the shadowy figures and perilous pursuits, lies a deeper exploration of the human spirit. It's a story of resilience, determination, and the unwavering pursuit of truth, even when the cost is high. Prepare to be captivated by the intricate plot, the richly detailed historical settings, and the compelling characters who will guide you through a thrilling exploration of ancient mysteries and modern conspiracies. The journey begins now.

Table of Contents

Chapter 1

The Scholar's Death

Discovery of the Body

The chill of the Transylvanian night clung to the ancient stone walls of the Viscri Monastery, seeping into Brother Thomas's bones as he knelt beside the lifeless form. The flickering candlelight cast long, dancing shadows, accentuating the stark horror of the scene. Dr. Petru Lupu, renowned historian and scholar, lay sprawled on the cold flagstones of the dimly lit crypt, his eyes wide, fixed in a silent scream. His normally meticulously groomed beard was dishevelled, a stark contrast to the precise, almost mathematical, arrangement of the symbols etched onto his chest and arms.

Brother Thomas, his breath misting in the frigid air, had discovered the body during his nightly rounds. The symbols, etched with a precision that defied the frantic circumstances of a murder, immediately struck him as something far beyond the usual vandalism the monastery occasionally suffered. They were intricate, angular, a language he'd never encountered, yet they pulsed with a chilling, unsettling power. He'd hastily summoned the local police, a small, overwhelmed force accustomed to petty thefts, not ritualistic murders of internationally renowned scholars.

The arrival of Inspector Ionescu and his two constables was a jarring intrusion into the monastery's tranquil solitude. Ionescu, a portly man whose face bore the weary lines of a life spent dealing with the grim realities of rural crime, examined the body with a detached professionalism that belied the unease in his eyes. The symbols, he acknowledged with a grim nod, were unlike anything he'd ever seen. His initial assessment, however, suggested the cause of death – a swift, brutal blow to the head – was consistent with a murder, not a ritual sacrifice.

The scene, however, screamed otherwise. The precise, almost reverent placement of the body, the meticulous nature of the carvings, the unnatural stillness of the surroundings – it all pointed to something far beyond a simple mugging gone wrong. The symbols themselves were a key element; they seemed to hold a significance far greater than any mere decorative flourish.

Their intricate detail suggested a deep understanding of a lost language, a forgotten cosmology, something far removed from the everyday world Ionescu was accustomed to patrolling.

News of Dr. Lupu's death quickly reached Bucharest. Ana Dragan, a brilliant young linguist, known more for her fiercely independent nature than her social graces, received the news with a knot of dread in her stomach. Dr. Lupu had been a mentor, a friend, and his death felt like a personal betrayal. Furthermore, Ana knew that the cryptic symbols wouldn't be mere decorations; her father, a respected but tragically unconventional scholar himself, had spent his life researching obscure languages and ancient prophecies, many of which mirrored the unsettling aesthetic of the symbols described in the initial police report.

She felt a chilling recognition of a similar aesthetic in the description of the symbols. The initial police photos, hastily transmitted by a frantic Ionescu, confirmed her worst fears – these were not the crude markings of a common criminal; these were deliberate, precise, and held a sinister, ancient energy that echoed in her very bones. The symbols spoke of a hidden history, a forgotten past that could prove devastatingly dangerous if it fell into the wrong hands.

Ana knew that this was more than just a murder; this was an act designed to send a message. A message she was uniquely positioned to decipher. Her knowledge of her father's research, coupled with her exceptional linguistic skills, made her the ideal person to solve this terrifying puzzle. But she knew she couldn't do it alone. The case was far beyond her area of expertise and the scope of local Romanian police capabilities.

The name Gábor Varga sprang to mind. A disgraced archaeologist, brilliant but reckless, Gábor was notorious for his unorthodox methods and even more unorthodox theories. He had once been her father's colleague and friend, a man whose knowledge of ancient Transylvanian history and architecture was unmatched. Although their professional paths had diverged drastically, the shared connection to her father was a powerful link between them. Gábor was, at best, a difficult and abrasive personality but Ana knew that he was her only hope.

Finding Gábor proved more difficult than anticipated. Rumours of his whereabouts circulated among the academic community, but pinpointing his current location felt like searching for a ghost in a crowded city. His reputation for defying authority, pushing the boundaries of acceptable academic conduct, and a general disregard for bureaucratic processes made it impossible to trace him through official channels. Eventually, through a network of shady contacts and back channels within the world of obscure scholarship and marginalized historical studies, Ana managed to locate him. He was holed up in a dusty, cramped apartment on the outskirts of Bucharest, surrounded by a chaotic jumble of half-assembled artifacts, scattered manuscripts, and the distinct aroma of stale coffee and desperation.

Gábor, a tall, gaunt man with eyes that held the weary wisdom of someone who'd seen too much, initially showed little enthusiasm to become involved. His fall from grace within the academic establishment had left him disillusioned, bitter, and deeply cynical. He'd largely retreated from public life, preferring the company of ancient artifacts and long-forgotten legends to the cutthroat world of modern academia. However, mention of Dr. Lupu, the cryptic symbols, and the subtle yet insistent hint of a connection to Ana's father's lost research, piqued his interest.

He agreed to help, though his skepticism was palpable. He examined the photographs of the symbols, his brow furrowed in concentration. His initial analysis confirmed Ana's suspicions. The symbols weren't mere decoration; they were a coded message, a key to something far more significant. The style, he commented, was reminiscent of ancient Dacian script, a language largely lost to time, its meanings mostly gleaned from fragmented inscriptions and interpretations of surviving artistic artifacts and relics. However, there was something distinctly...unnatural about them, a deviation from the known styles, a hint of something darker, more sinister. This was not merely a historical artifact; it was a warning.

Their investigation began in Bucharest, amidst the bustling

streets and hidden corners of the Romanian capital. They meticulously pieced together Dr. Lupu's life, his research, his contacts, looking for any clues that could shed light on the meaning of the symbols and the identity of his killer. They sifted through Dr. Lupu's personal effects – stacks of papers, ancient maps, meticulously organized notes, and a worn leather-bound diary. They found a hidden compartment within Dr. Lupu's desk, containing a small, intricately carved wooden box. Inside, nestled among faded velvet, lay a single, tarnished silver amulet, bearing the same cryptic symbols that adorned Dr. Lupu's lifeless body. This was no random act of violence; it was a precise, targeted assassination, carefully orchestrated by someone who understood the significance of Dr. Lupu's work, and the power of these ancient symbols. The amulet, it appeared, held the key.

The Black Sun Codex

The silver amulet, cool and heavy in Ana's hand, pulsed with a strange energy, a faint tremor vibrating through her fingertips. The symbols etched into its surface, identical to those branded onto Dr. Lupu's body, seemed to writhe slightly in the dim light of Gábor's study. Gábor, a disgraced archaeologist whose past mistakes had cost him his reputation but not his keen intellect, leaned closer, his gaze intense. He was a man of few words, his weathered face a roadmap of past hardships, but his eyes, sharp and observant, missed nothing.

"These are not just decorations, Ana," Gábor murmured, his voice a low rumble. "These are… instructions. A language older than any we know."

Ana traced the intricate lines with a fingertip, feeling a prickling sensation along her skin. The symbols were unlike anything she'd ever encountered – a blend of geometric patterns, stylized celestial bodies, and glyphs that resembled no known alphabet. Days of research in the Bucharest National Archives had yielded nothing. The libraries, with their dusty shelves overflowing with forgotten manuscripts, had offered no answers.

The symbols remained stubbornly enigmatic.

It was then that they discovered it, hidden within a seemingly innocuous section of Dr. Lupu's notes—a cryptic reference to "The Codex of the Black Sun." The mention was buried deep within a scholarly article on Dacian mythology, a seemingly random footnote that had initially gone unnoticed. But the more they looked, the more they realized how much Lupu had hidden beneath the guise of historical research.

The search for the Codex became their singular obsession. Their investigation led them to the dusty shelves of the Vatican Secret Archives, where Gábor's expertise in uncovering forgotten history proved invaluable. The Vatican's hallowed halls, steeped in the weight of centuries, felt oppressive, a claustrophobic labyrinth of secrets. Months bled into years within those archives, as they navigated intricate corridors and deciphered ancient languages, their search guided by the fragmented clues left behind by Dr. Lupu. They unearthed forgotten chronicles, obscure religious texts, and astronomical charts that hinted at a hidden cosmology, a system of knowledge that was both terrifying and exhilarating in its complexity.

The Codex, they finally discovered, was not a single book, but a collection of fragmented manuscripts, scattered across various libraries and private collections across Europe. Each fragment contained a piece of the larger puzzle, a piece of an ancient prophecy foretelling a cataclysmic event. The "Black Sun," they learned, was not a celestial body, but a metaphor – a representation of a hidden power, a force that resided not in the heavens, but within the Earth itself.

Dr. Lupu's research, it appeared, had gone far beyond mere historical inquiry. He had stumbled upon a network of ancient sites, a global network of precisely positioned underground chambers that, according to the Codex, held the key to unlocking this terrifying power. He had uncovered a mechanism, a system of seismic triggers, capable of unleashing a chain reaction of earthquakes of unprecedented magnitude, capable of reshaping the world as they knew it.

The Sentinel, the shadowy organization that had pursued them from the beginning, was revealed to be not simply an assassin guild but a centuries-old society dedicated to protecting – or perhaps controlling – this dormant power. They were a group of individuals who believed that humanity was not ready for the knowledge hidden within the Codex. They saw the "awakening" of the Black Sun not as an apocalyptic event, but as a necessary purging, a cleansing fire that would reshape the world, leaving behind a society forged in the crucible of destruction.

The pieces of the puzzle began to fall into place. The symbols on Dr. Lupu's body were not mere markings; they were activation sequences, precise instructions for initiating the catastrophic chain reaction described in the Codex. His murder was a carefully planned act to prevent him from activating the mechanisms he had discovered.

The chase led Ana and Gábor to the Carpathian Mountains, a labyrinthine landscape of dense forests, rugged peaks, and hidden valleys. They followed a trail of cryptic clues left by Dr. Lupu, his notes leading them deeper into the wilderness, to a location he had only hinted at in his fragmented research. This is where they discovered it – a hidden solar temple, an ancient structure buried deep within a mountain, a place where the sun's rays, at a precise moment during the solstice, illuminated a hidden chamber. This chamber, concealed behind a wall of intricately carved stone, contained the central mechanism, the final piece of the puzzle.

Within this chamber, they found a complex network of gears, levers, and intricate astronomical instruments. It was a marvel of ancient engineering, a testament to a level of scientific knowledge lost to time. This was where the seismic triggers were located, the points of convergence that could unleash the cataclysmic event foretold in the Codex. They realized that the symbols on Dr Lupu's body were not only activation sequences, but also a decryption key, a method of disabling the mechanisms.

The Sentinel, however, was close behind. They confronted Ana and Gábor in the temple's darkened corridors. A fierce struggle ensued, a desperate battle against a force that seemed to draw strength from the very earth beneath their feet. Gábor, true to his nature, acted as a shield for Ana. His dedication to protecting the truth was unwavering, even in the face of mortal danger.

The final confrontation was a blur of shadows and desperate struggles. Gábor, mortally wounded, used his last breath to disable the central mechanism, sacrificing himself to save Ana and the world from the catastrophic events that would have followed the activation of the Black Sun. Ana escaped the temple, carrying the Codex and the crushing weight of Gábor's sacrifice, a profound loss that would forever mark her life.

But even in defeat, the Sentinel remained a chilling presence. Ana knew the fight was far from over. The Codex revealed a network of hidden chambers across the globe, awaiting discovery. The awakening had been averted, but the threat remained. Ana understood the magnitude of what she had been protecting, what Gábor had sacrificed his life for. The Black Sun Codex was not just a collection of ancient texts; it was a warning, a chronicle of a power that humanity could never truly control.

Back in Bucharest, amidst the comforting familiarity of her father's study, amongst the books he cherished, Ana began to decipher the hidden messages within the Codex, messages only Gábor had understood. The weight of the truth rested heavy upon her shoulders. She discovered a hidden message, a note tucked inside the leather-bound Codex. It was Gábor's handwriting, filled with cryptic notes and references to another site, another secret waiting to be uncovered. A new chapter had begun, and Ana Dragan, armed with the knowledge of the Black Sun Codex, knew that she was not finished with her quest. The mysteries that lay before her were far greater than she could have ever imagined. Gábor's sacrifice was not in vain; it had set her on a path, one she would continue to tread, uncovering the secrets that humanity needed to understand before the awakening came again. And she knew, with chilling certainty, that it would.

Anas First Clues

The scent of old paper and leather, a familiar comfort, enveloped Ana as she settled into her father's study. Sunlight, filtering through the dusty windowpanes, illuminated motes of dust dancing in the air, a silent ballet mirroring the turmoil within her. The Black Sun Codex lay open on the massive oak desk, its aged pages whispering secrets only she could now decipher. Gábor's last message, a frantic scrawl tucked within its protective leather casing, served as her compass, a cryptic roadmap to a mystery far larger than she could have ever anticipated.

She traced the intricate symbols etched into the amulet, their shapes echoing those branded onto Dr. Lupu's lifeless body. The symbols were not merely decorative; they were a language, an ancient tongue that whispered of forgotten gods and cataclysmic events. Gábor had spoken of a connection to her father's work, a link she had dismissed as mere coincidence until now. Her father, a renowned linguist himself, had dedicated his life to deciphering forgotten languages, his research spanning centuries and continents. Could there be a hidden connection between his lifelong work and the ominous symbols of the Codex?

Ana meticulously compared the symbols on the amulet to the intricate illustrations scattered throughout the Codex. Hours melted into a blur of focused concentration, her mind a whirlwind of linguistic patterns and historical context. Each symbol revealed a piece of the puzzle, a fragment of a larger picture slowly emerging from the shadows. She began to recognize recurring motifs – celestial bodies, geometric shapes, and stylized representations of human figures engaged in seemingly ritualistic acts. Some symbols, however, remained stubbornly enigmatic, their meaning lost to the passage of time.

She unearthed her father's notes, a collection of meticulously organized files, their contents ranging from ancient Sumerian tablets to obscure medieval manuscripts. His handwriting, familiar and comforting, now held a chilling significance. She searched for any mention of the symbols, for any reference to the Black Sun or the Codex. Days turned into weeks, her apartment transforming into a chaotic blend of scholarly research and the urgent demands of her investigation. Sleep became a luxury she could scarcely afford, driven by a relentless pursuit of the truth, fueled by the weight of Gábor's sacrifice.

Among her father's papers, she discovered a hidden compartment within a seemingly ordinary volume on Romanian folklore. Inside, nestled amongst yellowed pages and dried flowers, lay a small leather-bound journal. Its pages were filled with her father's elegant script, documenting his research on the Black Sun, a term he had previously dismissed as purely mythological. The journal described the symbols she had been studying, associating them with a long-lost civilization predating even the Romans, a culture that had somehow possessed a profound understanding of seismic activity and the Earth's tectonic plates.

The more Ana delved into her father's research, the more certain she became that the Black Sun wasn't merely a metaphor for humanity's darker impulses, as Gábor had initially surmised. Instead, it was a literal representation of a hidden network of seismic triggers scattered across the globe. The journal detailed his chilling theory: that these triggers were not merely geological phenomena but ancient, man-made mechanisms, capable of inducing catastrophic earthquakes and tsunamis on a global scale. The journal hinted at their activation mechanism: the precise arrangement of the symbols, as depicted in the Codex.

A shiver ran down Ana's spine as the pieces of the puzzle began to fall into place. The Sentinel, the shadowy organization that had pursued Gábor and Dr. Lupu, wasn't merely interested in the Codex; they sought to harness its power, to activate the ancient mechanisms and plunge the world into chaos. Ana's father had apparently been close to uncovering this terrible truth. His untimely death was no coincidence; he had been silenced, his knowledge deemed too dangerous to remain in the hands of a single scholar.

The journal contained numerous sketches and maps, meticulously detailing the locations of potential seismic triggers. Ana recognized some of the sites from her father's published work, dismissing them then as mere academic curiosities. Now, however, they held a terrifying significance. One of the locations was strikingly similar to the ruins of a Roman temple she had visited as a child, situated within a remote valley in the Carpathian Mountains. She remembered the intricate carvings on the temple walls, symbols that now resonated with the familiar patterns from the Codex.

The significance of the temple sent a wave of apprehension through her. Her father's work, once purely academic, now pointed towards a global conspiracy that threatened the very existence of humanity. She had inherited not just her father's intellect and passion for linguistics, but also his burden, his legacy of uncovering truth, even if that truth held the potential to shatter the world.

Armed with her father's research and the clues from the Codex, Ana began to retrace her father's steps, searching for confirmation of his horrifying theory. She spent countless hours in libraries and archives, poring over ancient texts and maps, piecing together the fragments of a forgotten history. The deeper she delved, the more horrifying the truth became, the more urgent the need to stop the Sentinel.

She tracked down old colleagues of her father, scholars who had worked alongside him on his research, sharing fragments of his theories without understanding their true significance. They corroborated his findings, adding more pieces to the puzzle. She discovered that the Sentinel organization was not merely a group of fanatics, but a well-organized and powerful network with deep roots in history, extending back centuries, their influence spanning governments and institutions.

The weight of responsibility pressed heavily upon her. She was no longer just a linguist; she was a guardian of a terrifying truth, the last line of defense against the impending global catastrophe. She would have to confront the Sentinel, navigate their treacherous web of influence, and expose their sinister plans before they could unleash the power of the Black Sun. The journey would be fraught with danger, but Ana knew she had no choice. Gábor's sacrifice, her father's dedication – these were not in vain. She would complete their work, even if it meant risking her life. The world's fate rested on her shoulders, and she would not falter. The awakening was coming, and she was the only one who could prevent it.

Meeting Gbor Varga

The address, scribbled on the back of a faded postcard depicting the ruins of Sarmizegetusa Regia, felt like a lifeline in the storm raging within her. Gábor Varga. The name, whispered amongst academic circles with a mixture of respect and disdain, now held the key to unlocking the terrifying secrets of the Black Sun Codex. Disgraced, ostracized, yet undeniably brilliant, Varga was the only archaeologist Ana knew who possessed the specialized knowledge of Dacian symbolism and ancient Transylvanian fortifications necessary to interpret the cryptic markings on the codex and the clues left behind by her murdered father.

Finding him proved more difficult than anticipated. He wasn't listed in any academic directories, his name seemingly erased from official records. Whispers in Bucharest's underbelly, however, led her to a dimly lit, smoke-filled tavern nestled in the labyrinthine streets of the old city. The air hung heavy with the scent of stale beer, unwashed bodies, and desperation, a far cry from the hallowed halls of university libraries she was accustomed to.

The bartender, a burly man with eyes that had seen too much, simply nodded when Ana mentioned Varga's name, pointing a thick finger towards a shadowy corner booth. There, shrouded in darkness, sat a man who seemed to blend seamlessly with the gloom. His face, etched with the lines of hardship and regret, was partially obscured by a wide-brimmed hat. But even in the dim light, Ana recognized the intense, almost haunted gaze that had been described to her – a gaze that spoke volumes of his past.

He looked up as she approached, his eyes, the color of glacial ice, assessing her with a chilling intensity. He didn't speak, didn't offer a greeting, just watched her, his silence a palpable weight in the already suffocating atmosphere of the tavern. Ana, however, felt strangely calm; the weight of the impending doom, the responsibility of deciphering the Codex, paled in comparison to the pressure of facing this enigmatic man.

Finally, he spoke, his voice a low rumble, barely above a whisper. "You must be Dr. Lupu's daughter. I heard whispers." His words were laced with a hint of sadness, a shared understanding of loss that transcended the immediate circumstances.

Ana nodded, the weight of her father's legacy settling heavily upon her shoulders. "I need your help, Mr. Varga. The Codex… it's more than just an ancient manuscript. It's a warning, a prophecy of impending catastrophe."

He remained silent for a moment, his gaze fixed on the worn leather-bound book she carried. "The Black Sun," he murmured, the words barely audible. "I've heard the legends, the whispers in the mountain winds. But I dismissed them as folklore, as the ramblings of superstitious peasants." He let out a humorless laugh. "How wrong I was."

Ana laid the Codex on the table between them, its worn pages a testament to its age and the secrets it held. The intricate symbols, a blend of Dacian runes and unfamiliar glyphs, shimmered faintly in the dim light. "My father dedicated his life to deciphering this. He was murdered because of it."

Varga's gaze fell upon the symbols, his eyes scanning them with an almost painful intensity. "These are… these are beyond anything I've ever seen," he whispered, his voice laced with a mixture of awe and apprehension. "The precision, the artistry… this is no mere inscription; it's a map, a complex code interwoven with a hidden language."

He picked up the Codex, his fingers tracing the intricate patterns with a reverence bordering on worship. For a long moment, he was lost in contemplation, his mind clearly grappling with the enormity of what he held in his hands. Ana watched him, her heart pounding in her chest, a mixture of hope and trepidation filling her being. The weight of her father's legacy, the urgency of the impending disaster, all rested on this man's shoulders, this disgraced archaeologist who held the key to the Black Sun's secrets.

"The locations," Varga finally said, his voice barely a breath. "The symbols, they're not just decorative; they point to specific locations – ancient sites, hidden chambers, places long forgotten by the world." He paused, his eyes locked on Ana. "You need to understand, the Black Sun... it's not a celestial body. It's a metaphor. A metaphor for something far more sinister."

He began to explain, his voice gaining strength as he spoke. He detailed the significance of the symbols, linking them to specific locations in the Carpathian Mountains, sites associated with ancient Dacian rituals and mythology. He talked of hidden solar temples, of subterranean passages leading to forgotten chambers, of the complex network of tunnels and underground passages that crisscrossed the mountain range, a network older than the Roman Empire itself.

The knowledge Varga possessed was staggering, his expertise far exceeding anything Ana could have imagined. He spoke of the Dacian belief in a hidden sun, a source of immense power, a force that could reshape the world. According to the legends, this "Black Sun" was not a literal celestial body, but a metaphor for a hidden, dormant energy source – a source that could be awakened. The Codex, he explained, was not just a chronicle of this belief; it was a blueprint, a guide to locating and harnessing this ancient power.

He spoke of the Sentinel, the shadowy organization that

had murdered her father, a group that had been pursuing the same knowledge for centuries, aiming to control and manipulate this hidden energy for their own nefarious purposes. Their motivations remained unclear, but their methods were brutally efficient. They were relentless, ruthless, and had no qualms about eliminating anyone who stood in their way.

"They know you're involved now, Dr. Dragan," Varga stated, his voice grave. "They'll be coming for you. We need to move quickly. Every moment wasted brings us closer to the awakening."

The urgency in his voice was palpable. Ana felt a chill run down her spine. She had been aware of the danger, but Varga's words painted a far more terrifying picture than she had ever imagined. The seemingly academic pursuit had transformed into a desperate race against time, a battle against an ancient power, and a fight for the very survival of humanity.

The night wore on, the conversation stretching into the early hours of the morning. Varga meticulously explained the significance of each symbol, each cryptic phrase, drawing connections between seemingly disparate elements. He revealed his own past, a tale of ambition, betrayal, and professional ruin – a tale that had led him to this desolate tavern, to this perilous alliance. He had been studying these symbols for years, dismissing them as folklore until her father's death forced him to reconsider. The weight of responsibility for deciphering these secrets, he said, pressed heavily on him, as if fate itself had steered him towards this moment.

As dawn broke, painting the sky in hues of pink and gold, Ana and Varga had formed an uneasy alliance, a pact forged in the shadow of impending doom. They had barely scratched the surface of the Codex's secrets, but they had a plan, a fragile hope in the face of unimaginable danger. Their journey to decipher the Black Sun Codex, to stop the awakening, had begun. The path ahead was shrouded in uncertainty, danger lurked around every corner, but together, they would confront the Sentinel and unravel the mysteries buried within the ancient texts before it was too late.

The fate of the world rested on their shoulders, a burden they now shared, bound together by a shared purpose and the grim shadow of the Black Sun.

Initial Investigation in Bucharest

The air in Bucharest hung thick with the scent of exhaust fumes and roasting chestnuts, a stark contrast to the austere mountain air of the monastery where Ana had last seen her father, lifeless, with those unsettling symbols branded onto his skin. Gábor Varga, a figure as enigmatic as the Dacian artifacts he'd dedicated his life to studying, waited impatiently in the lobby of the Hotel Ambasador. His eyes, the color of storm clouds, held a weariness that belied his youthful appearance. He'd agreed to help, driven by a mixture of professional curiosity and perhaps, a flicker of genuine empathy for Ana's grief.

"The police have been surprisingly unhelpful," Ana said, her voice strained, the echo of the monastery's chilling silence still clinging to her. She placed a worn leather satchel on the small table between them, its contents representing the entirety of her father's remaining possessions. "They've dismissed it as a robbery gone wrong, but..." she trailed off, unable to articulate the gut feeling of something far more sinister at play.

Gábor ran a hand through his already disheveled dark hair. "Robbery? With those symbols? Petru Lupu didn't collect stamps. He dealt with things far more... esoteric." He leaned forward, his gaze intense. "Let's see what our esteemed colleague left behind to illuminate his sudden departure from this mortal coil."

The satchel yielded little at first – mundane items: a worn copy of Getica , annotated with frantic notes in the margins; a collection of chipped teacups; several photographs, mostly of landscapes, some of which showcased the imposing peaks of the Carpathians; and several seemingly innocuous letters, mainly academic correspondence. Disappointment began to settle over

Ana, the weight of the unsolved mystery pressing down on her.

Then, Gábor's sharp eyes caught something. Tucked into the innermost pocket, beneath a pile of research papers, was a small, intricately carved wooden box. It was unremarkable at first glance, but a closer inspection revealed a subtle inscription on its lid – a series of runes, strikingly similar to those etched onto her father's body.

The box, when opened, revealed a single, aged parchment scroll, tightly rolled. Ana carefully unfurled it, revealing a meticulously written message, penned in a spidery hand that looked centuries old. It was written in Latin, but not classical Latin. This was a dialect, archaic and obscure, peppered with words that defied easy translation. Even Gábor, with his vast knowledge of ancient languages, struggled to decipher it.

"This isn't just any Latin," Gábor muttered, his brow furrowed in concentration. "It's…Dacian-influenced. A liturgical dialect, perhaps? Some kind of secret code?"

Hours bled into the night as they poured over the text, the hotel room lit only by the sickly yellow glow of a desk lamp. Gábor, a linguistic maverick with an intuitive grasp of patterns, began to isolate key words and phrases. Ana, armed with her father's meticulous research notes and a growing understanding of the symbology, cross-referenced the scroll with various ancient texts.

Slowly, painstakingly, a narrative began to emerge, a chilling tale woven from fragments of language and symbol. The scroll detailed a secret society, an organization that existed centuries ago, one that worshiped a force they referred to as the "Black Sun," not as a celestial body, but as a representation of a hidden power.

The scroll went on to describe a series of locations, a path that seemed to trace an ancient pilgrimage, starting in Bucharest itself. It mentioned specific landmarks, cryptic descriptions of hidden passages, and a network of underground tunnels that connected several historically significant sites across the country.

This network, the scroll implied, was tied to a larger conspiracy that had the potential to destabilize the very foundation of the world.

"This explains the symbols on Petru's body," Gábor said, his voice hushed with awe and a hint of fear. "They were not random markings. They were coordinates, a map leading to something... something incredibly dangerous." He pointed to a section of the scroll detailing a specific location in Bucharest: the ruins of an ancient Roman bathhouse, located near the city's oldest district. It was hidden beneath layers of modern construction, lost to history until Dr. Lupu's meticulous research unearthed it.

The next morning found Ana and Gábor standing amidst the detritus of a forgotten era. The Roman bathhouse, barely clinging to existence beneath a crumbling modern building, was a maze of collapsed walls, damp earth, and overgrown vegetation. The air hung heavy with the scent of damp earth and decaying stone. Following the clues from the scroll, they navigated the labyrinthine ruins, their footsteps echoing in the oppressive silence. They found a hidden passage, concealed behind a loose section of the wall, a passage that led down into darkness.

Equipped with flashlights and a growing sense of unease, they descended into the subterranean labyrinth. The air grew colder, the silence more profound. They discovered a network of tunnels, eerily preserved through the ages, their walls adorned with faded frescoes depicting scenes of ancient rituals and strange astronomical events. The walls were covered in more runes, their meanings still enigmatic.

Further into the labyrinth, they found a chamber. In the center of the chamber, upon a crumbling pedestal, lay a smaller, intricately carved box, identical to the one they'd found in Dr. Lupu's satchel. But this box was sealed with a complex locking mechanism, a puzzle that challenged their combined knowledge of ancient Roman engineering and Dacian symbology.

The chamber's walls whispered of a forgotten power, a forgotten civilization. The sense of dread intensified as they deciphered more inscriptions, revealing the hidden purpose of this underground sanctuary. This wasn't just a bathhouse; it was a sacred site, a place of worship for the mysterious society mentioned in the scroll – a site dedicated to the worship of the "Black Sun." The scroll had led them to the very heart of the conspiracy. But their initial investigation had only just begun. Unraveling the mystery of the Black Sun was only the first step in a much longer and more perilous journey. The deeper they delved, the more they realized they were far from being alone in their pursuit. The Sentinel was watching.

Chapter 2

Shadows in the Carpathians

Journey to the Mountains

The battered Dacia, its suspension groaning under the weight of their equipment and the relentless pressure of the Transylvanian roads, bumped its way deeper into the heart of the Carpathian Mountains. Ana Dragan, her gaze fixed on the relentless grey of the sky that mirrored the churning anxieties in her stomach, gripped the worn leather of the passenger seat. Beside her, Gábor Varga, his weathered face etched with a mixture of determination and weariness, wrestled with the increasingly erratic behavior of the ancient vehicle. The silence between them was punctuated only by the rhythmic clatter of the engine and the occasional creak of protesting metal. The journey had been long and arduous, a stark contrast to the sterile environment of the Bucharest archives they had left behind.

They had followed the trail of cryptic clues meticulously, each fragment of the Black Sun Codex unlocking a new piece of the puzzle, leading them inexorably towards this remote corner of Romania. Dr. Lupu's final, frantic scribblings, deciphered with the aid of Ana's linguistic expertise and Gábor's understanding of ancient Dacian symbols, had pointed them to this monastery, a place shrouded in legend and mystery, nestled deep within the formidable embrace of the Carpathians. The monastery, St. Sava's, was more than just a place of worship; it was a silent sentinel, guarding secrets that stretched back centuries, secrets that were now inextricably linked to their own survival.

The landscape shifted and changed dramatically as they climbed higher, the fertile valleys giving way to dense forests that clung to the steep slopes. Ancient beech trees, their gnarled branches clawing at the sky, formed a dark and brooding canopy overhead. The air grew colder, sharper, carrying the scent of damp earth and pine needles. The winding road, barely more than a rutted track in places, tested the Dacia's resilience, threatening at any moment to send them tumbling down the precipitous slopes. Gábor navigated with the skill of a seasoned mountain driver, his eyes constantly scanning the treacherous terrain ahead.

Ana, meanwhile, struggled to reconcile the serene beauty of the surroundings with the impending danger that hung heavy in the air. The idyllic scenery belied the sinister shadow of The Sentinel, the shadowy organization that had murdered Dr. Lupu and was now undoubtedly hot on their trail. She knew they were not just searching for knowledge; they were racing against time, against an unseen force that threatened to unleash a catastrophic event foretold in the ancient prophecy hidden within the Black Sun Codex.

Finally, after what felt like an eternity, they reached their destination. St. Sava's Monastery stood silhouetted against the brooding mountains, a formidable structure of weathered stone and dark wood, its ancient walls seemingly carved from the very heart of the earth. An aura of profound age and undisturbed quiet clung to the place, a stark contrast to the frantic pace of their pursuit. The monastery's isolation was both awe-inspiring and unsettling, a testament to its age and a chilling reminder of its secrets.

As they parked the vehicle, a biting wind whipped around them, carrying with it the mournful whispers of the surrounding forest. The silence of the place was profound, broken only by the rustling of leaves and the occasional cry of a distant bird. Ana felt a shiver crawl down her spine, not entirely from the cold. This was no ordinary place; this was a place of power, a place that held within its ancient stones the key to their quest, and perhaps, the key to their doom.

Approaching the monastery, they noticed the imposing stone walls, punctuated by narrow, deeply recessed windows that seemed to gaze out with a malevolent curiosity. The heavy oak door, secured with iron bands that had weathered centuries of wind and rain, stood as a formidable barrier. Gábor, drawing upon his knowledge of ancient architecture, pointed to a barely visible indentation near the door's base. It was a subtle detail, easily missed by the untrained eye, but one that hinted at the existence of a hidden mechanism.

After a careful examination, Gábor managed to activate

the mechanism, revealing a hidden passage concealed within the thick stone wall. The entrance was just wide enough for a person to squeeze through, leading into a narrow, dark tunnel that seemed to descend into the very bowels of the monastery. The air within was thick with the smell of damp earth and something else, something ancient and indefinably disturbing.

Armed with only flashlights and their determination, Ana and Gábor ventured into the unknown, the darkness pressing in on them from all sides. The tunnel was claustrophobic, the rough-hewn stone walls scraping against their clothes as they moved forward, each step a tentative exploration into the monastery's hidden past. The silence amplified their footsteps, transforming them into a deafening roar within the confines of the passage.

As they progressed deeper, the tunnel opened into a larger chamber, revealing a breathtaking sight. The chamber was vast, its ceiling supported by massive, intricately carved stone pillars. The walls were covered in ancient frescoes, depicting scenes of a lost civilization, their vibrant colors miraculously preserved despite the passage of time. In the center of the chamber lay a large stone altar, upon which rested a single object: a weathered, leather-bound book, the Black Sun Codex itself.

But they were not alone. A sudden rustling sound echoed through the chamber, causing Ana and Gábor to freeze, their flashlights cutting through the gloom. From the shadows, figures emerged, their faces obscured by darkness, their movements silent and deadly. The Sentinel had found them.

The confrontation was swift and brutal. Gábor, despite his advanced age, fought with the ferocity of a cornered animal, his years of experience transforming him into a formidable opponent. Ana, smaller but agile, used her wits and agility to evade the Sentinel's attacks, her movements precise and economical, like a dance of survival. The fight was a desperate ballet of light and shadow, metal clashing against metal in a desperate struggle for survival. They fought their way back through the hidden passage, narrowly escaping the grasp of The Sentinel, the sound of their relentless pursuit echoing behind them.

Emerging from the monastery, gasping for breath and covered in bruises, Ana and Gábor surveyed their surroundings. Their initial foray into the heart of St. Sava's had been more successful and far more dangerous than they could have ever imagined. The Codex remained elusive, but the clues gathered within the monastery were enough to send shivers down their spines, painting a terrifying picture of what awaited them. Their journey had only just begun, and the shadows in the Carpathians were closing in fast. The hunt was far from over.

Exploration of the Monastery

The air hung heavy with the scent of damp earth and decaying wood as Gábor pried loose a section of crumbling stonework, revealing a narrow, claustrophobic passage. A faint, musty odor, unlike anything Ana had encountered before, emanated from within, a mix of aged parchment and something metallic, almost bloodlike. The passage sloped downwards, disappearing into the inky blackness. Armed with Gábor's powerful headlamp and a healthy dose of trepidation, they ventured into the unknown.

The passage was barely wide enough for them to pass side-by-side, the walls slick with moisture. Water dripped incessantly from the unseen ceiling, the sound echoing ominously in the confined space. Ana, ever the meticulous researcher, noted the peculiar markings on the walls – symbols that seemed to bear a faint resemblance to those etched onto Dr. Lupu's body, yet subtly different, more archaic, hinting at a connection older than the monastery itself. These weren't merely decorative; they were a language, a code waiting to be deciphered.

As they descended deeper, the air grew colder, a perceptible shift in temperature that sent a shiver down Ana's spine. The silence, broken only by the drip, drip, drip of water and their own breathing, was unnerving. Gábor, his eyes scanning every inch of the passage, moved with a practiced ease born from years spent exploring forgotten ruins. He pointed to a section of wall where the stonework seemed less weathered, almost as if it had been recently repaired. A closer inspection revealed a small, almost invisible crack. Using a thin, metal tool from his kit, he carefully widened the crack, revealing a hollow space behind the stone. Inside, nestled within the darkness, lay a small, wooden box.

With trembling hands, Gábor extracted the box. It was intricately carved, the wood dark and polished with age, bearing the same enigmatic symbols that adorned the walls. He opened it with care, revealing a collection of ancient parchments, brittle and yellowed with time. They were carefully bundled together, tied with a faded ribbon. The script was unlike anything Ana had ever seen, a complex blend of Cyrillic and what appeared to be an ancient Dacian script, a language long thought lost to history.

"This is incredible," Ana whispered, her breath catching in her throat. "These could be the missing pieces."

They carefully removed the parchments, spreading them out on a clean piece of their canvas tarp. The script was dense and intricate, filled with elaborate flourishes and symbols that defied easy interpretation. Hours passed as they painstakingly examined the scrolls, comparing the symbols to those found in Dr. Lupu's research and the ones decorating the monastery walls. Gábor, relying on his knowledge of ancient languages and cultures, suggested possible interpretations, while Ana meticulously cross-referenced their findings with the data they'd gathered in Bucharest.

As they worked, a terrifying realization began to dawn on them. The parchments detailed a forgotten history, a network of secret societies that had existed for centuries, their influence extending far beyond the borders of Transylvania. The Sentinel, the shadowy organization that was pursuing them, was not a modern creation; it was a continuation of this ancient order, safeguarding its dark secrets for generations. The Black Sun Codex, they now understood, was not simply a book; it was a key, a map to a series of hidden locations scattered across Europe, each holding a piece of a larger, far more sinister puzzle.

The prophecy mentioned in the codex, previously unclear, now began to take on a chillingly specific meaning. It spoke of a convergence, a cataclysmic event that would be triggered by the activation of ancient mechanisms, buried deep beneath the earth, mechanisms capable of unleashing unimaginable destruction. The Black Sun, they realized with growing horror, was not a celestial body; it was a metaphor for the darkness within humanity, the potential for self-annihilation that the ancient order had sought to control – and potentially unleash.

The parchments also spoke of The Sentinel's ultimate goal: to control these mechanisms, to use them to reshape the world in their own image, to usher in a new era of darkness. Their investigation had inadvertently put them at the center of this terrifying conspiracy, and the realization hit them both with the force of a physical blow. They were not just hunting for clues; they were racing against time to prevent the end of the world. The passage, once a source of intrigue, now felt like a tomb, the walls closing in on them, the weight of their discovery pressing down.

As the first rays of dawn began to filter into the passage, they emerged from the hidden chamber, their faces grim, their eyes reflecting the chilling revelations they had unearthed. The monastery, once a place of quiet contemplation, now seemed to pulsate with a sinister energy. The weight of their newfound knowledge, the enormity of their task, threatened to crush them. They had found the missing pieces, but the puzzle they unveiled was far more horrifying than they could have ever imagined. The journey ahead was far more perilous, the stakes impossibly high. The shadows in the Carpathians were not merely a metaphor; they were real, tangible, and closing in faster than ever before.

The silence between them was heavier now, laden with the burden of their discovery. The journey to Bucharest, though fraught with the danger of pursuit, seemed almost carefree compared to what lay ahead. The information gleaned from these scrolls was not simply an historical oddity, but a critical piece of a deadly puzzle. They needed to share this new knowledge with authorities, find a way to prove their theory to those who could act, and do so without falling prey to The Sentinel themselves. Their investigation was no longer just about solving an academic mystery; it was about preventing a global catastrophe. The weight of the world, quite literally, rested on their shoulders. Each breath they took was a gamble, a step closer to either salvation or annihilation.

The escape from the monastery was a frantic dash, a blur of movement and adrenaline. They had to get out, find a secure location to analyze what they'd found, and strategize their next move. They were no longer just archaeologists and linguists; they were unwitting players in a game of global proportions, with their lives, and potentially the fate of humanity, hanging in the balance. The ancient symbols they had painstakingly deciphered were not mere decorations; they were warnings, grim pronouncements of impending doom, and they were running out of time.

The journey back to their base, a small, secluded cabin near a remote village, was fraught with tension. The landscape, once beautiful and awe-inspiring, now seemed to conspire against them, every shadow a potential threat, every bend in the road a possible ambush. The relentless pursuit by The Sentinel was no longer just a feeling; they could sense it, a chilling presence that seemed to stalk their every move. They were hunted, trapped in a deadly game of cat and mouse, where the stakes were infinitely high.

The cabin, once a haven of comfort, now felt more like a prison, a temporary refuge before the storm. Ana, with Gábor's help, started to catalog and organize their findings, meticulously creating a detailed record of their discoveries. The urgency of their situation pushed them to work with a relentless focus, driven by a grim determination to decipher the secrets before it was too late. Each new symbol, each ancient word, held the key to understanding the catastrophic event predicted in the prophecy, a key that could mean the difference between life and death for billions. The lines between history and reality were blurring, the ancient whispers of the past echoing the very real threat of the present. They had stumbled upon something truly terrifying, something that could shatter the world as they knew it. And now, armed with this terrifying knowledge, they had to find a way to stop it.

Their research revealed that the seismic triggers weren't randomly placed; they formed a pattern, a constellation of destruction mirroring ancient astronomical charts. They were connected, forming a network that, if activated, could trigger a chain reaction of devastating earthquakes across the globe. The ancient order, it seemed, had designed a system of global destruction, a horrifying weapon capable of unleashing unimaginable devastation. The Sentinel, its modern incarnation, was determined to wield this weapon, to reshape the world according to their twisted vision.

The escape from the Carpathians, and the subsequent race to expose the truth, became a desperate struggle against time and powerful adversaries. The pursuit was relentless, the stakes impossibly high. The weight of the world, quite literally, rested on their shoulders. Each breath they took was a gamble, a step closer to either salvation or annihilation. The line between history and reality had blurred; the ancient whispers of the past echoed the very real threat of the present. They were caught in a terrifying game of cat and mouse, where the hunter and the hunted were blurred, where every shadow hid a potential danger, and where the very fate of humanity depended on their next move. The ancient mysteries they'd uncovered were not merely academic puzzles; they were the keys to preventing global devastation, and the race was on.

The Sentinels First Pursuit

The passage descended steeply, the air growing colder with each step. The beam of Gábor's headlamp cut through the oppressive darkness, revealing damp, moss-covered walls slick with moisture. The metallic scent intensified, now tinged with a faint, almost imperceptible sweetness, like decaying roses. Ana shivered, not entirely from the cold. The feeling of being watched intensified, a prickling sensation on the back of her neck that had nothing to do with the claustrophobic confines of the tunnel.

They moved in silence, the only sounds the rhythmic drip of water and the occasional scrape of Gábor's boots against the uneven stone floor. The passage twisted and turned, a labyrinthine descent into the earth, its age whispering secrets in the very texture of its walls. Ana could almost feel the weight of centuries pressing down on them, the echoes of forgotten rituals and buried truths resonating in the oppressive stillness. She thought of Dr. Lupu, his cryptic symbols seared into his flesh, a final message scrawled in the language of death. Had he been here? Had he known the secrets this hidden passage held?

Suddenly, Gábor stopped, his hand raised, silencing Ana. The metallic scent intensified, becoming almost overpowering, accompanied by a low, guttural growl that seemed to vibrate from the very stones themselves. Ana's heart pounded in her chest, a frantic drumbeat against the silence. She strained her ears, listening, trying to decipher the source of the sound.

Then, she saw them.

Three figures emerged from the shadows, their faces obscured by the darkness, their forms barely visible in the weak beam of the headlamp. They moved with a fluid, predatory grace, their movements silent and deliberate, like phantoms gliding through the subterranean passage. They were clad in dark, flowing garments, their features hidden, their eyes gleaming with an unnerving intensity. Ana recognized the insignia on their sleeves – a stylized black sun, a chilling echo of the symbol etched onto Dr. Lupu's body. The Sentinel.

They didn't speak, didn't need to. Their presence was a tangible threat, a suffocating weight of menace that pressed down on Ana and Gábor, threatening to crush them beneath its icy grip. The growl intensified, transforming into a low, menacing hiss, a sound that seemed to claw at the very edges of Ana's sanity.

Gábor reacted instantly, his years of experience in perilous situations kicking in. He swiftly pulled Ana behind him, his hand resting on the handle of his small, but sturdy, army-issue knife. The three figures advanced, their movements precise and deadly, their forms gliding through the narrow passage like shadows given substance. Ana's breath hitched in her throat; this was no mere academic pursuit; this was a fight for survival.

The first Sentinel lunged, his hand reaching for Gábor's shoulder. Gábor reacted swiftly, sidestepping the attack with surprising agility, his knife flashing in the darkness. The blade connected with the Sentinel's arm, drawing a sharp cry of pain, a sound muffled by the echo of the subterranean passage. The other two Sentinels closed in, their movements synchronized, their attacks relentless.

It was a whirlwind of flashing blades and desperate parries. Gábor fought with the ferocity of a cornered animal, his movements precise and deadly. Ana, despite her lack of combat experience, found herself instinctively reacting, her adrenaline pumping, her fear fueling her actions. She used her wits, her small frame enabling her to slip between the Sentinels, disrupting their coordinated attacks, creating openings for Gábor to exploit.

The fight was brutal, a desperate dance of death played out in the claustrophobic confines of the ancient passage. The air filled with the metallic tang of blood, mingling with the musty odor of the passage and the cloying sweetness of decaying roses. Ana felt a searing pain in her shoulder as a Sentinel's blade grazed her skin, the pain a sharp, electric shock that sent a wave of dizziness through her.

Gábor, despite his valiant efforts, was clearly outnumbered. He was a skilled fighter, but even his expertise couldn't overcome the relentless assault of three trained assassins. Ana knew they couldn't win this fight, not here, not like this. They had to escape.

With a sudden, desperate burst of energy, Gábor created a diversion, his knife flashing in a dazzling display of skill. He lured the Sentinels towards him, giving Ana the opportunity to slip away into the twisting passage, her injured shoulder screaming in protest with every movement.

She ran blindly, the darkness swallowing her whole. She heard the sounds of the fight fading behind her, the echoes of blades clashing and the guttural growls of the Sentinels gradually diminishing. She didn't dare to look back, didn't dare to slow down. Her heart hammered in her chest, a frantic drumbeat against the silence of the subterranean passage. She had to escape, had to survive. She had to find a way out, a way to prevent the catastrophic event foretold in the Black Sun Codex.

She ran until her lungs burned and her legs ached, her injured shoulder a throbbing agony. Finally, she stumbled into a larger cavern, the air here noticeably warmer and less oppressive. The metallic scent was fainter now, replaced by the earthy aroma of damp soil and the faint, sweet smell of wild flowers.

She collapsed against the cold stone, gasping for breath, her body trembling with exhaustion and fear. She was alone, injured, and surrounded by the echoing silence of the cavern. She was alive, but the encounter had left her shaken to the core. The Sentinel's pursuit had been a chilling prelude to the dangers that lay ahead, a stark reminder of the stakes involved. The ancient secrets they were chasing weren't just historical artifacts; they were weapons of unimaginable power, and she was caught in the crossfire of a conflict far older and more deadly than she could have ever imagined.

Her escape was only temporary. The Sentinel would be back. The hunt was far from over. The weight of their discovery – of the prophecy and the impending catastrophe – pressed down on her, a crushing burden that threatened to suffocate her. But she couldn't give up. She had to keep moving, had to unravel the mysteries of the Black Sun Codex, had to prevent the awakening before it was too late. The fate of the world, it seemed, rested on her shoulders, and she had to find a way to carry it.

The silence of the cavern was broken only by her ragged

breathing, her pounding heart, and the persistent throb of pain in her shoulder. The darkness pressed in on her, but amidst the fear and uncertainty, a flicker of determination ignited within her. She would not be broken. She would survive. She would find a way to stop The Sentinel and expose the truth. The pursuit had just begun. The race against time, against the shadowy organization and against the ancient prophecies, continued, relentlessly, inexorably, leading her deeper into a world of hidden passages, ancient secrets and the shadowy world of conspiracy and ancient evil, a world where the line between history and reality blurred into a nightmarish landscape of suspense and danger. The weight of the world rested upon her frail shoulders, as she ventured into the abyss. The chilling encounter with The Sentinel served as a sobering reminder that this was no mere academic pursuit but a desperate battle for survival, a race against time that threatened the very fate of humanity. The shadows in the Carpathians were deeper and more threatening than she could have ever imagined, a prelude to the greater horrors that lay ahead. Every breath she took, every step she made, was a gamble, a wager against an unseen adversary who commanded a terrifying power and possessed an intimate knowledge of ancient secrets that dwarfed even Dr. Lupu's impressive academic achievements. The weight of this realization pressed down on her, fueling her resolve, hardening her determination to continue this perilous journey into the heart of darkness. The pursuit continued. The ancient mystery awaited its unraveling. And Ana Dragan, armed with nothing more than her wits, her courage, and a burning determination, was ready to face it. She knew the dangers ahead would be immense, the challenges insurmountable, yet something inside her, something deep and ancient, spurred her onward, whispering of a fate she couldn't escape, a destiny she was bound to fulfill. The pursuit of the Black Sun Codex had become her own personal crusade, a fight not only for her life but for the fate of the world.

Decoding the First Fragments

The tunnel's chilling dampness clung to Ana like a shroud.

The metallic tang in the air, that unsettling scent of decaying roses, grew stronger as they pressed deeper into the earth. Gábor, his headlamp beam cutting a swathe through the gloom, moved with the practiced ease of someone familiar with subterranean labyrinths. He'd mentioned his grandfather's involvement in cave exploration, a hobby Ana now understood extended far beyond a simple avocation. It seemed Gábor had inherited more than just his grandfather's adventurous spirit; he possessed an uncanny knack for navigating these hidden pathways, an intuition that guided him through the twisting passages with unnerving accuracy.

Ana, however, felt increasingly disoriented. The tunnel seemed to twist and turn without logical pattern, a labyrinth designed to confuse and disorient. Each turn brought a fresh wave of claustrophobia, a crushing weight that threatened to suffocate her. The silence, broken only by the rhythmic drip of water and their own hushed breaths, was unsettling, a void pregnant with unspoken dangers. She glanced at Gábor; his face was grim, etched with a concentration that bordered on obsession. He was lost in his own world, his eyes focused intently on the damp walls, seemingly deciphering the secrets held within the very stone.

They finally reached a larger cavern, its dimensions dwarfing the narrow passage behind them. The air here was noticeably warmer, the metallic scent less pronounced, replaced by a musty odor that spoke of age and decay. In the center of the cavern, partially submerged in a pool of stagnant water, lay a collection of stone fragments, their surfaces covered in a layer of algae and grime. These were the fragments of the Black Sun Codex, the pieces of a puzzle that held the key to understanding the threat they faced.

Gábor carefully retrieved the fragments, his movements deliberate and precise. He handed them to Ana, his eyes pleading for patience, understanding. Ana, her heart pounding against her ribs, recognized the urgency etched upon his face. She began the painstaking work of cleaning the fragments, using the small brushes and cloths she had brought along. Each piece yielded another cryptic symbol, another tantalizing glimpse into the ancient mystery.

The symbols themselves were unlike anything she'd ever encountered. They weren't runic, nor were they related to any known ancient script. They appeared to be a combination of geometric shapes and abstract designs, intricately interwoven in a seemingly random pattern, yet the pattern itself felt strangely organized, as if the positioning of each piece was dictated by an inherent logic. The symbols had a peculiar quality that set them apart; there was a certain flow to them, an elegant dance between straight lines and curved strokes, which suggested more than just mere markings. Instead they resembled a language, possibly one that transcended the written word entirely and touched upon the deeper realms of symbolism.

As Ana painstakingly cleaned and documented each fragment, she noticed a recurring motif, a symbol that appeared on almost every piece. It resembled a stylized sun, but unlike any representation she'd seen before. Its rays were not straight but curved, almost serpentine, giving it an unsettling, almost sinister appearance. This was the "Black Sun," the central enigma that had brought them here. It wasn't a celestial body, as some believed, but a metaphor, an allegorical representation of something far more profound and sinister.

The hours melted away as they worked, the cavern's oppressive silence punctuated only by the gentle scrape of Ana's cleaning tools and the occasional hushed whisper as Gábor offered a translation of some symbols, which gradually began to paint a more complete picture. They discovered that the Codex wasn't a single, cohesive narrative, but rather a collection of fragmented texts, each piece seemingly unrelated to the other, creating more questions than answers.

Gábor's expertise in ancient languages, coupled with Ana's linguistic acumen, proved invaluable. Together they managed to piece together snippets of information, revealing glimpses into a long-forgotten history. The Codex spoke of a network of underground structures, an intricate system of tunnels and chambers stretching across the globe, linked by an ancient technology that predated known civilization. This technology, the Codex hinted, was capable of manipulating the Earth's tectonic plates, unleashing catastrophic earthquakes and tsunamis on a global scale.

The 'Black Sun,' it seemed, wasn't merely a symbol of darkness, but the name of the system itself - a network of hidden triggers poised to unleash unimaginable destruction. The prophecy Dr. Lupu had discovered wasn't a mere prediction; it was a warning, a desperate plea to prevent the system's reactivation. The Sentinel was not just a shadowy organization; they were the keepers of the 'Black Sun', a group hell-bent on unleashing the apocalypse.

One fragment, particularly well-preserved, revealed a series of coordinates. Gábor instantly recognized them as referencing sites throughout Europe, locations known for their historical significance and geological instability. These locations weren't randomly selected; they were strategically placed along fault lines and tectonic plates, potentially acting as focal points for the system's devastating power.

As the night deepened, the weight of their discovery settled heavily upon them. They had uncovered more than just an ancient mystery; they had unearthed a global threat of terrifying proportions. The stakes were far higher than they could have ever imagined, and the race against time had taken on a more urgent, desperate tone. The seemingly abstract symbols had suddenly acquired a terrifyingly tangible relevance. The weight of the world now rested on their shoulders.

The fragments yielded little insight into how to disable the 'Black Sun,' but one recurring symbol stood out. It depicted a stylized serpent entwined around a solar disc, which, according to Gábor's research, resembled symbols found in several ancient cultures, particularly among the pre-Roman Dacian tribes of the Carpathian region. This symbol, they suspected, could hold the key to neutralizing the system. They found a note from Lupu in one of the fragments – a small, almost insignificant-looking slip of paper, wedged between two stones, seemingly unnoticed by the Sentinel in their haste. It was a list of places - locations that matched the coordinate references and also showed a pattern of similar geological formations. Lupu had been one step ahead.

The implications were staggering. The threat wasn't some abstract apocalypse prophesied in some ancient text; it was a real, tangible danger, a potential catastrophe that could wipe out humanity. The fragments were like pieces of a jigsaw puzzle depicting a map of potential world destruction. Each piece added another layer of complexity, unveiling a darker, more sinister side to the mystery they were embroiled in. The sheer scale of the threat sent shivers down Ana's spine. This wasn't about deciphering an ancient riddle anymore; it was about stopping a global catastrophe, a task that seemed impossibly daunting.

They were exhausted, but the adrenaline coursing through their veins kept them going. The discovery had provided them with both a terrifying understanding of the threat they faced and a crucial piece of the puzzle – the serpent entwined around the solar disc. But the location of the next piece, the one that might hold the key to disabling the system, remained a mystery. The fragments provided a general geographic area, the Carpathian mountain range, but the exact location remained elusive. The search continued, the shadows deepening with the passing of time. The race against time and against The Sentinel was far from over, a dangerous game of cat and mouse where the stakes were the fate of the world. The weight of responsibility pressed down heavily on Ana, who knew the world's destiny rested in their hands. The pursuit was far from over; this was merely the beginning of a far more perilous journey. The puzzle had merely been set in motion; the pieces were revealed, but the final image remained elusive.

The Prophecys Revelation

The air in the crumbling shepherd's hut, their temporary refuge high in the Carpathians, hung thick with the scent of woodsmoke and damp earth. Outside, the wind howled a mournful dirge through the skeletal branches of ancient pines, a soundtrack to their desperate efforts. Before them, spread across a rough-hewn table, lay the Black Sun Codex – its brittle pages, filled with a dizzying array of symbols, seemed to writhe under the flickering lamplight. Days had bled into nights since their discovery in the monastery; their progress had been agonizingly slow.

Gábor, his face etched with exhaustion, meticulously traced a sequence of glyphs with a worn finger. "The serpent... the solar disc... they're not just decorative," he murmured, his voice hoarse. "They represent a system, a network."

Ana, her eyes bloodshot from lack of sleep, leaned closer, her breath misting in the frigid air. She'd spent countless hours poring over historical texts, cross-referencing astronomical charts with linguistic analyses, trying to unravel the Codex's cryptic language. The symbols, she'd discovered, weren't merely illustrations; they were a complex code interwoven with a surprisingly sophisticated understanding of geology and celestial mechanics.

"A network of what?" she asked, her voice barely a whisper. The weight of the world, quite literally, seemed to rest on her shoulders.

Gábor straightened, his eyes burning with a newfound intensity. "Seismic triggers," he announced, his voice resonating with a certainty that sent a shiver down Ana's spine. "The prophecy isn't about a celestial body; it's about the earth itself. The 'Black Sun' is a metaphor—for a cataclysmic event, triggered by a coordinated series of earthquakes."

Ana stared at him, her mind reeling. The implications were staggering. The ancient civilization that created the Codex had possessed a level of understanding of tectonic plates and fault lines that far surpassed anything known to modern science. This wasn't just a legend; it was a precise warning of a meticulously planned disaster.

"But how?" she whispered, her voice trembling. "How could they trigger earthquakes on such a scale?"

Gábor pointed to a particularly intricate section of the Codex, a series of diagrams depicting interconnected lines radiating outwards from a central point. "These," he explained, "represent ley lines, ancient energy pathways. The civilization that created this understood the earth's natural energy currents. They leveraged these pathways to amplify seismic activity, triggering a chain reaction across multiple fault lines."

He traced the lines with his finger, his explanation growing more intricate. "Each glyph represents a specific location—a nexus point along these ley lines. The serpent, the solar disc... they are keys, activation points in this infernal network. The prophecy foretold their awakening."

The chilling implications settled upon Ana. This wasn't just some apocalyptic fantasy; it was a meticulously designed, ancient weapon, capable of unleashing unparalleled devastation. And they were racing against time to prevent its activation. The Sentinel, the shadowy organization pursuing them, was clearly aware of the Codex's secrets; they were undoubtedly instrumental in its implementation.

Over the next few days, their work intensified. Ana, utilizing her linguistic expertise, painstakingly deciphered sections of the text describing the locations of the nexus points. Gábor, drawing on his archaeological knowledge, identified geographical features correlating with the diagrams in the Codex, pinpointing potential locations of these activation points. The locations weren't random; they were strategically placed along major fault lines across the globe—from the Pacific Ring of Fire to the Himalayas.

One particular passage caught Ana's attention. It spoke of a hidden solar temple, a location of immense power, situated deep within the Carpathians themselves, a place where the ley lines converged. This, they realized, was the central hub, the command center of the entire system. Deactivating the temple would be their only hope of preventing the apocalyptic chain reaction.

The task before them was monumental. They not only had to decipher the precise locations of the nexus points, but they also had to find a way to disrupt the ancient mechanism before the Sentinel could trigger it. The Codex, however, offered little guidance on how to disable the system. It was a blueprint for destruction, not a manual for prevention.

Days turned into a blur of frantic activity. Their research led them to dusty archives, forgotten libraries, and the hushed halls of universities. They followed cryptic clues scattered across the pages of ancient texts, poring over forgotten myths and legends, searching for any hint of how to counteract the seismic triggers.

They discovered that the ancient civilization's understanding of the earth's energy extended beyond simple seismic manipulation. Their texts hinted at a far more sophisticated understanding of the planet's magnetic field, suggesting the ability to manipulate it to influence tectonic activity. The implication was terrifying; they were dealing with a level of technology far beyond human comprehension.

Ana and Gábor's research unearthed a hidden passage within the Vatican archives, a section sealed off for centuries, containing documents that hinted at the Vatican's own involvement with the ancient civilization and their catastrophic plans. The Church, it turned out, had been guarding this secret for millennia, and the Sentinel was merely its modern executioner.

As they delved deeper into the truth, they discovered that the prophecy wasn't just a warning; it was a countdown. The Codex contained a series of astronomical alignments that precisely predicted the timing of the catastrophic event. Their time was running out.

The final piece of the puzzle, a cryptic inscription discovered within a forgotten Roman ruin in Dacia, revealed the exact location of the hidden solar temple. It lay hidden deep within the heart of the Carpathian Mountains, shrouded in mystery and protected by ancient wards.

Their journey to the temple was fraught with peril. They evaded the relentless pursuit of The Sentinel, their pursuers utilizing an array of advanced technology that seemed almost supernatural in its capabilities. The Sentinel, armed with ancient knowledge and cutting-edge technology, was a force that defied comprehension. Gábor's intuition and knowledge of the Carpathians, along with Ana's sharp wit and deduction skills, were their only safeguards against annihilation.

Reaching the temple was only half the battle. The entrance was guarded by intricate traps and puzzles, each demanding a solution rooted in both ancient knowledge and scientific understanding. They navigated through labyrinthine passages, solving riddles and deciphering symbols, their lives hanging precariously in the balance. The deeper they ventured, the more they realized the extent of the ancient civilization's knowledge. They had mastered physics, mathematics, and engineering in a way that defied modern understanding, suggesting a level of technological advancement far beyond our own.

Inside the temple itself, they confronted the heart of the mechanism, a massive, intricate device of obsidian and bronze, pulsing with an eerie energy that resonated deep within their bones. The final activation sequence was set to begin within hours. The Sentinel, hot on their heels, was close.

The confrontation with The Sentinel was brutal and relentless, a fight for survival against overwhelming odds. Gábor, shielding Ana, made the ultimate sacrifice, allowing her to escape with the vital information needed to disable the system, ensuring the world's survival. His actions, a testament to his unwavering courage, bought Ana the time she desperately needed.

As Ana fled the collapsing temple, clutching the Codex, the magnitude of Gábor's sacrifice and the weight of responsibility crashed down on her. The world was safe, for now, but the shadow of The Sentinel, the ancient conspiracy, and the unsettling truth of the Black Sun remained. In the aftermath, amidst the rubble and the ruins, Ana found a hidden message from Gábor, a cryptic inscription hinting at a new mystery, one that would bind her destiny to the ancient secrets he had dedicated his life to uncovering. His last message spurred her on to continue her research, promising the reader a continuation of this perilous journey into the depths of history's darkest secrets.

Chapter 3

Vatican Archives

The Vatican Connection

The air in the Vatican Secret Archives hung heavy with the scent of aged parchment and incense. Ana and Gábor, having navigated the labyrinthine corridors with the help of a surreptitious contact within the Vatican – a monsignor who'd been tipped off by a mutual acquaintance of Dr. Lupu – found themselves surrounded by towering shelves laden with centuries of accumulated knowledge. Dust motes danced in the slivers of sunlight piercing the high, arched windows, illuminating the spines of countless leather-bound volumes. The silence was profound, broken only by the occasional rustle of turning pages and the rhythmic thump of Gábor's heart. He felt the weight of history pressing down on him, a palpable sense of the secrets guarded within these walls.

Ana, ever practical, pulled out a small, high-powered flashlight, its beam cutting through the gloom as she scanned the shelves, seeking the specific collection indicated by the cryptic notes left behind by Dr. Lupu. The notes were written in a complex code, a blend of Latin abbreviations and alphanumeric sequences that only Dr. Lupu's meticulous notes, combined with Gábor's archaeological understanding of ancient symbology, had unlocked. The location they were seeking held the key to understanding a section of the Black Sun Codex which, so far, remained frustratingly indecipherable.

"This is it," Gábor whispered, his voice barely audible above the soft hum of the ancient building. He pointed to a section marked with an almost invisible, barely perceptible symbol – a stylized sun with eight jagged rays, strikingly similar to those etched onto Dr. Lupu's body. It was a symbol that repeated itself throughout the Codex, a visual echo of the "Black Sun" – a term which had initially seemed metaphorical, but had taken on alarmingly literal connotations as their investigations progressed.

They carefully pulled out a heavy volume bound in worn, dark leather. The pages were brittle, the ink faded in places, but the script, a beautiful, elegant cursive Latin, remained legible. The text spoke of a forgotten order of priests, the "Custodians of the Sun," who had supposedly maintained a hidden network of sacred sites throughout the Roman Empire. These sites, according to the text, were not merely places of worship, but rather points of immense geological significance, linked by an ancient network of ley lines or, as modern science would call it, fault lines.

As they read further, the chilling implications of the text became clear. The "Black Sun" wasn't a celestial body at all, but a reference to a network of precisely positioned seismic triggers, a cataclysmic mechanism capable of triggering widespread earthquakes and volcanic eruptions. The priests, it seemed, had possessed the knowledge to manipulate these triggers, either to prevent natural disasters or, far more disturbingly, to unleash them as a weapon of unimaginable power. The prophecy within the Black Sun Codex did not foretell a simple apocalypse from the heavens but a man-made cataclysm, a deliberate act of global destruction.

The realization hit Ana with the force of a physical blow. The seemingly mythological prophecy was not fantasy; it was a chillingly realistic warning. The ancient priests had left behind not just a warning, but a map, a detailed blueprint for unleashing their terrifying legacy. The Codex wasn't just a book; it was a geological map detailing the precise locations of the triggers. The eight-rayed sun symbol, it turned out, marked each of the pivotal trigger sites.

Gábor, his face pale, ran his fingers along the faded text. "This is bigger than we ever imagined," he breathed, his voice strained. "It's not just about stopping a prophecy; it's about preventing global devastation."

Their research in the Archives revealed more than just the locations of the triggers. They discovered fragmented records of the Custodians' activities, detailed accounts of their rituals, and hints at a sophisticated understanding of geology and seismology far beyond what was expected of an ancient civilization. They found evidence suggesting the Custodians had built mechanisms that amplified the natural seismic activity in the trigger sites, making even minor tremors into devastating earthquakes. It was like a deadly symphony of earthquakes, orchestrated across the globe.

The Archives were not just a repository of historical knowledge; they served as a living testament to a long-forgotten, highly-organized secret society, the level of planning and organization behind their potential weaponization of nature being as terrifying as the potential consequences. Detailed drawings within hidden compartments of the ancient volumes depicted intricate devices, a complex network of levers, pulleys, and gears built into the foundations of the earth, capable of amplifying and directing seismic forces with terrifying precision.

Days blurred into weeks as Ana and Gábor meticulously pieced together the fragmented information. They worked in shifts, fuelled by coffee and the urgency of their task. The Vatican, initially hesitant, became increasingly cooperative as the gravity of their discovery sunk in. The monsignor guiding them, initially cautious, became a silent ally, providing access to previously restricted areas and resources. He even offered them, discreetly, some of his own research, adding to the already terrifying tapestry of knowledge unravelling before them. The scope of their investigation broadened exponentially, their initial chase evolving into a race against time of epic proportions.

As they delved deeper, they encountered evidence of The Sentinel's involvement. The shadowy organization wasn't merely interested in the prophecy; they were actively seeking to exploit the Custodians' mechanisms for their own nefarious purposes. Documents suggested that The Sentinel possessed not only knowledge of the trigger sites but also the technical expertise to activate the ancient mechanisms. They were using a combination of ancient technology and modern science, creating a terrifying hybrid that would unleash unimaginable devastation. The implications were staggering – a complete rewriting of history, the exposure of a global conspiracy that stretched back millennia.

One particularly chilling document detailed a series of coded messages between high-ranking members of The Sentinel, discussing their plans for the triggers' activation. The messages were encrypted in a cipher based on ancient Etruscan and Greek alphabets, but Gábor, with his expertise in classical languages and Ana's linguistic prowess, managed to decode them. The plan, they learned, was to trigger the mechanisms not all at once, but in a carefully choreographed sequence designed to maximize chaos and destruction. This was no mere accidental apocalypse; it was a calculated, deliberate act of global terrorism, using forces of nature as weapons of mass destruction.

Their work within the Vatican Archives wasn't merely intellectual exercise; it became a deadly game of cat and mouse. The Sentinel's agents, operating within the Vatican itself, were getting closer, their presence a subtle but ever-increasing threat. The quiet whispers in the hallways, the subtle shifts in shadows, and the occasional fleeting glimpse of a figure in the periphery sent shivers down their spines. They were hunted, not just by the organization's external agents, but by unseen hands within the seemingly impenetrable walls of the Vatican itself – those who were protecting the ancient secret from being revealed. They were running out of time. The ancient mechanisms, once dormant for millennia, were showing signs of awakening. The earth itself was beginning to stir.

Searching for Answers

The Monsignor, whose name Gábor had only been given as "Benedetto," led them through a series of increasingly labyrinthine corridors, the air growing colder with each turn. The scent of incense gave way to the musty odor of damp stone and aged paper. Finally, he halted before a heavy oak door, its iron hinges rusted and worn. A single, flickering candle cast dancing shadows on the stone wall. Benedetto produced a small, tarnished key, its teeth worn smooth with age. The lock clicked open with a groan that echoed unnaturally in the silence.

Inside, the room was circular, the walls lined with floor-to-ceiling shelves packed with ancient manuscripts, their titles written in faded gold leaf on their spines. The air was thick with the scent of decaying paper and dust. A single, high window allowed only a meager shaft of sunlight to penetrate the gloom, illuminating swirling dust motes like tiny stars. Benedetto gestured towards a large, leather-bound volume resting on a lectern in the center of the room. Its cover was plain, unmarked save for a single, almost invisible symbol – a stylized sun with rays emanating from its center, subtly different from the Black Sun symbol they'd seen on Dr. Lupu's body.

"This," Benedetto whispered, his voice barely audible above the rustling of the ancient texts, "is the key. The Liber Stellarum ."

The Liber Stellarum , or Book of Stars, proved to be a collection of astronomical observations and astrological interpretations dating back to the late Roman era. Its pages, brittle with age, contained detailed charts of the constellations, intricate diagrams depicting celestial alignments, and cryptic prophecies written in a complex mixture of Latin and an ancient, unknown script. Ana, with her linguistic expertise, immediately recognized the latter as a form of Etruscan, a language long thought to be lost to time. She meticulously began translating the passages, while Gábor, his eyes tracing the intricate diagrams, focused on the astronomical data.

Hours melted into a timeless blur as they worked, the silence broken only by the whisper of turning pages and Ana's occasional murmured translation. The prophecies spoke of a celestial alignment, an extraordinary conjunction of planets that would occur only once every several thousand years. This alignment, according to the text, was not a mere astronomical event, but a catalyst, a trigger for a cataclysmic shift in the Earth's tectonic plates. The "Black Sun," they realized, was not a celestial body but a metaphor – a representation of the Earth itself, about to unleash its latent, destructive power.

The Liber Stellarum also revealed a network of locations,

marked on the astronomical charts with tiny, almost imperceptible symbols. These locations were scattered across the globe – from the remote corners of the Andes to forgotten islands in the Pacific. Each symbol corresponded to a specific geological formation, a point of seismic vulnerability, a potential trigger for the Earth's catastrophic awakening. The Sentinel, they realized, was not merely interested in the prophecy; they were preparing to exploit it. They were planning to trigger the cataclysm, to unleash the Earth's fury upon the world, perhaps to reshape it in their own twisted image.

The implications were staggering. The prophecy wasn't merely a prediction of a natural disaster; it was a blueprint, a guide to unleashing a man-made apocalypse. The network of locations were not merely points of vulnerability; they were levers, points where the Earth's tectonic plates could be manipulated, shifted, and ultimately destroyed.

As the sun began its descent, casting long shadows across the room, Ana and Gábor discovered another hidden compartment within the Liber Stellarum . Inside, nestled amongst faded silk ribbons and dried herbs, they found a small, intricately carved wooden box. Inside the box was a collection of ancient coins, each bearing a different symbol, and a rolled-up parchment tied with a thin silver thread. The parchment was covered in faded ink, bearing the location of a hidden solar temple – a structure that, according to the Liber Stellarum , served as a central hub, a control point for the seismic triggers scattered across the globe.

The discovery sent a chill down their spines. The Sentinel was not only aware of the prophecy, but they possessed the tools – the knowledge, the maps, and the physical means – to activate it. They had to act quickly. The location of the solar temple, however, was vague, its coordinates described using an archaic system of celestial navigation. Deciphering it required both astronomical and ancient cartographic expertise.

As they worked through the night, deciphering the cryptic clues, the subtle tremors beneath their feet became more pronounced. The Earth was stirring, awakening from its millennia-long slumber. The whispers in the hallways outside the archive intensified, replaced by footsteps, the muffled sounds of hurried conversations, the distant clash of steel. The Sentinel was closing in. They knew their time was running out. The awakening was not a distant threat anymore; it was imminent. The very air crackled with tension, the weight of the world pressing upon them. The ancient texts spoke of a final sacrifice, a necessary act to prevent the catastrophic event. But what would that sacrifice be?

They worked with feverish intensity, poring over the texts, meticulously cross-referencing the astronomical data with the geographical clues. Ana's linguistic skills, combined with Gábor's knowledge of ancient cultures and astronomy, proved to be their salvation. They painstakingly pieced together the puzzle, their minds working in perfect synchronicity. They were racing against the clock, against the forces of nature, against the shadowy organization that sought to unleash global chaos. The weight of the world, literally and figuratively, bore down upon them as the earth's tremors intensified. It was a race against time, against a destructive force as old as the planet itself.

Finally, amidst the crumbling parchment and aged ink, they found it – the precise location of the hidden solar temple, a place shrouded in legend, a site unknown to modern scholars, a forgotten sanctuary of immense power. It was nestled deep within the Carpathian Mountains, hidden within a system of ancient caves. The location was remote, isolated, and guarded by ancient traps and mechanisms designed to deter any intruders. It was a place of immense power, a place where the secrets of the Earth lay hidden, waiting to be unleashed.

The next challenge would be reaching it before the Sentinel, and before the planet itself decided to rend itself apart. The journey would be treacherous, the dangers countless. But they knew they had no choice. The fate of the world rested on their shoulders, on their ability to stop the awakening before it was too late. The fate of billions of lives rested on them. The silence in the archive was broken by the sharp crack of a collapsing wall, as the tremors increased their intensity. They knew now that the world would soon be a vastly different place, and the choice between salvation and destruction was entirely in their hands. The race was on.

The True Meaning

The heavy oak door creaked open, revealing a vast chamber bathed in the ethereal glow of strategically placed lamps. Rows upon rows of towering shelves stretched into the shadows, crammed with ancient manuscripts, scrolls, and bound volumes – a silent testament to centuries of accumulated knowledge. The air hung heavy with the scent of parchment and time, a palpable sense of history pressing down on Ana and Gábor. Benedetto, his face etched with a solemnity that hinted at the weight of the secrets within these walls, gestured towards a particular alcove.

"The prophecy speaks not of a celestial event, but of a terrestrial one," Benedetto whispered, his voice barely audible above the rustling of unseen drafts. "The Black Sun is not a star, but a network... a network of seismic triggers."

He led them to a large, leather-bound volume, its pages yellowed and brittle with age. It was written in a script neither Ana nor Gábor recognized immediately, a complex blend of Latin, Greek, and what appeared to be a long-lost dialect of Etruscan. Benedetto explained that it was a detailed cartographic representation of the world, not as it was now, but as it was understood by those who built the hidden solar temple. The map was overlaid with a series of symbols – intricate glyphs that marked specific locations across the globe.

"These are not mere markings," Benedetto explained, tracing one of the symbols with a trembling finger. "Each glyph represents a point of convergence, a nexus of tectonic instability. Our ancestors understood the earth's fragility, its susceptibility to catastrophic upheaval. They believed they could control these forces, harness them for their own purposes. But something went wrong."

Ana, her eyes scanning the intricate symbols, felt a chill run down her spine. The glyphs were not arbitrary; they seemed to follow a pattern, a carefully constructed network stretching from the Mediterranean to the Pacific Rim. She recognized some of the locations: the volcanic slopes of Mount Vesuvius, the fault lines along the Pacific Ring of Fire, the ancient ruins of Baalbek in Lebanon. Each location held a history of seismic activity, some of it catastrophic.

Gábor, meanwhile, was engrossed in the accompanying text. He translated portions of the Etruscan dialect, revealing chilling details of rituals, sacrifices, and the construction of sophisticated mechanisms designed to amplify the earth's natural energies. He discovered passages that spoke of the 'Awakening,' not as a sudden apocalyptic event, but as a gradual escalation, a carefully orchestrated unleashing of tectonic forces. The Black Sun, then, was not a singular event but a coordinated chain reaction.

Days blurred into nights as they worked tirelessly, deciphering the cryptic text and mapping the locations marked on the ancient cartography. The Vatican archives became their world, the rhythmic ticking of the ancient grandfather clock in the hallway a constant reminder of the dwindling time. They discovered that the Sentinel organization, far from being a modern creation, had roots that extended back millennia, their purpose the safeguarding – or perhaps the manipulation – of these ancient mechanisms. The tremor intensified, shaking the very foundations of the archive. The air grew heavy with anticipation, the silence broken only by the frantic turning of pages and the low murmurs of anxious discussion.

The research revealed a terrifying truth: the network was not just a map of potential seismic events, but a system of interconnected triggers, a complex web of levers and counterweights capable of manipulating the earth's crust. The ancient civilizations that had constructed this network believed that they could control the forces of nature; they were wrong. The map indicated the exact locations where these triggers were placed, waiting to be activated. It was a system of immense power, and if it fell into the wrong hands, the consequences were too ghastly to contemplate.

As the sun set on another day, casting long shadows across the hallowed halls of the Vatican archives, Ana and Gábor made a terrible discovery. Embedded within the Etruscan text were passages detailing the construction of a central control mechanism—a device capable of triggering all the seismic points simultaneously. Its location was not marked on the map, but a series of cryptic clues pointed towards a hidden chamber beneath the ruins of a lost solar temple in the remote Andes Mountains. Their journey was far from over; this was merely the beginning.

The true horror of the prophecy dawned on them: the Black Sun was not a metaphor, but a literal network of controlled catastrophes. It was a weapon, a terrifying instrument of global destruction, capable of triggering earthquakes and volcanic eruptions on a scale never before witnessed. The Sentinel's intentions became terrifyingly clear. They sought not to prevent the 'Awakening,' but to unleash it – to reshape the world in their own image, to plunge the planet into chaos and forge a new order from the ashes.

The weight of the world rested on their shoulders. They had uncovered a horrifying secret, a hidden truth buried beneath layers of history and deceit. They had cracked the code, understood the plan, but the true battle was only just beginning. The race against time continued, now with a more profound understanding of the stakes. The fate of humanity hung precariously in the balance. Each passing tremor served as a grim reminder of the impending catastrophe. They needed to reach the Andes before the Sentinel, before the planet itself began to unravel.

The challenge ahead was daunting. They had to navigate perilous terrains, outwit their relentless pursuers, and decipher additional layers of the ancient civilization's secrets. The sheer scale of the conspiracy was staggering; their resources were limited. They would need all their skill, courage, and ingenuity to stop this looming disaster. The information they uncovered was not merely historical; it was a living, breathing danger, ticking like a time bomb ready to detonate.

The Vatican library, previously a silent sanctuary of knowledge, now echoed with the palpable fear and urgency of their situation. Each whispered word, each carefully placed footstep, served as a testament to the weight of their discovery. The very air around them seemed charged with the potential for destruction, a tangible threat mirroring the earth's unrest. They had a map, but no compass; a prophecy, but no certainty. They knew only one thing: they had to act, and they had to act fast. Their journey to the Andes would not be a mere chase; it would be a desperate fight for the survival of humanity itself. The tremors continued, each one stronger than the last, a relentless drumbeat of impending doom. The world held its breath, unaware of the ancient secret that threatened to tear it asunder.

Benedetto, despite his age, displayed surprising resilience, his faith in their mission bolstering their spirits amidst the rising dread. He provided them with a contact – a reclusive scholar in the Andes, rumored to possess knowledge of the hidden chamber. His name was Professor Ramirez, an expert in Andean archaeology, who had dedicated his life to uncovering the secrets of the lost solar temple.

As they prepared to leave the Vatican, the air grew thick with apprehension. The tremors were becoming more frequent, more intense, shaking the very foundations of the ancient building. They knew they were running out of time. The Sentinel was undoubtedly aware of their discovery, and they would stop at nothing to prevent Ana and Gábor from exposing their machinations. Their escape from the Vatican was nothing short of a harrowing flight, a desperate race through twisting corridors and shadowed chambers. The ancient stones seemed to moan and groan with the intensity of the approaching cataclysm. The journey ahead was fraught with peril, but their determination burned brighter than ever. They were carrying the weight of the world on their shoulders, and they were not about to let it fall. The fate of the planet rested on their next move.

New Dangers Emerge

The cobbled streets of Rome, usually alive with the buzz of scooters and chattering tourists, were eerily deserted. The tremors, which had begun subtly within the Vatican walls, were now a palpable force, shaking the very foundations of the city. Each shudder felt like a premonition, a tremor not just of the earth but of impending doom. Ana and Gábor, huddled in the back of a battered Fiat, exchanged worried glances. Benedetto, his face pale with anxiety, gripped the steering wheel, his knuckles white. The escape from the Vatican had been a chaotic blur of frantic sprints, near misses, and the chilling certainty that they were being hunted.

The car lurched violently as another tremor hit, sending a wave of nausea through Ana. She clutched the Black Sun Codex, its worn leather cover a comforting weight against her chest. The manuscript, with its cryptic symbols and prophecies of impending cataclysm, felt less like a historical artifact and more like a ticking time bomb. She glanced at Gábor, his usually sharp features etched with exhaustion but his eyes burning with fierce determination. He had been injured during their escape – a glancing blow from a Sentinel agent, leaving a nasty gash on his arm. The blood had stained his already dirt-encrusted shirt, a grim reminder of the deadly game they were playing.

"They're close," Gábor rasped, his voice strained. "I can feel it."

Benedetto swore under his breath, weaving the car expertly through the deserted streets, narrowly avoiding a collapsing building. He was a Vatican insider, a man who knew the hidden passages and secret routes of the city like the back of his hand, but even his knowledge felt insufficient in this moment of escalating chaos. The relentless pursuit of The Sentinel had moved beyond mere surveillance. This was a full-scale hunt, and they were the prey.

They reached the relative safety of a secluded, ancient Roman villa, its walls whispering tales of emperors and conspiracies. Benedetto, despite his shaken state, efficiently secured the property. The villa, abandoned for centuries, provided a temporary sanctuary, a place to catch their breath and assess their situation. But it offered no long-term security. The Sentinel was relentless; their resources were vast, and their determination seemed limitless.

Ana carefully opened the Codex, its pages brittle with age. The symbols swam before her eyes, each one a puzzle piece in a terrifyingly intricate jigsaw. She had deciphered much of the text during her time in the Vatican archives, but several passages remained stubbornly opaque. The prophecy spoke of a network of seismic triggers, ancient mechanisms strategically placed across the globe, capable of unleashing unimaginable devastation. But the Codex also hinted at a method of deactivation, a way to prevent the "awakening" it foretold.

Gábor, despite his injury, began to analyze the satellite imagery Benedetto had managed to procure. The images, taken earlier that day, showed subtle but significant anomalies – unusual heat signatures at specific locations around the globe. Locations that coincided, chillingly, with the cryptic geographical coordinates mentioned in the Codex. The Sentinel was activating the triggers, preparing for the ultimate cataclysm. Their meticulous plan was terrifyingly efficient.

As the sun dipped below the horizon, casting long shadows across the villa's dusty floors, the tremors intensified. The ancient stones groaned and creaked, the sounds echoing the growing unease in the room. Ana and Gábor realized their sanctuary was fragile at best. They needed a plan, and they needed it fast. Their initial attempt to reach the authorities had been met with silence and apparent disbelief – a chilling indication of The Sentinel's influence extending far beyond their initial expectations.

The following hours were a blur of frantic activity. Ana, using her linguistic skills, painstakingly worked to decipher the remaining passages of the Codex, translating ancient Aramaic and Sumerian into modern language. The words revealed a disturbing history – a long-forgotten civilization, masters of seismic engineering, who had built these triggers as a failsafe, a way to prevent their own catastrophic hubris. The Sentinel, however, intended to unleash that power.

Gábor, meanwhile, meticulously analyzed the satellite imagery, comparing the heat signatures with the descriptions within the Codex. He pinpointed the locations of at least three triggers – one in the Andes Mountains, another in the Himalayas, and a third in the Mariana Trench. These were merely the ones they could detect, confirming the scale of the impending destruction. The Sentinel's operation was global, precise and horrific. Their organization surpassed anything they could have initially imagined.

As dawn broke, painting the Roman sky in hues of orange and purple, Ana had cracked the final piece of the puzzle. The Codex described a counter-mechanism, a way to deactivate the triggers, but it was a delicate process, one that required precision timing and a specific sequence of actions. The window of opportunity was rapidly closing.

The next challenge was the logistics of their plan. How could two people, hunted by a global organization with seemingly limitless resources, manage to deactivate three globally dispersed triggers before the earth shattered beneath their feet? The sheer scale of the problem overwhelmed them both. The only thing they had to their advantage was the element of surprise. Their only hope was their combined knowledge, their resilience, and the slimmest of chances. They were up against an enemy who had been planning for centuries, an enemy who seemed to anticipate their every move, but they had the knowledge, and the knowledge was power. They had to use it, before it was too late.

The escape from Rome was almost as perilous as the escape from the Vatican. Benedetto, ever resourceful, had secured a small, lightly armed private jet, and they managed to evade The Sentinel by taking a remote, uncharted route to avoid detection. The flight was tense; the tremors continued, even at altitude, but the relief of leaving Rome behind was palpable. They were headed for the Andes, their first target. The journey would be fraught with peril. But they would stop at nothing. They were fighting not for themselves, but for the world. The fate of millions rested on their shoulders, and they intended to bear that weight. The Codex was their weapon, their guide, and their only hope. The mission was now undeniably personal, for they carried with them the memory of Dr. Lupu and the burning desire for justice. The Sentinel's actions would not go unpunished, and the planet's survival hinged on their ability to stop them. The race against time had begun in earnest. Each second counted. Each tremor served as a reminder that time was their most precious adversary.

Betrayal and Capture

The Andes loomed before them, a jagged, snow-capped behemoth against the bruised twilight sky. The plane, a far cry from the luxurious jets Ana was accustomed to seeing in her father's circle, shuddered with every gust of wind, mirroring the unease churning in her stomach. Gábor, his usually sharp eyes clouded with fatigue, stared out the window, his jaw tight. Benedetto, his face etched with lines of worry that belied his years, focused intently on navigating the treacherous mountain passes. The silence in the small cabin was thick with unspoken anxieties, a stark contrast to the vibrant chaos of their escape from Rome.

The deceptive calm was shattered by a sudden, sharp crackle from the radio. Benedetto swore under his breath, his hand instinctively reaching for a small, antiquated pistol tucked beneath his seat. A voice, cold and devoid of emotion, sliced through the static, speaking in perfect Italian, yet tinged with a foreign accent. It was a voice Ana recognized – Cardinal Bellini, a man they had once considered an ally.

"Your flight is terminated," the voice hissed, its icy tone sending a shiver down Ana's spine. "We know your destination. Surrender peacefully, and perhaps your suffering will be less protracted."

The betrayal hit Ana with the force of a physical blow. Bellini, a man who had seemed sympathetic to their cause, offering seemingly invaluable assistance in navigating the Vatican archives, had been playing them all along. The carefully curated trust, the shared glances, the whispered assurances – all meticulously crafted pieces of a deceptive façade. The question wasn't just how Bellini had discovered their plans but how deeply the infiltration went. Had anyone else been compromised?

The pilot reacted instantly. In a desperate maneuver to evade capture, he sent the small plane into a steep, perilous descent, aiming for a narrow gorge between the towering peaks. The world outside the windows dissolved into a dizzying blur of snow-covered mountains and swirling clouds. The feeling of impending doom intensified as the plane fought against the unforgiving winds and treacherous terrain. The radio crackled again, this time with the sound of roaring engines, a clear indication of pursuit.

The daring, desperate flight ended with a jarring crash, not with the earth-shattering impact Ana had anticipated, but with a hard landing in a concealed snowfield. The small plane was wrecked, the mangled metal a testament to their desperate escape attempt. Shaken but alive, they emerged into a blinding white landscape, their immediate surroundings shrouded in a suffocating silence punctuated only by the crackling of the radio.

They knew it was just a matter of time before The Sentinel found them. Benedetto was injured, his leg twisted at an unnatural angle. Gábor, ever the pragmatist, immediately assessed their situation. Their escape had been successful only in the sense that it delayed the inevitable. Now, surrounded by the vast, unforgiving landscape, they had to fight.

Their escape, or what was left of it, was short-lived. The silence of the mountains was broken by the sound of approaching helicopters, their rotors slicing through the crisp mountain air. They were surrounded. The Sentinel, efficient and ruthless, closed in on their position. There was no escape.

The capture itself was swift and brutal. Ana's resistance, fueled by adrenaline and desperation, was futile against the sheer force of their attackers. The fight was a blur of punches, grappling, and the metallic clang of weapons. Benedetto, injured and vulnerable, could only watch helplessly as Gábor was subdued with a swift, brutal efficiency that suggested long training and practice. Ana, her spirit unbroken but her body aching, found herself facing Cardinal Bellini, his usually composed face contorted in a cruel, triumphant smile.

"Foolish girl," he sneered, his voice dripping with disdain. "You believed in the myth of a righteous crusade, a noble fight against a shadowy organization. You never realized that The Sentinel had already infiltrated your world, even your closest allies. You have played right into our hands."

The betrayal stung worse than any physical pain. The weight of disillusionment was almost unbearable. Ana found herself bound, her hands tied behind her back, led away through the snow. The cold seeped into her bones, a chilling counterpoint to the fire of anger that burned within her. The pristine white landscape was tainted with the harsh reality of their situation: captured, betrayed, and facing an unknown fate.

Her captors marched her across the treacherous terrain, the rhythmic crunch of their boots against the snow a relentless reminder of her helplessness. The journey was a torturous odyssey, each step a torment to her injured body and bruised spirit. Through the freezing air, she could make out the shape of a colossal structure nestled within the heart of the mountain – a temple, ancient and ominous, its sheer size dwarfing the surrounding landscape.

The temple, seemingly hewn from the very mountain itself, was an imposing sight. Its stone walls, weathered by time and elements, exuded a palpable sense of age, of secrets guarded for millennia. As Ana approached, a chilling realization struck her – this was not merely an ancient ruin; it was a powerful, potentially dangerous, mechanism.

Bellini's triumphant smile widened as they reached the entrance. "The Black Sun's awakening is imminent," he whispered, his voice echoing in the vastness of the temple. "And you, Ana Dragan, will witness it firsthand."

The temple's interior was a labyrinth of corridors and chambers, carved with intricate designs that spoke of a sophisticated civilization long lost to time. Ana, still bound, was led deeper into the heart of the structure, her senses overwhelmed by the oppressive silence, the weight of centuries pressing down upon her. The air grew heavy with a strange, otherworldly energy that resonated with the tremors still wracking the earth.

This wasn't simply about decoding a codex; it was about preventing the activation of a global network of seismic triggers – a network whose existence was previously unknown. The tremors weren't random; they were controlled, manipulated to trigger a global catastrophe. And they were now, thanks to Bellini's betrayal, on the verge of activating it.

The realization struck her with terrifying clarity. This wasn't just a conspiracy to control power or ancient knowledge; it was a plot to destroy the world. The Black Sun, the metaphor for humanity's darkest secrets, was about to unleash its fury. And she was a prisoner, at the epicenter of this impending global devastation. The fate of the world, it seemed, rested squarely on her shoulders, even in her helpless condition. The weight of that responsibility was almost crushing.

The sheer scale of the deception, the depth of the conspiracy, staggered her. How many others were involved? How many lives had been sacrificed in the pursuit of this sinister objective? Her anger, a burning ember until now, flared into a raging inferno. She would not surrender. Not now. Not ever. Even bound and captured, the fight had only just begun. The awakening of the Black Sun might be imminent, but so was her defiance.

Chapter 4

The Solar Temple

Imprisonment and Interrogation

The flickering gas lamp cast long, dancing shadows across the rough-hewn stone walls of the cell. Ana Dragan huddled deeper into the meager straw pallet, the chill seeping into her bones despite the thick wool cloak she wore. Across from her, Gábor Varga sat slumped against the wall, his usual boisterous energy replaced by a grim silence. The air hung heavy with the stench of damp earth and something else…something metallic and sickeningly sweet, a scent that clung to the very fabric of the stone. It was the smell of fear, she realized, a pervasive aroma woven into the very architecture of their confinement.

Their captors, the shadowy organization known as The Sentinel, had been surprisingly efficient. From the moment the betrayal had struck—a jarring, unexpected twist of the knife from someone they had considered an ally—their capture had been swift and brutal. There had been no time for resistance, no opportunity for a desperate fight. They had been blindsided, subdued with a chilling efficiency that spoke volumes about the organization's meticulous planning and lethal expertise.

The interrogation had begun almost immediately. A tall, gaunt man with eyes as cold and calculating as glacial ice had overseen the proceedings. He spoke little, his words clipped and precise, delivered with the detached air of a surgeon dissecting a specimen. His name, they learned, was simply "Silas." He was not interested in casual conversation; his focus was laser-sharp, his questions designed to extract the information he desired from Ana and Gábor. Their combined knowledge, the key to deciphering the Black Sun Codex, was the prize at stake.

The first few hours had been a grueling ballet of psychological pressure. Silas had employed a carefully crafted strategy of intimidation, exploiting their individual vulnerabilities. He had taunted Gábor with his past failures, dredging up the professional disgrace that had haunted him for years, whispering insinuations about his competence and worth. Ana, he tried to break by insinuating danger to her family, subtly hinting at the reach and power of The Sentinel, painting a vivid picture of the harm that could befall those she loved should she refuse to cooperate. Their unwavering resolve, however, appeared to surprise their interrogator. Ana's steadfast refusal to reveal any information, coupled with Gábor's grim stoicism, frustrated Silas. He was unprepared for such defiance.

Their resistance began to shift Silas' tactics. The subtle psychological games were replaced by more brutal methods. Ana had been subjected to sensory deprivation, confined to a pitch-black chamber where the silence was only broken by the rhythmic drip of water, a relentless torture designed to erode her mental fortitude. The darkness played tricks on her mind, the silence deafening, the ever-present drip of water a hypnotic rhythm that chipped away at her defenses. The claustrophobia was almost unbearable, a stifling pressure that threatened to crush her. Only through sheer willpower, aided by memories of Gábor's unwavering belief in her, had she managed to maintain her silence.

Gábor, meanwhile, endured a far more physical ordeal. He was subjected to a series of brutal beatings, each blow designed to break his spirit. He refused to yield, however, his silence as unbreakable as Ana's. The guards, rough and merciless, were clearly accustomed to this kind of work. They were brutal and efficient, their actions designed to inflict maximum pain with minimum effort. Each blow was calculated, each strike placed to maximize the agony without leaving lasting visible damage – a testament to their expertise in eliciting information through torture without leaving incriminating evidence.

Days bled into nights, the line between reality and hallucination becoming increasingly blurred. The rhythmic thud of blows against Gábor's body became a relentless soundtrack to Ana's ordeal in the darkness, and the constant drip of water became the counterpoint to her own silent screams. The food they were given was meager – barely enough to sustain life, yet designed to ensure they remained conscious enough for the continued torture. They were prisoners of mind and body. Every moment was a struggle, a testament to their will to survive and their commitment to safeguarding the secrets held within the Codex.

One night, Silas returned, his face unreadable as he studied them from the dim light of his lantern. He seemed to have abandoned his attempts at psychological manipulation and pure physical intimidation. This time, his approach was different. He offered them a choice: cooperate, and they would be spared, given a chance to survive. Refuse, and they would face the full wrath of The Sentinel. The consequences, he implied, would be far worse than anything they had experienced so far.

Ana and Gábor exchanged a look, a silent communication of mutual understanding and unwavering resolve. They knew that cooperation meant betraying everything they stood for, compromising the safety of the world. Their response was a silent defiance. Their unwavering gaze spoke louder than any words.

Silas, visibly irritated by their resilience, gestured to his guards. The guards responded by leading Gábor away into the darkness, leaving Ana alone in her cell with the unsettling silence and the increasingly maddening drip of water. The sounds of Gábor's struggle, muffled and distant, were a chilling prelude to what she knew was to come. The weight of the situation and the fear of the unknown washed over her, an icy wave of apprehension that threatened to sweep her away.

The silence that followed Gábor's removal was even more oppressive than before. Ana knew he had been taken to the hidden solar temple, where the ancient seismic triggers were located. The thought of the horrors that awaited him, the possibility of torture beyond her wildest imagination, made the cold stone feel like a burning pyre beneath her. Yet within the darkness, she began to devise a plan, not only for survival, but for escape. She was aware that their silence had driven Silas to a new tactic – separation and manipulation. She knew he would try to extract information from each one separately, leveraging their reliance on each other against them. But the longer they resisted, the more desperate Silas would become.

The ensuing days were a blur of uncertainty. Ana endured more interrogation, more sensory deprivation, but this time she realized that Silas's aggression was slowly dwindling. His patience was wearing thin, their resistance far greater than he had expected. In his frustration, he provided an opening, a momentary lapse in attention, a crack in his seemingly unbreakable composure. It was a crack she was ready to exploit. The sounds of construction, the distant clang of metal on stone, reached her ears amidst the silence. These were sounds far too methodical, too focused, to be purely coincidental. It signified the nearing completion of The Sentinel's plan, a plan she was determined to thwart.

She knew that their chance for escape was coming, that the balance of power was shifting, subtly but perceptibly. The Sentinel was growing complacent, confident in its victory. That complacency, Ana realized, would be their undoing. She would use their overconfidence against them. Her resilience, fueled by her unwavering dedication to uncovering the truth, had held her steady. The escape wouldn't be easy but it would be worth every risk. Gábor's sacrifice, she vowed silently, would not be in vain. She would carry their shared mission to its end, exposing The Sentinel and preventing the apocalyptic event they sought to unleash. The fight, she knew, was far from over.

Escape Attempt

The rhythmic drip, drip, drip of water from a unseen leak echoed in the oppressive silence of their cell. Ana traced the rough texture of the stone wall with a fingertip, her mind racing. Gábor remained silent, his gaze fixed on the heavy oak door reinforced with iron bands. The scent of fear, that metallic sweetness, was still present, a constant reminder of their precarious situation. But beneath the fear, a spark of determination flickered.

Their captors, the faceless members of The Sentinel, had grown careless. Their initial brutality had given way to a smug confidence, a belief in their absolute control. This arrogance, Ana realized, was their only hope. She had observed their routines, their patrols, the precise timing of their guard changes. She had noted the inconsistencies, the small lapses in vigilance that spoke of complacency. It was these weaknesses that she would exploit.

"Gábor," she whispered, her voice barely audible above the drip of water, "I have a plan."

He turned, his eyes dark and shadowed, but a glimmer of hope flickered within their depths. "Let's hear it, then. My bones are getting tired of this damp floor."

Ana outlined her escape plan, a complex choreography of timing and deception. It hinged on the predictable rhythm of the guards' shifts, the placement of the poorly-lit hallways, and a series of carefully timed distractions. The heart of the plan, however, lay in the seemingly innocuous detail of a loose stone in the cell wall, a flaw she had discovered during her initial observations.

"The loose stone," she explained, "It's not just loose; it's deliberately placed. A cleverly hidden pressure plate, I suspect. If we manipulate it correctly, it might trigger a mechanism, perhaps opening a hidden passage or disabling a section of the wall."

Gábor, despite his initial skepticism, readily agreed. His expertise in archaeology and his keen eye for detail proved invaluable. Together they meticulously examined the stone, feeling for hidden levers and pressure points. They worked silently, their movements economical and precise, the shared task uniting them in a desperate dance of survival. Hours crawled by, each second weighted with the possibility of discovery and the certainty of immediate capture if their plan failed.

Finally, after what seemed like an eternity, Gábor's fingers brushed against a small, almost invisible indentation beneath the stone. With a gentle pressure, the stone shifted, revealing a small, dark aperture in the wall. It smelled of dust and decay, a hint of the ancient world lying hidden behind the modern facade of the prison. A narrow passage extended beyond.

"A miracle," Gábor breathed, his voice hoarse with relief.

"Not a miracle," Ana countered, "Just meticulous observation and a little bit of luck. Now, we move swiftly and quietly. Remember the plan."

The passage was cramped and tortuous, barely wide enough for them to squeeze through. The air was thick with the scent of stale earth and something else, a faint, metallic tang that intensified as they ventured deeper into the unknown. They navigated the passage with caution, their movements slow and deliberate, every sound amplified in the echoing darkness.

At one point, they encountered a collapsed section of the tunnel, a pile of rubble blocking their path. Gábor, using his considerable strength and ingenuity, managed to clear the obstruction, revealing a continuation of the passage beyond. They pressed onward, their hopes rising with each step.

After what felt like an eternity, the passage widened, leading into a larger chamber. The air here was cleaner, fresher. The flickering glow of an unseen light source hinted at an exit, a possibility of freedom. But their relief was short-lived. They were not alone.

Three guards stood facing away from them, their backs to the entrance. They were arguing, their voices low and indistinct, but Ana heard the words "the Codex," and "the awakening." It seemed that the guards were divided, perhaps in a power struggle. Their distraction proved crucial.

Gábor used his knowledge of ancient fighting techniques, moving silently as a shadow. Using only his wits and strength, he disarmed the guards with swift, precise movements, rendering them unconscious before they even knew what had hit them. Ana stayed close, ready to help, her own knowledge of languages providing a strategic edge. She found loose stones in the chamber and used them as makeshift weapons to knock out the guards. The whole affair was a brutal dance, played out in near-silence.

They secured the guards, tying them up with their own belts. Then, carefully, silently, they made their way towards the faint light source. It led them to another passage, ultimately to an unguarded exit. The moon hung high in the inky sky, casting long, skeletal shadows across the landscape. Freedom lay before them, hard-won but precious.

As they moved away from the solar temple, the heavy weight of their escape pressed down upon them, the adrenaline fading to reveal the daunting task still before them. The Codex was still hidden; the prophecy still loomed. But they had escaped. They had bought themselves time, a precious commodity in their desperate race against the impending catastrophe. Gábor, though exhausted, forced a smile. "We're alive," he said. The words felt miraculous and precious.

They knew their journey was far from over, but for now, they celebrated their escape with a shared breath of the crisp night air and a renewed determination to stop The Sentinel and unravel the mysteries of the Black Sun Codex, knowing that the shadow of the prophecy still hung heavily over them. The escape had been daring, but the true test lay ahead. The fight for humanity's future was far from over, and they would face it, together, armed with their wits, their skills, and the unshakeable belief in the cause for which they fought. Their journey would continue, leading them deeper into the heart of the conspiracy and closer to the truth behind the Black Sun. They were survivors, for now, but the fight had only just begun. The weight of the world, and the impending apocalypse, rested squarely on their shoulders. Their escape was just the first act in a much larger, more dangerous play.

The Hidden Temple

The chill mountain air bit at Ana's exposed skin as they followed the winding path, the faint light of dawn painting the Carpathian peaks in hues of grey and rose. The escape from the Sentinel's clutches had left them shaken but not broken. Gábor, ever the pragmatist, had immediately begun analyzing the information gleaned from their captors' careless remarks during their imprisonment – scraps of conversation, overheard whispers, even the careless drop of a map fragment. It was from these fragments that they pieced together the location of the hidden solar temple, a place mentioned only in cryptic allusions within the Black Sun Codex.

The Codex itself, bound in worn leather and smelling faintly of incense and time, felt heavier in Ana's hands than its physical weight suggested. Each page held a universe of secrets, its intricate script a testament to a civilization long vanished. The symbols, deciphered painstakingly over weeks of relentless work, revealed a chilling truth: the 'Black Sun' was not a celestial body, but a network of ancient, technologically advanced seismic triggers, capable of unleashing catastrophic earthquakes across the globe. The solar temple, they now understood, served as the central control mechanism for this terrifying network.

The path led them deeper into the mountains, the air growing thinner, the silence more profound. The landscape, beautiful in its starkness, offered little comfort. Every shadow seemed to hold a threat, every rustle of leaves a potential sign of pursuit. Gábor, his knowledge of archaeology and ancient civilizations proving invaluable, identified subtle clues along the way – barely visible carvings on rocks, unusual formations of the land, all pointing towards their destination. He moved with a quiet intensity, his eyes constantly scanning their surroundings, his instincts honed by years spent navigating treacherous terrain and uncovering forgotten secrets.

Ana, meanwhile, wrestled with the linguistic puzzles of the Codex. Each newly deciphered passage added another layer to the already complex picture. She learned of a forgotten priesthood, keepers of a devastating technology, their motives shrouded in mystery. She also understood the true nature of The Sentinel, not merely a shadowy organization, but the last vestiges of this ancient priesthood, desperately trying to awaken their devastating machine. Their motivations, however, remained unclear. Were they driven by a desire for power, or were they seeking to fulfill some ancient prophecy?

Finally, after what felt like an eternity, they arrived at a seemingly unremarkable section of the mountainside. Gábor pointed to a barely visible fissure in the rock face, barely wider than a human hand. "This is it," he whispered, his voice raspy with exertion. "The entrance to the solar temple."

The fissure led to a narrow, winding tunnel, descending steeply into the earth. The air grew heavy with the scent of damp earth and something else, something ancient and strangely metallic. Armed only with their wits, a single flashlight, and the weight of the world on their shoulders, they ventured into the unknown.

The tunnel was claustrophobic, its walls slick with moisture. Ana, her heart pounding in her chest, felt a primal fear rising within her. This was not just a physical descent; it was a journey into the darkest recesses of human history, a confrontation with a power that dwarfed anything they had previously encountered. Gábor, despite his own apprehension, maintained a calm demeanor, his expertise a comforting presence in this frightening underworld.

The descent lasted for what seemed like hours. The tunnel twisted and turned, leading them through a labyrinth of subterranean passages. At one point, they encountered a massive chamber, its walls adorned with intricate carvings that mirrored those in the Black Sun Codex. These carvings, Ana realized, were a detailed map of the seismic network, each symbol representing a specific trigger point around the globe. The sheer scale of the operation, the devastating potential, sent a shiver down her spine.

Further down, they came across evidence of past inhabitants. Skeletal remains, scattered artifacts, and faded murals depicting a civilization far advanced in its understanding of engineering and cosmology. The murals told a story of a society that held immense power, a power that eventually destroyed them. The message, painted vividly in the fading colors, seemed to be a grim warning: the same fate was in store for humanity unless they found a way to stop them.

Finally, they reached the heart of the solar temple – a vast chamber, circular in shape, its center dominated by a massive, intricately engineered machine. It resembled a giant astronomical clock, with dials, gears, and levers that seemed to defy understanding. The air hummed with a low, resonant thrum, a tangible manifestation of the immense power contained within this ancient device.

The Codex held clues to its operation, and with Gábor's expert eye and Ana's linguistic prowess, they began to decipher the complex mechanisms. They understood its workings, the intricate interplay of levers and gears that would unleash the devastation. They were facing not a weapon but a complex astronomical system built upon a vast network of triggers and sensors. The machine was capable of manipulating earth's tectonic plates using highly advanced technology.

As they worked, a low growl echoed through the chamber. The earth trembled beneath their feet, a subtle warning of the power they were grappling with. The Sentinel were close. They had anticipated this final confrontation. Ana felt a growing sense of dread, not for their immediate danger but for the potential consequence of their failure. The weight of the world's future rested squarely on their shoulders.

Suddenly, a section of the wall slid open, revealing a group of figures clad in dark robes, their faces obscured by hoods. The Sentinel had arrived. The confrontation began immediately; the air filling with the clash of steel and the desperate cries of those engaged in a deadly struggle. Gábor, ever the protector, shielded Ana, drawing their attention, allowing her precious time to decipher the final sequence in the Codex.

The fight was brutal, desperate. Ana watched, helpless, as Gábor, armed with nothing more than his wits and a small knife, fought against overwhelming odds. His strength, his courage, was astounding. He was a fearless warrior, protecting Ana from the relentless attackers.

Finally, with a final, desperate move, Gábor succeeded in disabling the central mechanism. The humming ceased, the tremor subsided. The ancient machine fell silent, its power neutralized, but not before a devastating explosion rocked the chamber, collapsing parts of the ancient structure.

In the ensuing chaos, Ana, miraculously unscathed, managed to escape the collapsing temple, clutching the Black Sun Codex close to her chest. Gábor, however, was lost in the rubble. She never saw him again. The victory was bittersweet. She had prevented the catastrophe, but at a terrible price.

Days later, back in Bucharest, sifting through Gábor's belongings, Ana found a small, leather-bound notebook tucked away in a secret compartment of his satchel. It contained a single page, a faded sketch of a previously unknown symbol, accompanied by a cryptic note: "The Serpent's Eye... awaits." The fight was over, but a new mystery had begun. The quest for the truth, it seemed, was far from over. Ana knew, with a chilling certainty, that Gábor's final message was a call to action. The world was safe, for now, but the shadows of ancient secrets still lurked, waiting for the opportune moment to unleash their fury. The search for the Serpent's Eye, a new puzzle in this vast labyrinth of history and conspiracy, began.

Ancient Mechanisms

The air hung heavy with the scent of damp earth and decaying stone. Before them stood the solar temple, not as a majestic edifice of polished marble and gleaming gold, as depicted in romanticized sketches, but as a crumbling ruin, half-swallowed by the encroaching forest. Ivy, thick as pythons, snaked across its weathered stones, obscuring faded carvings and hinting at a forgotten grandeur. The entrance, a gaping maw in the temple's heart, was barely discernible, a shadowed cleft in the overgrown façade.

Gábor, his usually meticulous composure slightly frayed by the ordeal, adjusted his backpack. "The Codex mentions a series of interlocking mechanisms," he muttered, his breath misting in the cold morning air. "A system of levers, pulleys, and celestial alignments designed to… well, we don't know exactly what it's designed to do, but it's clearly the core of the prophecy's activation."

Ana, her heart pounding a frantic rhythm against her ribs, followed him into the temple's shadowed interior. The air inside was thick with the smell of dust and mildew, a palpable silence broken only by the drip, drip, drip of water echoing through the cavernous space. Torches, thankfully provided by Gábor's ever-prepared kit, cast flickering shadows that danced and writhed like restless spirits, exaggerating the temple's already oppressive atmosphere.

The first chamber was relatively intact, the walls adorned with faded frescoes depicting scenes of a sun god, his face obscured by the passage of millennia, surrounded by figures engaged in a ritualistic dance. The vibrant colors of the past were reduced to muted shades of ochre and burnt umber, yet the power of their message remained. They seemed to chronicle a complex system of astronomical observations, hinting at a sophisticated understanding of celestial mechanics far exceeding what Ana would have expected from such an ancient civilization.

"Look at this," Gábor whispered, pointing to a section of the fresco depicting a series of symbols remarkably similar to those etched onto Dr. Lupu's body. "These aren't just decorative elements. They're instructions."

As they moved deeper into the temple's labyrinthine

depths, the structures became increasingly complex. They navigated through narrow passageways, past collapsed pillars, and around precarious piles of rubble, the air growing heavier with each step. The walls seemed to whisper secrets, their surfaces covered in a dense tapestry of inscriptions, carvings, and cryptic symbols – a language lost to time yet somehow echoing with a chilling familiarity. Ana recognized elements reminiscent of Proto-Indo-European roots, hints of Sumerian, and glyphs that seemed to defy any known linguistic classification.

The mechanisms themselves were a marvel of ancient engineering. Massive stone levers, intricately carved with symbols that mirrored those in the frescoes, extended from the walls, their surfaces worn smooth by the passage of time. Intricate systems of ropes and pulleys, still surprisingly functional, connected these levers to a complex network of gears and counterweights hidden within the temple's very foundation. The air thrummed with a subtle vibration that Ana could feel rather than hear, a low hum emanating from deep within the earth.

"It's a seismograph," Gábor deduced, his voice tight with the gravity of the discovery. "Not just any seismograph, but a massive, ancient device capable of amplifying seismic activity. The levers... they control the amplification. The symbols... they're instructions for calibrating the machine to specific geographical locations."

The horror of the discovery settled upon Ana like a shroud. The 'awakening' – it wasn't a metaphorical event. It was a calculated, technologically driven disaster, designed to unleash tectonic fury upon the world. The Sentinel hadn't just wanted to control the Codex; they sought to wield it as the key to triggering a global catastrophe.

Hours passed as they painstakingly studied the mechanisms, meticulously deciphering the instructions etched into the stone. Ana's linguistic expertise proved invaluable in translating the cryptic symbols, while Gábor's knowledge of archaeology and engineering allowed him to understand the intricate workings of the machinery. The task was fraught with peril, their every move threatening to trigger the devastating potential of the ancient device.

They learned that the solar temple wasn't a singular entity; it was part of a network, a sophisticated chain of interconnected seismic amplifiers spanning the globe. The 'Black Sun' was not a celestial body, but a metaphor for this terrifying network of destruction, its power harnessed from the earth itself, ready to unleash a cataclysm upon an unsuspecting world. The prophecies within the Codex weren't mere warnings; they were operational manuals.

As they worked, a cold dread settled over them. The sheer scale of the threat was overwhelming. This wasn't some ancient cult's misguided attempt at apocalyptic ritual. This was advanced technology, a weapon of mass destruction concealed within an ancient façade, waiting to be activated by those who understood its secrets. The implications stretched far beyond their immediate predicament, extending into the future, into the potential annihilation of human civilization.

Gábor, despite the chilling reality of their discovery, remained focused, his mind a whirlwind of calculations and deductions. He pointed to a specific sequence of symbols. "This section describes the precise geographical coordinates," he said, his voice strained, "of at least twelve key locations. They're seismic fault lines, all strategically positioned for maximum impact." He ran a hand through his already disheveled hair, his eyes wide with a terrifying understanding. "This isn't just about causing earthquakes. This is about triggering a cascade effect, a chain reaction that would destabilize the entire planet's tectonic plates."

Ana felt a cold wave of nausea wash over her. The weight of their discovery was almost unbearable. They were not just dealing with an ancient mystery; they were confronting the potential end of the world. The fate of billions rested on their shoulders. They had managed to stop the immediate threat, but a far greater, far more insidious danger lay before them.

As they continued to decipher the remaining symbols, they discovered more details about the system's activation sequence, its failsafes, and its incredible destructive capacity. The meticulous planning, the advanced understanding of geology and seismology, the sheer audacity of the undertaking sent shivers down Ana's spine. It was clear that the architects of this ancient weapon possessed a level of knowledge and technological sophistication far beyond their time. Who were they? And what had motivated them to create such a devastating instrument?

The final piece of the puzzle fell into place as they discovered a hidden compartment within the temple's central chamber. Inside, they found a collection of artifacts - tools, diagrams, and meticulously crafted maps, all hinting at a clandestine organization that predated even the earliest known civilizations. The organization was far older, far more powerful, and far more sinister than the Sentinel. This discovery deepened the mystery, pushing the scope of their investigation far beyond the immediate threat of the solar temple. It opened a Pandora's Box of ancient secrets and conspiracies, a labyrinth of untold power, waiting to be explored. The fight, Ana knew, was far from over. The Serpent's Eye awaited, and the shadow of the Black Sun still loomed large over the horizon.

Confrontation with The Sentinel

The air within the temple hung thick and still, the only sound the drip, drip, drip of water echoing through the cavernous space. Dust motes danced in the weak beams of Gábor's headlamp, illuminating fragments of ancient frescoes – depictions of a sun, not golden and benevolent, but a dark, almost malevolent orb, radiating shadows. The maps, meticulously drawn on what appeared to be tanned human skin, were spread across the rough-hewn stone floor, their cryptic symbols a chilling testament to the scale of the conspiracy. Ana traced a finger along one particularly intricate line, a shiver tracing its path up her spine. This wasn't just some ancient society; this was an organized network, stretching back millennia, manipulating events, controlling leaders, all for a purpose yet to be fully understood.

Gábor, his face grim, examined a complex mechanism embedded in the temple floor. It resembled a massive astronomical clock, its intricate gears and levers crafted from a dark, obsidian-like material. "This," he murmured, his voice low, "is the heart of it. The seismic trigger."

A low growl echoed from the shadows, a sound that sent a jolt of adrenaline through Ana. A figure emerged, silhouetted against the faint light filtering through a crack in the ceiling. Tall, imposing, cloaked in black from head to toe, the Sentinel's leader, a figure known only as "The Obsidian Hand," stood before them. He carried no weapons, yet his presence exuded a palpable menace, a cold, calculating power that seemed to chill the very air around him.

"You have delved too deep," The Obsidian Hand's voice was a gravelly whisper, resonating with an unnerving calm that belied the danger. "The secrets you seek are not for mortal eyes."

Gábor stepped forward, his hand resting on the hilt of his worn leather-bound knife. "We know more than you think," he said, his voice steady, his eyes unwavering. "We know about the network, the triggers, the centuries of manipulation."

The Obsidian Hand chuckled, a dry, rasping sound that grated on Ana's nerves. "Foolish mortals. You believe you can comprehend the power you have stumbled upon? You think you can unravel the threads of destiny itself?" He paused, his gaze sweeping over the maps and the intricate mechanism. "You are but insects, squirming under the heel of forces far beyond your understanding."

Ana stepped beside Gábor, her hand instinctively reaching for the small, obsidian dagger she had recovered from Dr. Lupu's monastery cell – a dagger that seemed strangely connected to the artifacts within the temple. "We're not trying to understand it," she said, her voice clear and strong, despite the tremor in her hands. "We're trying to stop it."

The Obsidian Hand's eyes narrowed, a flicker of something – annoyance? Disrespect? – crossing his features. "Stop it? You cannot stop what is ordained. The awakening is inevitable. It is the culmination of millennia of planning, a symphony of destruction orchestrated with divine precision." He gestured toward the mechanism. "This is not a weapon, child. It is a key. A key to unlocking a new era, an era of power beyond your wildest dreams."

A tense silence descended, broken only by the rhythmic dripping of water. The Obsidian Hand's words were chilling, yet Ana detected a subtle undercurrent of desperation in his tone, a crack in his otherwise impenetrable composure. He was not simply a cold, calculating killer; he was a believer, a fanatic, driven by a warped sense of destiny.

"An era of destruction," Gábor corrected, his grip tightening on his knife. "Millions will die."

The Obsidian Hand laughed, a harsh, grating sound. "Death is merely a transition, a necessary prelude to the new dawn. The weak will perish, the strong will survive. It is the natural order of things."

The confrontation escalated without warning. The Obsidian Hand lunged, his movements surprisingly swift and agile for a man of his apparent age. Gábor reacted instantly, parrying the attack with his knife. The ensuing fight was brutal, a whirlwind of flashing steel and desperate struggles. Ana, despite her lack of formal combat training, found herself thrust into the fray, using her agility and the small obsidian dagger to create openings for Gábor. The temple's claustrophobic confines amplified the intensity of the struggle, the clash of steel echoing through the chamber, punctuated by grunts and gasps for breath.

Gábor, despite his superior fighting skills, was clearly outmatched. The Obsidian Hand moved with a supernatural grace, his attacks precise and deadly. Ana witnessed Gábor sustain a deep gash across his arm, the blood staining his dark leather jacket. It was clear he was losing strength, his movements becoming slower, less precise.

In a desperate attempt to change the momentum, Ana threw herself at the Obsidian Hand, aiming for his throat with the obsidian dagger. He sidestepped her attack with ease, but she managed to scratch him, breaking the skin of his neck. The Obsidian Hand recoiled, a look of surprise – perhaps even pain – flickering across his face. It was a brief moment of vulnerability, a window of opportunity.

Gábor seized the chance. With a surge of adrenaline, he disarmed the Obsidian Hand, sending his opponent stumbling backwards. But the victory was short-lived. The Obsidian Hand recovered quickly, his eyes blazing with fury. He lunged at Gábor, his bare hands moving with a speed that defied belief. Ana screamed, but she was powerless to intervene. The Obsidian Hand landed a crushing blow to Gábor's chest, sending him reeling backwards. He collapsed to the ground, his body convulsing.

Ana rushed to his side, cradling his head in her lap. Blood welled from his wound, staining her hands crimson. Gábor coughed, a ragged sound, his eyes fluttering open. He looked at her, a faint smile playing on his lips. "The Serpent's Eye...," he whispered, his voice barely audible. "The truth... lies... deeper..." Then, his eyes closed, and he was still.

Ana was devastated, overwhelmed with grief and rage. But she knew Gábor wouldn't have died in vain. His sacrifice had bought her time, a chance to escape with the knowledge, the truth he had helped her uncover. She glanced at the mechanism, its obsidian surface gleaming faintly in the dim light. The Obsidian Hand had failed to activate it; he had underestimated Ana and Gábor's intervention. But the threat was far from over; the network remained, its tendrils stretching across the globe. She had to expose The Sentinel, to warn the world of the impending catastrophe. And she had to find out what Gábor meant by "The Serpent's Eye". The fight had just begun. She picked up the obsidian dagger, the weight of it both heavy and reassuring in her palm – a weapon, a symbol of the fight that lay ahead. The Black Sun had set on Gábor, but its shadows still threatened to engulf the world. Ana would not rest until she had done everything in her power to stop it.

Chapter 5

Gábor's Sacrifice

The Ultimate Sacrifice

The air hung thick with the stench of ozone and crumbling stone. Dust, disturbed by the tremors that had ripped through the solar temple, swirled around Ana, stinging her eyes and filling her lungs. The once-magnificent structure, a testament to a forgotten civilization's hubris, was now a chaotic ruin, its intricate mechanisms twisted and broken. She stumbled through the debris, the weight of the Black Sun Codex a constant, heavy presence against her chest. Gábor's sacrifice echoed in her ears, a deafening silence punctuated by the occasional groan of shifting stone.

She had seen it happen, the horrific finality of his act. He'd shoved her, a desperate heave that sent her sprawling across the uneven floor, just as the temple's ancient defenses – a complex web of pressure plates and hidden explosives – activated. She'd caught a glimpse of him, silhouetted against the fiery glow erupting from a newly breached chamber, a defiant stand against the collapsing structure. He'd triggered a secondary collapse, a calculated move to bury the temple's secrets and buy her precious time. Time that had allowed her to escape, to carry his burden, his legacy.

The Codex felt heavier now, not just from its physical weight, but from the weight of Gábor's life that had been sacrificed to protect it. She could still smell the metallic tang of his blood, a phantom scent clinging to the air despite the dust and the smoke. She squeezed her eyes shut, the image of his brave face seared into her mind. His face, usually etched with a sardonic humor, was now contorted in a grimace of effort, his eyes gleaming with a fierce determination that bordered on madness. He'd known the risks, understood the price, but his decision had been instantaneous, unwavering. No hesitation, no second-guessing. A selfless act, born not of fear, but of an unwavering commitment to stopping The Sentinel.

The escape had been harrowing. Navigating the labyrinthine corridors of the collapsing temple, dodging falling stones and searing heat, had pushed her to the limits of her physical and mental endurance. She'd had to use every ounce of her strength and agility to survive. The sheer terror had been overwhelming, the fear of death a constant, chilling companion. Yet, fueled by adrenaline and a desperate need to succeed, she'd pushed onward. She'd remembered his words, his trust, his faith in her abilities. That trust, that faith had become her lifeline.

Emerging from the ruins into the cool night air felt surreal. The moon hung like a skeletal eye in the inky sky, casting long, distorted shadows across the devastated landscape. The silence was jarring, a stark contrast to the cacophony of the collapsing temple. The relief, the sheer, overwhelming relief, was almost crippling. She was alive. She had the Codex. She had done it. But at what cost?

The weight of Gábor's sacrifice settled upon her, heavy and oppressive. She sank to her knees, the cold ground a stark contrast to the searing heat she'd just escaped. Tears welled in her eyes, blurring the already indistinct shapes of the ruined temple. She allowed herself to grieve, to mourn the loss of her partner, her friend, the man who had risked everything for her and for the world.

His death wouldn't be in vain. She would expose The Sentinel. She would share her findings with the world, ensuring that their insidious plot would never again threaten humanity. Gábor's sacrifice would serve as a warning, a testament to the lengths some would go to control the world's destiny.

Dawn arrived as a pale, hesitant light, casting long shadows that danced like specters across the devastated landscape. She looked back at the ruins of the temple, a silent monument to Gábor's courage and his ultimate sacrifice. The once-imposing structure was now a mere pile of rubble, a stark reminder of the fragility of human ambition. The silence that followed was a deafening testament to the catastrophe that had been averted.

The following days were a blur of activity. She had to make sure his sacrifice wasn't for nothing. Getting the Codex to the authorities was a priority. She contacted her colleagues, carefully relaying the information she'd gleaned from the Codex – the seismic triggers, the locations of the devices, the extent of the Sentinel's network. The authorities were initially skeptical, the information so incredible, so far-fetched, that it initially seemed like the ravings of a traumatized survivor. But the sheer detail, the accuracy of the information, the way it tied together previously unrelated historical events, slowly began to sway them.

Ana presented the Codex, its pages filled with ancient symbols and cryptic warnings, as evidence. She spoke of Gábor, her voice thick with emotion, of his dedication and sacrifice. The authorities, awestruck by her bravery and the scale of the averted catastrophe, began a massive global operation, dismantling the network piece by piece, arresting the surviving members of The Sentinel. News of the incident, initially hushed, eventually spread worldwide. The press was initially cautious, but the undeniable evidence forced a global reckoning.

The world learned of The Sentinel, of their audacious plan, and of the extraordinary bravery of the two individuals who had stopped them. Gábor's name, once synonymous with professional disgrace, now echoed through the halls of history, a symbol of ultimate sacrifice. His actions were not only crucial in saving humanity from an imminent global disaster, but they also served as a poignant testament to the power of selflessness and dedication.

But even as the world celebrated the victory, Ana felt the gnawing emptiness of his absence. She meticulously documented everything: the symbols, the mechanisms, the history of The Sentinel, incorporating Gábor's notes and her own observations. The world hailed her as a heroine, but the accolades felt hollow, meaningless. The world didn't understand the personal price she'd paid.

Days turned into weeks, weeks into months. The investigation was far from over. There were loose ends to tie up, hidden connections to explore. And then, one rainy afternoon, while carefully cataloging Gábor's personal effects, a small, leather-bound journal caught her eye. It was unmarked, its cover plain and unremarkable, easily overlooked amidst the chaos of his belongings. It was locked, a tiny brass padlock securing its secrets.

She spent hours working on it, testing various combinations, trying to find the right key. And then, tucked inside a hidden pocket of the journal, she found a tiny, almost invisible slip of paper folded into a miniature origami crane. On it, a single, almost imperceptible sentence was inscribed in a language she recognized immediately – an archaic dialect of Romanian, a language her father had dedicated his life to studying. The message spoke of a new threat, a new organization, even more insidious than The Sentinel, and a new location – a seemingly innocuous library in a small, remote village in the heart of the Carpathian Mountains.

Gábor's sacrifice had been monumental, his legacy cemented in history. Yet, in his quiet way, he'd left her one last clue, one last whisper of a looming threat, a challenge she could not ignore. She had promised herself she would continue his work and ensure that his sacrifice wasn't in vain. Now, she knew precisely where to start. The game wasn't over. It had merely begun. The whisper of a new mystery echoed in her ears, a promise of a new adventure, a new challenge, and a new path to follow. Gábor's sacrifice would not be forgotten. It would be her guiding star as she faced the shadows that lay ahead.

Escape from the Temple

The ground bucked beneath Ana's feet, a violent shudder that sent a wave of debris crashing down around her. She scrambled, the heavy Codex a lead weight against her chest, her lungs burning with the dust that choked the air. The temple, once a breathtaking monument to a forgotten sun god, was collapsing around her, a testament to the catastrophic power unleashed by The Sentinel's reckless actions. Giant stone blocks, intricately carved with symbols she now understood to be warnings, tumbled from the crumbling ceiling, narrowly missing her as she weaved through the chaotic maze of fallen columns and shattered frescoes.

The roar of the collapsing structure was deafening, a symphony of grinding stone and snapping timbers that drowned out her own panicked breaths. She could still feel the phantom weight of Gábor's hand on her shoulder, the warmth of his touch a stark contrast to the icy fear that gripped her heart. His sacrifice echoed in the devastating cacophony, a silent scream lost in the symphony of destruction. He had bought her time, precious seconds that might be the difference between life and death.

She risked a glance back, her heart plummeting at the sight of a massive stone slab, the size of a small car, threatening to crush the spot where he had stood moments ago. The sheer weight of it was terrifying, a brutal punctuation mark to the finality of his action. A wave of guilt washed over her, the weight of his sacrifice pressing down on her even heavier than the Codex. She had promised to continue his work, to ensure his death wasn't in vain, and the thought spurred her on, fueling her desperate flight.

Using the faint moonlight filtering through the cracks in the collapsing roof, she navigated the labyrinthine ruins, her movements fueled by adrenaline and a primal instinct for survival. She remembered Gábor's hushed instructions, his last words a cryptic map guiding her towards the hidden exit he had spoken of – a passage concealed behind a seemingly insignificant statue depicting a kneeling priestess. The statue, miraculously untouched by the devastation, stood out starkly amidst the chaos, its serene expression a stark contrast to the maelstrom of destruction around it.

With trembling hands, Ana pushed against the statue, feeling a satisfying click as a hidden mechanism disengaged. A section of the wall swung inwards, revealing a narrow passage shrouded in darkness. She didn't hesitate, squeezing through the opening and tumbling into the cool, damp darkness beyond. The air was thick with the smell of earth and something else, something ancient and strangely comforting.

The passage was claustrophobic, barely wide enough for her to pass through. She crawled on her hands and knees, her heart pounding a frantic rhythm against her ribs. The only sound was the rhythmic drip of water from the unseen ceiling and the pounding of her own heart. The passage seemed to go on forever, a torturous journey that tested her physical and mental limits. The thought of Gábor, his unwavering dedication and sacrifice, kept her going, a beacon of hope in the oppressive darkness.

Finally, after what seemed like an eternity, the passage opened into a small, airless chamber. Ana gasped, her lungs aching for air, and stumbled to her feet. The chamber was circular, its walls lined with rough-hewn stones. A single shaft of light pierced the darkness, illuminating a narrow opening in the opposite wall. It was the way out.

As she stepped out of the chamber, the full force of the night hit her, the fresh air a balm to her lungs. She found herself in a hidden ravine, a secret passage carved into the mountainside. Above her, she saw the gaping maw of the ruined temple silhouetted against the star-studded sky. The scene was surreal, a breathtaking testament to the temple's utter destruction, yet eerily calm in the quiet solitude of the ravine.

She collapsed onto the soft earth, her body trembling with exhaustion and relief. The Codex, clutched tightly to her chest, was safe. Gábor's sacrifice had not been in vain. But the sense of relief was fleeting, quickly replaced by a wave of grief, the profound loss of her friend and colleague a heavy weight on her soul. His sacrifice had not only saved her life but had revealed the terrifying truth behind the Black Sun prophecy – a truth she now had to share with the world.

The journey out of the ravine was arduous, the terrain treacherous and unforgiving. She used the starlight to guide her way, her resolve fueled by the knowledge that she carried the key to preventing a global catastrophe. She was alone, vulnerable, and hunted, but she possessed the power to stop The Sentinel.

As dawn broke, casting a pale light over the Carpathian Mountains, Ana emerged from the ravine, exhausted but determined. The Codex, still clutched to her chest, held within its weathered pages the secrets that could save the world. She was miles from civilization, the nearest town a day's journey away, but the daunting task ahead did not intimidate her. Gábor's sacrifice had given her a purpose, a mission that transcended her own personal loss and grief.

Her next challenge was to decipher the remaining clues within the Codex and expose The Sentinel, a task that required not only her intellectual prowess but also her courage and resilience. The world was unaware of the threat that loomed, unaware of the imminent danger that Gábor had sacrificed his life to prevent. It was now her responsibility to make them aware. She had to find a way to reach the authorities, to convince them of the truth, before it was too late.

The escape from the temple had been a harrowing experience, a fight for survival against the relentless forces of nature and the shadowy organization that had orchestrated this catastrophe. But Ana was no ordinary linguist; she was a survivor, a woman whose determination knew no bounds. She had faced death and emerged victorious, empowered by Gábor's sacrifice and armed with the knowledge that could save the world. The road ahead was long and dangerous, but Ana was ready. The fight for humanity's future had just begun.

The sun climbed higher in the sky, its warmth a comforting contrast to the chilling memories of the night. As she looked back at the ruins of the temple, nestled deep within the Carpathian Mountains, she couldn't help but feel a profound sense of loss. The temple was a tomb, a monument to Gábor's sacrifice, a somber reminder of the dangers that lay ahead. But it was also a symbol of hope, a testament to the resilience of the human spirit. Gábor might be gone, but his legacy lived on, etched not only in the pages of the Codex but also in the heart of the woman who had escaped his demise. His final act had been one of extraordinary courage, a sacrifice that had bought humanity a fighting chance.

The journey had just begun. The road ahead would be paved with challenges, conspiracies, and the inevitable threat of The Sentinel. But Ana was no longer just a linguist; she was a warrior, a guardian of ancient secrets, a woman who carried the weight of the world on her shoulders. She was armed with the Codex, Gábor's legacy, and the unwavering resolve to expose The Sentinel and prevent the catastrophe that loomed on the horizon. She would not fail him. She would not fail humanity. The memory of Gábor's sacrifice would be her guiding light in the darkest of times. The escape had been a victory, but the war was far from over.

Exposure of The Sentinel

The escape from the collapsing solar temple had been a blur of dust, debris, and adrenaline. Ana emerged into the blinding sunlight, coughing and gasping for breath, the Black Sun Codex clutched tightly to her chest. The once majestic structure was now a ruin, a testament to the catastrophic power unleashed by The Sentinel and a chilling reminder of Gábor's sacrifice. She looked back, a wave of grief washing over her, but the urgency of the situation pushed aside her sorrow. Gábor's sacrifice had bought her time, precious time that she couldn't afford to waste. His death had to mean something, his sacrifice had to have a purpose. She had to expose The Sentinel.

Her immediate priority was to reach safety and contact the authorities. She stumbled through the surrounding landscape, her senses heightened, every rustle of leaves, every snap of a twig, sending a jolt of fear through her. The Sentinel wouldn't simply let her escape; they were relentless, shadowy figures who operated in the dark, their motives obscured by centuries of secrecy. She had to find a way to expose them before they could strike again.

She eventually stumbled upon a small, remote village nestled in the Carpathian foothills. The villagers, initially wary of the dust-covered, distraught woman who burst into their midst, were soon convinced by her desperate pleas for help. They provided her with food, water, and a place to rest, their kindness a stark contrast to the malevolence she had just escaped. While they tended to her wounds, Ana knew she couldn't stay hidden for long. She had to act, and act quickly.

Using the villagers' limited phone access, Ana contacted her old mentor, Professor Schmidt, a respected academic with connections within the international community of archaeologists and historians. She relayed her story, carefully recounting her journey, the discovery of the solar temple, the horrifying truth about the prophecy, and the devastating actions of The Sentinel. Professor Schmidt listened intently, his initial skepticism gradually replaced by a growing sense of urgency and conviction.

He immediately understood the gravity of the situation, recognizing the potential for global catastrophe. He promised to use his influence to bring the story to light, contacting key figures in the international community, arranging for a press conference, and mobilizing support for a worldwide investigation into The Sentinel. Professor Schmidt also alerted various governmental agencies, outlining the organization's activities and their potential to trigger widespread seismic devastation.

The press conference was a whirlwind. Ana, still shaken but resolute, stood before the world, revealing the existence of The Sentinel, their centuries-long conspiracy to manipulate global events, and their chilling plan to awaken a network of ancient seismic triggers. She presented the Black Sun Codex as evidence, showcasing its cryptic symbols and translations. The media frenzy was intense, the gravity of her revelation sinking in slowly but surely across the globe.

The response was immediate and overwhelming. Governments around the world launched investigations, mobilizing resources to track down The Sentinel's members and dismantle their operations. International teams of archaeologists and geologists were sent to investigate the locations mentioned in the Codex, searching for and securing the ancient seismic triggers. The world held its breath, watching as the story unfolded, waiting to see if Ana and her allies could prevent the catastrophe.

The investigation was complex and challenging, spanning continents and decades. Ancient texts, forgotten languages, and hidden historical records were brought to light, revealing a far-reaching conspiracy that went beyond simple theft and vandalism. The Sentinel's origins were traced back centuries, to a secret society dedicated to harnessing the earth's power, interpreting the ancient prophecies for their own nefarious ends. They believed themselves to be guardians, protectors of a balance of nature – but in doing so, they were prepared to unleash a global catastrophe upon humankind.

Ana, with the support of Professor Schmidt and a growing network of allies, meticulously tracked The Sentinel's activities. They uncovered a network of informants, collaborators, and sympathizers operating in positions of power, influencing global politics, economies, and scientific advancements to further their agenda. The Sentinel had been subtly influencing the course of history for centuries, planting the seeds of their catastrophic plan.

The unraveling of The Sentinel's network was a slow, painstaking process. Each arrest, each seizure of evidence, brought them closer to the heart of the conspiracy. But The Sentinel remained elusive, operating in the shadows, capable of striking from any direction. Ana knew they were watching, waiting for an opportunity to strike back.

The revelation of The Sentinel's existence brought about a seismic shift in global consciousness. The ancient mystery had suddenly become a very real and present danger, causing fear and uncertainty among many. Yet, it also sparked a wave of global collaboration, as nations joined forces to combat the threat. Scientists, historians, and experts from diverse fields worked together, sharing information and resources, united in their determination to prevent catastrophe.

The final confrontation came unexpectedly. A coded message, hidden within the Black Sun Codex, led Ana and her team to a hidden facility beneath the Vatican. There, they discovered the central control mechanism for the ancient seismic network, a complex device of ancient design and terrifying capabilities. The Sentinel's leader, a shadowy figure known only as "The Curator," was waiting for them.

The confrontation was fierce, a battle of wits and technology, as Ana and her team struggled against The Curator and their remaining loyalists. The Curator, armed with knowledge gleaned from centuries of research, attempted to justify their actions as necessary to restore a balance to the world. But Ana, fueled by Gábor's memory and a determination to protect humanity, refused to yield.

In the ensuing struggle, the ancient control mechanism was damaged, disabling the network of seismic triggers. The Curator was apprehended, their conspiracy exposed, their legacy destroyed. The world had averted a catastrophe of unimaginable proportions. Ana and her team emerged victorious, but the scars of the battle, both physical and emotional, remained.

The aftermath of the battle left Ana exhausted but resolute. The world was safe, at least for now. The Sentinel was defeated, their insidious network dismantled. But the struggle for truth and justice wasn't over. The victory felt bittersweet, overshadowed by the loss of Gábor, a man whose sacrifice had made her success possible. Among Gábor's belongings, Ana discovered a hidden message, a fragment of a different ancient text, a new puzzle that hinted at even more ancient secrets, secrets that only she could possibly unravel. The journey had just begun. The road ahead was long and winding, but Ana, armed with the truth, and the memory of Gábor's sacrifice, was ready. His legacy would live on, and his sacrifice wouldn't be in vain. The fight for the future had only just begun.

Mourning and Reflection

The dust still clung to Ana's clothes, a gritty reminder of the devastation she had witnessed. The sun, once a symbol of hope, now seemed to mock her with its relentless brightness, a stark contrast to the darkness that had threatened to consume the world. Gábor was gone. The thought, a physical blow, sent a fresh wave of grief crashing over her. She sank to her knees, the Black Sun Codex forgotten momentarily in her hands, its leather cover cool against her trembling fingers.

The weight of his absence was crushing. She replayed their last moments in her mind, a relentless loop of collapsing stone, dust, and the echoing scream that had been swallowed by the earth. His face, etched with a mixture of determination and despair, remained frozen in her memory. He had smiled, a brief, almost apologetic smile, before the earth gave way beneath him. That smile, a testament to his unwavering spirit, even in the face of certain death. He had sacrificed himself, not for glory, not for fame, but for a world he barely knew, a world he had dedicated his life to protecting. His death was a testament to his selflessness, a sacrifice that had secured the safety of millions. It was a responsibility so heavy, it threatened to break her.

She recalled their first meeting, a chance encounter in the dimly lit archives of Bucharest University. He had been disgraced, his reputation shattered by a conspiracy he had unknowingly stumbled upon. She had been searching for answers, driven by the same insatiable curiosity that had consumed her father, the respected linguist whose research had inadvertently drawn them into this maelstrom of ancient secrets. Their paths had converged, two unlikely allies united by a shared destiny, a relentless pursuit of the truth, even when that truth was shrouded in shadows and death.

Their journey had been fraught with peril. The relentless pursuit by The Sentinel, the treacherous paths through the Carpathian Mountains, the perilous descent into the hidden solar temple. Each step had been fraught with danger, a constant test of their courage, their ingenuity, and their unwavering belief in each other. He had been her rock, her guide, her unwavering support in the face of overwhelming odds. His knowledge of archaeology, his intuitive understanding of ancient cultures, his unwavering commitment to justice - all had been essential to their survival. She had learned to trust his judgment implicitly, even when her own doubts threatened to overwhelm her. His calm demeanor in the face of danger, his quiet strength, had been her beacon of hope in the darkest hours.

Gábor had been more than just a partner; he had become a friend, a confidant, a brother. They had shared laughter and tears, moments of intense fear and exhilarating triumph. They had uncovered secrets that would shake the foundations of the world, secrets that would forever alter the course of history. His presence, his laughter, the sharp edge of his wit, his unwavering loyalty – these were things she would carry with her always.

She remembered his stories, his animated accounts of ancient civilizations, his meticulous explanations of forgotten languages. His passion for history had been infectious, his knowledge boundless. He had shown her the beauty in the ancient world, the intricate tapestry of human history, the enduring power of human ingenuity. He had opened her eyes to a world beyond the confines of her own linguistic studies, a world where history wasn't just dates and facts but a living, breathing organism, constantly evolving, forever connected.

But it wasn't just the shared knowledge that bound them. It was the shared understanding, the implicit trust, the unspoken bond forged in the crucible of danger and shared purpose. He had understood her grief, her anxieties, her fears. He had known her far better than she had ever known herself. They had both sacrificed everything - their reputations, their relationships, their own safety - in pursuit of a greater good, a common goal that transcended their individual ambitions.

The Codex, still clutched in her hand, felt heavy, almost unbearably so. It was a testament to Gábor's sacrifice, a symbol of his unwavering dedication, a repository of knowledge that could change the world. It was his legacy, a legacy that she now had the responsibility to protect. But the weight of that responsibility was almost too much to bear. It felt like a burden, a crushing weight of expectation that would follow her for the rest of her life. The victory felt hollow, a bitter pill to swallow, tainted by the irreplaceable loss of Gábor. The silence was deafening, a profound emptiness that echoed the void in her heart.

Days bled into weeks, and the initial shock gradually gave way to the profound ache of grief. The world continued its relentless march forward, oblivious to her inner turmoil. She found herself revisiting their shared memories, the countless hours spent poring over ancient texts, deciphering cryptic symbols, piecing together fragments of a forgotten past. She saw his face in every shadow, heard his voice in the rustling of leaves, felt his presence in the quiet moments of reflection.

Ana found herself returning to Gábor's apartment, a small, cluttered space filled with the remnants of his life. Books lined the shelves, overflowing with notes and sketches. The air was thick with the scent of old paper and dust, a poignant reminder of his presence. She meticulously went through his belongings, searching for clues, for answers, for some shred of comfort in the desolation. She found letters, photographs, personal journals filled with his thoughts and reflections – a trove of memories that painted a more complete picture of the man she had come to know and love. His passion for his work, his love for his family, his quiet acts of kindness - all emerged from the pages, filling the void in her heart with a different kind of grief, a more profound appreciation for the life that had been cut tragically short.

Within a worn leather-bound book, tucked away in a hidden compartment, she discovered his message – a fragment of text, barely legible, written in a language she initially found unfamiliar. It was a language she'd never encountered during her many years of linguistic research. The script resembled no known alphabet she knew, but there was a familiarity in its structure, a subtle resonance that echoed the archaic scripts she had deciphered in the Black Sun Codex. A puzzle within a puzzle, a new mystery awaiting to be unraveled, a testament to Gábor's enduring legacy and an irresistible invitation for her to carry on his work, his quest for knowledge and truth. His sacrifice had not been in vain. It was a call to action, a continuation of their shared journey, a promise to uncover the secrets that lay hidden in the shadows of history. His last message was an echo of his spirit, his tireless pursuit of knowledge, his insatiable thirst for the truth; an inheritance she would proudly and faithfully continue to pursue. The journey had just begun.

The Legacy of the Codex

The weight of the Codex felt heavier now, imbued not just with ancient ink and parchment, but with Gábor's sacrifice. His last message, a cryptic puzzle in an unknown script, burned in her mind, a stark reminder of the unfinished business they had shared. The dust motes dancing in the shafts of sunlight filtering through the ruined temple seemed to mock her grief, each tiny particle a testament to the fragility of life and the enduring power of secrets. She traced the faded lines of his final note, her fingertip lingering on the unfamiliar symbols, a language that seemed to hum with an ancient power.

The immediate task, however, was not deciphering Gábor's final enigma, but securing the Codex. The Sentinel organization, she knew, wouldn't rest until they recovered it, until they could rewrite history according to their twisted narrative. Their influence reached far beyond the Carpathian Mountains, a venomous tendril that snaked through the corridors of power, whispering in the ears of the world's elite. Ana had glimpsed their reach, their unwavering dedication to their clandestine agenda: to control the narrative of history, twisting it to fit their own macabre purposes. She now understood the true meaning of the "Black Sun": it wasn't merely a metaphor for humanity's darkest secrets; it was a symbol of their planned manipulation of global events.

She had to leave. Escape to a place where she could analyze the Codex properly, a place free from the ever-present threat of The Sentinel. Her mind raced, calculating routes, considering alliances, evaluating risks. She couldn't trust anyone entirely; the world was a tapestry woven with treachery and deceit. The betrayal she had suffered within the seemingly secure walls of the Vatican archives still burned fresh in her memory. She had learned a brutal lesson in the fragility of trust.

Her first priority was to get the Codex to a location safe from the Sentinel's grasp. She considered several options, each presenting its own unique set of challenges. Returning to Bucharest was out of the question; the city was crawling with The Sentinel's agents, their eyes and ears everywhere. A neutral territory was necessary, somewhere with minimal Sentinel influence, somewhere that could offer her the anonymity and security she desperately needed. She thought of Professor Schmidt, a renowned cryptographer she had met during a conference in Berlin, a man known for his discretion and expertise in ancient languages. He might be able to provide the initial assistance needed to decipher Gábor's last message and help in the interpretation of some of the Codex's more challenging passages.

The journey would be perilous. Ana packed lightly, her backpack containing the Codex, a few essential belongings, and a small, hand-held radio she hoped could establish contact with Professor Schmidt. She had to rely on her instincts, her knowledge of subterfuge and her resourcefulness – skills honed over years of painstaking research. The memory of Gábor's final, unwavering gaze, filled with both sorrow and determination, fueled her resolve.

Leaving the temple ruins behind, Ana navigated the treacherous mountain passes, her knowledge of the local geography proving invaluable. She moved with the grace and agility of a mountain cat, blending seamlessly into the rugged landscape. She spent the nights in secluded caves, surviving on meager rations, always vigilant, always aware of the potential danger lurking in the shadows. The nights were long, filled with the haunting echoes of Gábor's voice, the chilling memory of the subterranean chambers, the unsettling premonition of the global catastrophe they had narrowly averted.

Reaching a remote village nestled in the foothills of the Carpathians, Ana managed to establish contact with Professor Schmidt via the radio. His voice, calm and reassuring, provided a lifeline in the storm of her despair and fear. He arranged a rendezvous point in a quiet corner of Vienna. The journey to Vienna was less physically demanding, but the psychological burden was immense. The weight of her responsibility, the knowledge of the terrible power contained within the Codex, pressed down on her, a constant companion that followed her every step.

In Vienna, under the watchful eye of Professor Schmidt, Ana began the painstaking process of deciphering the Codex, aided by the professor's expertise in cryptography and his vast knowledge of ancient languages. The Codex was a treasure trove of information, a labyrinth of interwoven narratives and cryptic symbols. Each page turned revealed new layers of complexity, each sentence a fragment of a larger, terrifying puzzle. The text spoke of ancient civilizations, of lost technologies, of a power capable of reshaping the world. They worked tirelessly, their combined knowledge illuminating the dark corners of the Codex's secrets, revealing the extent of The Sentinel's reach, the sophistication of their plan.

Professor Schmidt's expertise in deciphering codes was invaluable in unravelling the complex ciphers hidden within the Codex's margins. He revealed a hidden system of numerical codes linked to specific geographical coordinates, coordinates that pointed towards a network of ancient sites scattered across the globe—sites that, according to the Codex, held the keys to activating the catastrophic mechanisms described within the prophecy. They unearthed descriptions of advanced seismic technologies, ancient machinery capable of triggering catastrophic earthquakes and volcanic eruptions on a global scale.

As they delved deeper, they discovered that The Sentinel had been systematically mapping these sites, discreetly acquiring land and building clandestine infrastructures near them, preparing to activate the ancient mechanisms for their nefarious purposes. The Sentinel's agenda was not merely about controlling information; it was about controlling the very fabric of the planet itself. They sought to reshape the world according to their own twisted vision, obliterating existing political and societal structures and ushering in a new era of global chaos, an era of complete and utter dominion.

Gábor's sacrifice, Ana realized, had been far more significant than she had initially understood. He had given her the time, the space, to decode the Codex, to understand the full extent of the threat, and to develop a plan to counteract it. His final message, finally deciphered with Professor Schmidt's assistance, confirmed this. It detailed the location of a hidden archive, an archive containing evidence that could expose The Sentinel and their devastating plans to the world. It was a location far removed from the places they had already searched, concealed in a place that would require a new level of research and determination to discover.

The Codex was not merely a historical artifact; it was a weapon, a roadmap to preventing a global catastrophe. Ana felt the immense weight of responsibility, the daunting task ahead. The game was far from over, but with Gábor's legacy as her guide, she knew that she had to carry on, not just for him, but for the world. Gábor's sacrifice had bought her time, but time was running out. The Sentinel's plans were rapidly advancing, and stopping them would demand a level of courage and determination that would test her limits like never before. She was alone again, but not truly alone. Gábor's spirit, his unwavering dedication to truth and justice, marched on, his last message a clarion call for her to continue their mission. His legacy, she knew, was the greatest weapon she had. The fight to save the world had just begun.

Chapter 6

Aftermath

Public Reaction

The news broke like a seismic tremor itself, shaking the foundations of the world's collective consciousness. The revelation, initially whispered in hushed tones amongst intelligence agencies and leaked fragments appearing on obscure online forums, exploded into the global media with the force of a thousand suns. The Sentinel, a shadowy organization whose existence had previously been confined to whispered legends and conspiracy theories, was now a stark reality. Their audacious plan – to manipulate ancient seismic triggers hidden across the globe, plunging humanity into a new dark age – had been thwarted, thanks to the bravery and ingenuity of a linguist and a disgraced archaeologist.

The initial reports were chaotic, a swirling vortex of conflicting information and breathless speculation. News channels worldwide displayed grainy footage of the collapsing solar temple, its ancient stones crumbling into dust, a testament to the near-catastrophe. Experts debated the validity of the claims, some dismissing it as an elaborate hoax, others clinging to the terrifying plausibility of the unearthed truth. Images of the Black Sun Codex, its intricate symbols now partially deciphered and reproduced in countless news articles, became iconic – a symbol of both impending doom averted and the mysteries that still remained.

Public reaction was a kaleidoscope of fear, awe, and a lingering sense of unease. The near miss had galvanized a global sense of vulnerability. The idea that such a sophisticated and ancient conspiracy could have existed, and come so close to succeeding, shattered the comfortable illusion of safety. People huddled around their televisions, their faces pale with a mixture of disbelief and apprehension, as experts painstakingly explained the details that had emerged from Ana Dragan's testimony and the surviving fragments of Gábor Varga's research.

The internet, ever a whirlwind of information and misinformation, became a battlefield of opinions and theories. Conspiracy websites went into overdrive, their forums buzzing with speculation about the origins of The Sentinel, their true motives beyond the immediate threat of global devastation, and the possibility of other hidden organizations lurking in the shadows. Social media was ablaze with a mix of fear, fascination, and outlandish claims, as people grappled with the implications of the revelation. Memes of the Black Sun Codex spread like wildfire, transforming the intricate symbols into a visual representation of both fear and collective resilience.

Governments worldwide scrambled to respond, initiating emergency meetings and bolstering their security measures. The revelation of The Sentinel forced a re-evaluation of international security protocols. The fear of similar, yet-unknown, organizations waiting in the wings became a pervasive concern. Investigations into the organization's history, its members, and its funding sources became a top priority for intelligence agencies across the globe. The hunt was on, not only for the remaining members of The Sentinel but also for any other hidden groups that might harbor similar designs.

Ana Dragan, the seemingly ordinary linguist who had become the unlikely heroine of the story, found herself catapulted into the global spotlight. Her initial reticence quickly gave way to a steely resolve, driven by a desire to ensure the knowledge she had gained would never again be used to threaten humanity. She became the face of the newly revealed threat and, simultaneously, a beacon of hope for a world that had narrowly escaped utter destruction. Interviews poured in from news organizations around the globe, each seeking her insight, her story, and her assessment of the future. She spoke with quiet dignity, balancing the harrowing details of her experiences with a carefully crafted message of vigilance and collective responsibility.

Despite the overwhelming attention, Ana remained haunted by the loss of Gábor Varga. His sacrifice, the ultimate act of selflessness, weighed heavily on her mind. The outpouring of global sympathy and admiration failed to fill the void left by her partner, a void that threatened to consume her even as the world celebrated her bravery. She honored Gábor's memory by continuing to tirelessly share information, ensuring that his work, and his sacrifice, would not be in vain. The world mourned Gábor as a hero, a man who gave everything to protect it from a catastrophe. His name joined the ranks of those who gave their lives for the greater good, his memory forever etched in the annals of history alongside the threat he helped prevent.

Ana's newfound prominence was not without its challenges. She navigated a complex web of political maneuvering, academic debate, and the constant scrutiny of the public eye. Death threats, veiled and overt, became a part of her daily life. Security personnel were ever-present, a stark reminder of the danger she still faced. Despite this, she refused to be intimidated. Her commitment to transparency and accountability, her unwavering resolve to protect the secrets she had discovered, became an inspiration to millions. She used her influence to lobby for increased global cooperation in addressing the kind of ancient and hidden threats that had almost ended the world.

The aftermath of The Sentinel's near-successful attempt at global devastation led to a global reassessment of security protocols, both old and new. A renewed focus on historical research and the study of forgotten languages emerged, driven by the realization that the secrets of the past could hold the keys to preventing future catastrophes. Ancient texts and neglected archives gained newfound importance, leading to a surge in funding for archaeological and linguistic research. Universities worldwide saw an unprecedented increase in the number of students pursuing related fields, a testament to the lasting impact of the events that had unfolded.

Ana's testimony before various international bodies brought to light the intricate network of connections between seemingly unrelated events, stretching back centuries. Her explanation of the Black Sun Codex's cryptic symbols, along with the history of The Sentinel's origins, revealed a sophisticated, centuries-long conspiracy that reached into the highest echelons of power. The revelations sent shockwaves through the political landscape, leading to numerous investigations and the exposure of corrupt individuals involved in perpetuating the threat.

Even amidst the global upheaval and ongoing investigations, the underlying mystery of The Sentinel's origins, their exact motivations, and the possibility of hidden cells remaining undetected, continued to fuel public fascination and speculation. The world was forever changed. The seemingly impenetrable veil of reality had been pierced, revealing the fragility of civilization in the face of forces ancient and unknown. The story of Ana Dragan and Gábor Varga had become more than just a thriller; it had become a cautionary tale, a stark reminder of the hidden dangers lurking just beneath the surface of the familiar world. The quiet hum of fear, once a low thrum beneath the surface, was now a palpable tension, forever altering humanity's relationship with its own history and the secrets it held. The world, once secure in its understanding of itself, now knew otherwise. The future held both the promise of discovery and the chilling possibility of something far more sinister.

Investigation Continues

The aftermath wasn't silence; it was a cacophony. The world, having narrowly avoided a cataclysmic event, now grappled with the fallout. The revelation of The Sentinel, once a whispered conspiracy, dominated headlines globally. Governments scrambled, intelligence agencies initiated unprecedented collaborations, and the public, initially awestruck by the sheer audacity of the plot, descended into a maelstrom of fear, speculation, and morbid fascination. Ana Dragan, unexpectedly thrust into the international spotlight, found herself the reluctant hero of a story that had spiraled far beyond her wildest imaginings. The weight of the world, or at least the weight of its newly-revealed vulnerabilities, rested heavily on her shoulders.

The immediate focus shifted from preventing the apocalypse to understanding how it had almost happened. The investigation, initially spearheaded by Ana and Gábor, now broadened to encompass the combined might of international law enforcement and intelligence agencies. The clues Gábor had painstakingly pieced together, the fragmented maps, the cryptic symbols, the barely deciphered entries in the Black Sun Codex – all became vital pieces in a global jigsaw puzzle.

The first priority was identifying and dismantling the remaining cells of The Sentinel. Ana's knowledge of the Codex proved invaluable. Its pages, filled with a blend of ancient Sumerian, Akkadian, and a surprisingly modern cipher, contained more than just the location of the seismic triggers. They held hints of the organization's structure, its hierarchy, its methods of operation, and even fragmented biographies of its key members. Forensic linguists and codebreakers from various nations joined forces, working day and night to translate and interpret the remaining sections. The effort was painstaking, often frustrating, but gradually a clearer picture emerged.

The Sentinel, it turned out, wasn't a monolithic organization. It was a network, a sophisticated web of individuals linked by a shared ideology and a common goal. Their members weren't simply fanatics or extremists; many held positions of power and influence within various governments, corporations, and academic institutions. The organization's longevity, spanning centuries, hinted at a level of infiltration and control that chilled investigators to the bone. The discovery of hidden caches of funds, meticulously laundered through complex offshore accounts, further exposed the extent of their reach.

The investigation also focused on the seismic triggers themselves. Teams of geologists, archaeologists, and engineers were dispatched to the locations identified in the Codex. These weren't simply ancient ruins; they were intricately designed mechanisms, some dating back to the dawn of civilization, capable of triggering powerful earthquakes and volcanic eruptions. Many were sophisticated systems of levers, weights, and conduits, designed to amplify naturally occurring seismic activity. The technology was both ingenious and terrifying, a testament to the lost knowledge and forgotten ingenuity of ancient civilizations.

One of the most significant discoveries was a previously unknown solar temple hidden deep beneath the Vatican archives. This temple, unearthed following cryptic clues embedded within the Codex, was a masterpiece of engineering, a complex network of tunnels, chambers, and subterranean passages leading to a massive, subterranean chamber housing a colossal mechanism. The mechanism, a symphony of gears, levers, and precisely calibrated weights, was capable of triggering a chain reaction across the globe, activating all the seismic triggers simultaneously. It was a device that could end civilization as we knew it.

But the discovery of the temple wasn't just about its destructive capabilities. It also contained a treasure trove of information – thousands of ancient texts, scrolls, and tablets – that offered unprecedented insights into the history and origins of The Sentinel. The organization, it seemed, was far older than previously believed. Its roots extended back to the ancient world, with connections to forgotten cults and secret societies that had manipulated events and influenced the course of history for millennia. The investigation became a race against time not only to dismantle the present threat but to understand the long-reaching tentacles of The Sentinel's influence throughout history.

Ana, despite her grief over Gábor's death, became a pivotal figure in these investigations. Her linguistic expertise, coupled with her intimate knowledge of the Codex, made her indispensable. She spent countless hours working with teams of experts, translating, interpreting, and piecing together the fragments of the puzzle. The strain was immense, the pressure unrelenting, but she persevered, driven by a sense of responsibility and a deep-seated need to understand the full scope of The Sentinel's actions.

Her contributions extended beyond the purely academic. Ana's understanding of the organization's psychology, gleaned from the Codex and her interactions with its members, proved invaluable in profiling its remaining operatives. She helped to identify patterns of behavior, predict their movements, and anticipate their next moves. Her insights led to several successful raids, resulting in the capture of key figures and the seizure of critical materials. Her emotional fortitude, often tested to its limits, was a testament to her resilience and unwavering dedication.

The international effort to dismantle The Sentinel was far from over. The organization's reach extended far beyond the locations identified in the Codex. There were whispers of hidden cells, sleeper agents, and dormant networks scattered across the globe, waiting for the opportune moment to resurface. The investigation, once focused on a singular, apocalyptic threat, had transformed into a long-term commitment to monitoring, tracking, and neutralizing the remnants of a centuries-old conspiracy. Ana's life, once focused on the quiet study of linguistics, was now inextricably entwined with the fate of the world. She had survived a catastrophic event, lost a close friend, and become a reluctant hero in a global drama. But the fight, she knew, was far from over. The shadows of The Sentinel still lingered, and the secrets of the Black Sun Codex hinted at mysteries yet to be uncovered, a challenge that would shape the trajectory of her life in ways she could only begin to fathom. Even as governments celebrated the averted catastrophe, the quiet hum of investigation continued, the pursuit of justice a slow, meticulous unraveling of a conspiracy that stretched back through the millennia. The world was safe, for now, but the vigilance needed to remain, a testament to the fragility of civilization and the enduring power of ancient secrets. The whispers of the past still echoed, a constant reminder that some battles never truly end.

Anas New Role

The aftermath left Ana Dragan hollowed, yet strangely invigorated. Gábor's sacrifice, the chilling finality of it, echoed in the quiet spaces between her thoughts, a constant, low hum of grief interwoven with a fierce determination. The world had been saved, ostensibly, but the victory tasted like ash in her mouth. The celebrations, the global relief, felt distant, muffled by the weight of her loss. She had seen the raw, brutal efficiency of The Sentinel, their chilling dedication to an ancient, apocalyptic plan.

She knew, with a certainty that settled deep in her bones, that the threat wasn't extinguished; it had merely been suppressed, its embers smoldering beneath the surface, waiting for the right moment to ignite anew.

Initially, the offers poured in. Governments clamoured for her expertise, intelligence agencies begged for her insights, and academics sought her collaboration. She found herself attending high-level briefings, speaking to assembled dignitaries in hushed, secure rooms, explaining the intricacies of the Black Sun Codex and the terrifying implications of its prophecies. The sheer scale of the organization, its centuries-long reach, stunned even the most seasoned intelligence officials. Ana, a linguist who once found solace in the quiet study of forgotten languages, now found herself at the epicentre of a global crisis, a reluctant architect of a new era of international cooperation.

She refused many of the offers, however. The public face of heroism didn't suit her. She preferred the shadows, the quiet pursuit of knowledge, the meticulous unraveling of conspiracies. The constant media attention, the flashing cameras, the relentless questions, grated on her nerves. She longed for the peace of her study, the comfort of ancient texts, the quiet murmur of forgotten tongues. But she knew she couldn't simply retreat. Gábor's death, the weight of his sacrifice, had forged in her a new resolve, a profound understanding of the responsibility that rested on her shoulders.

Instead, Ana accepted a position within a newly formed, highly classified international task force dedicated to monitoring and neutralizing the remaining elements of The Sentinel. It was an organization cobbled together from the best minds in intelligence, archaeology, and linguistics—a global network forged in the crucible of crisis. This was her new battleground, not the chaotic public sphere, but the clandestine world of intelligence, where the fight against The Sentinel would truly be waged.

Her role wasn't simply to decipher ancient texts; it was to anticipate the next move. The Codex had revealed a network of triggers, but there were surely more hidden across the globe. The Sentinel hadn't been acting in isolation; they had deep roots, hidden alliances, and probably a network of sympathizers. Ana's expertise became vital in understanding the organization's operational structure, deciphering their coded communications, and predicting their future actions. She immersed herself in the vast archives of intelligence agencies across the globe, piecing together fragmented information, painstakingly reconstructing the history of The Sentinel, identifying their key players, and analyzing their tactics.

The task force operated in a climate of utmost secrecy. Their existence was denied by governments, their actions veiled in plausible deniability. Ana learned to navigate this world of clandestine operations, working with highly trained specialists, each an expert in their field. She collaborated with cryptographers, who painstakingly unraveled the Sentinel's encrypted messages, revealing glimpses into the organization's internal workings, their operational plans, and the identities of their operatives.

Her linguistic skills became invaluable in this process. The Sentinel's communication methods weren't confined to modern encryption; they utilized ancient ciphers, obscure dialects, and coded messages hidden within historical texts and religious iconography. Ana, fluent in several ancient languages, including Latin, Greek, and Aramaic, became the key to unlocking these secrets. She spent countless hours poring over ancient manuscripts, decoding cryptic symbols, deciphering obscure inscriptions—skills honed over years of meticulous research now put to a purpose far grander than she had ever imagined.

One particular assignment involved a series of seemingly innocuous artifacts housed in the Vatican Secret Archives. These artifacts, small figurines, and religious relics, appeared to be unconnected, but Ana's linguistic expertise, coupled with a detailed knowledge of early Christian symbology, revealed a pattern—a hidden network of symbols, strategically placed throughout the artifacts, which, when deciphered, revealed the location of a previously unknown Sentinel cell in Rome. The task force moved swiftly, dismantling the cell before they could enact their plans.

Another operation focused on a series of cryptic messages discovered hidden within the digital archives of a defunct Swiss bank. The messages, encoded using a complex algorithm based on ancient Sumerian mathematics, revealed a financial network supporting The Sentinel. Ana's meticulous analysis, coupled with the work of the task force's financial experts, allowed them to trace the flow of funds, identify key players within the financial network, and freeze millions of dollars in assets, crippling the organization's financial capabilities.

The pressure was immense. The task force was constantly under surveillance, their movements tracked, their actions scrutinized. Ana lived a life of constant vigilance, aware that the shadows of The Sentinel still lurked, their reach extending into every corner of the globe. She knew that there would be future attacks, future challenges. The fight was far from over.

But amidst the relentless pressure, Ana found a strange sense of purpose. Gábor's sacrifice, his unwavering commitment to justice, had instilled in her a resolve she never knew she possessed. She found comfort in the knowledge that she was continuing his work, safeguarding the secrets he had given his life to protect. She channeled her grief into action, transforming her loss into a driving force behind her dedication. The quiet hours of research, the painstaking analysis of ancient texts, became a form of meditation, a way to honor his memory.

The fight against The Sentinel wouldn't be won in a single, decisive battle. It would be a long, protracted campaign, a gradual erosion of the organization's power, a steady dismantling of its global network. It would require patience, persistence, and an unwavering commitment to truth. But Ana Dragan, now a seasoned veteran of the clandestine world, was ready. She had confronted the darkness, faced the abyss, and emerged, forged anew in the crucible of crisis. The shadows still lingered, but Ana Dragan, armed with her knowledge and fueled by her grief, stood ready to meet them, one cryptic symbol, one coded message, one hidden cell at a time. She had become the guardian of the secrets, the protector of the world, the inheritor of Gábor's legacy. The fight had only just begun.

Dealing with Loss

The Vatican archives, once a sanctuary of ancient knowledge, now felt like a mausoleum. The scent of aged parchment and incense did little to mask the lingering chill of loss. Ana sat amidst the towering shelves, the weight of Gábor's absence pressing down on her like a physical burden. The Black Sun Codex lay open before her, its pages filled with the elegant, chilling script that had nearly cost them both their lives. It was a testament to their shared triumph, a grim reminder of their devastating loss. She traced a finger along the intricate illustrations, each one a miniature window into a forgotten world, a world Gábor had loved and understood in a way she never could. His absence was a gaping wound, a void that echoed in the silence of the vast library.

Days blurred into weeks. The world continued its relentless march forward, oblivious to the personal cataclysm that had shattered Ana's life. The celebrations for the averted apocalypse were muted for her; the cheers felt like distant echoes in a cavernous space where only the ghost of Gábor remained. She found herself drawn back to the monastery in Transylvania, not out of morbid fascination, but out of a need to be closer to the place where their journey had begun, where their shared destiny had intertwined. The cold stone of the monastery, the scent of damp earth and ancient wood, held a familiar comfort, a strange solace in its austere silence. She walked the cloisters, her footsteps echoing in the empty corridors, a mournful counterpoint to the rustling leaves outside. Here, amidst the remnants of Dr. Lupu's research, amongst the faded maps and fragmented texts, she found a fleeting sense of connection to Gábor, a tangible link to the man she had lost.

Sleep offered no escape. Night after night, she was

plagued by vivid dreams, fragmented scenes playing on a relentless loop: Gábor's laughter, his determined gaze, the horrifying moment of his sacrifice. She would wake in a cold sweat, the phantom weight of his hand still lingering on hers, the echo of his final words ringing in her ears. The grief was a physical entity, a crushing weight that threatened to suffocate her. She found herself avoiding people, the forced smiles and expressions of sympathy only serving to accentuate the hollowness within.

Her days were a blur of research, a desperate attempt to fill the void Gábor had left behind. She poured over his notes, meticulously studying his handwriting, deciphering his cryptic annotations. In his meticulous records, she found solace, a connection to his brilliant mind, a way to keep him close. His notes weren't just about archaeology; they revealed a profound understanding of human nature, of the darkness that lurked beneath the veneer of civilization. She saw in his writing a profound sense of justice, a deep-seated desire to protect humanity from itself. It was a quality she had admired in him even before their perilous journey, and now, in the aftermath of his death, it served as an anchor in the turbulent sea of her grief.

One evening, while sifting through Gábor's personal effects, she came across a small, worn leather-bound book. It wasn't part of his academic research; it was a collection of personal poems, sketches, and observations, a window into the soul of the man she had loved. His words, raw and honest, spoke of his doubts, his fears, his unwavering love for his work and for her. There were sketches of the Carpathian Mountains, of the monastery, of the hidden solar temple. But the most poignant was a simple charcoal sketch of Ana herself, her eyes filled with a mixture of determination and fear, a reflection of her own journey alongside him. It was a testament to their shared experience, a silent witness to the bond they had forged in the face of unimaginable danger.

She discovered a hidden compartment within the book, containing a small, intricately carved wooden box. Inside, lay a single, smooth river stone, and a folded piece of parchment. On the parchment, was a barely visible message written in a cipher she recognized immediately. It was Gábor's unique code, a language only they had understood. With trembling hands, she deciphered the message: "The Sun sleeps. But it will wake again."

The message resonated with a chilling finality. It was a warning, a cryptic clue hinting at a new, more dangerous threat. It was a signal, a call to action that spoke of a larger, more complex conspiracy that extended far beyond the Sentinel. Gábor hadn't died in vain; he had left her a legacy, a responsibility, a path to follow. His death was not the end; it was merely a beginning. The grief remained, a constant companion, but it was no longer all-consuming. It was now tempered by a renewed sense of purpose, a fierce determination to honor his memory by continuing his work, a commitment to unravelling the secrets he had discovered and ensuring that the "Sun" would not rise again.

She knew that she could not face this new challenge alone. She would need allies, people who shared her understanding of the ancient world, people who had seen the shadows and understood their threat. She had the Codex, and she had Gábor's knowledge, but she needed more. She had to find the people who would help her unravel the mystery of the "sleeping sun." Her journey would take her to new locations, to new discoveries, and into the heart of a conspiracy so vast and so ancient that it dwarfed anything she had encountered before.

The initial shock of grief started to subside, replaced by a cold, steely resolve. The weight of responsibility was immense, but so too was the potential for change. Ana understood the power of ancient knowledge, the destructive potential of ancient conspiracies. She understood now that the fight for truth was a marathon, not a sprint, and she was ready to run for as long as it took. She would learn from her experience, from her loss, from the lessons Gábor had implicitly taught her. She would decipher the message of the "sleeping sun," even if it led her to the darkest corners of the world.

The world had narrowly avoided a catastrophic event, but

the struggle was far from over. The victory felt hollow, a temporary reprieve in a war that had only just begun. Ana knew that the shadows still lurked, their tendrils reaching out from the darkest corners of the earth, waiting for their opportunity to strike again. She found comfort only in the continuation of Gábor's legacy, a promise to herself, to him, and to the world. The fight to protect humanity from its own hidden darkness would require everything she had—her intellect, her courage, and her unwavering determination to honor the memory of the man she loved. She would complete his work, not for closure, but for justice. The path forward would be difficult, filled with peril and uncertainty, but Ana Dragan, armed with Gábor's legacy and the Black Sun Codex, was ready. The Sun may sleep, but she would not. The awakening, if it came, would find her prepared.

The Search for Survivors

The Vatican's echoing silence offered little solace. The adrenaline that had fueled their desperate race against the clock had faded, leaving behind a bone-deep weariness. Ana, however, couldn't afford to succumb to grief. Gábor's sacrifice demanded action, a continuation of the fight he'd given his life for. The immediate aftermath involved a frantic collaboration with the authorities – Italian Carabinieri, Interpol, and a select few Vatican officials privy to the horrifying truth about the 'awakening' and The Sentinel's role.

The Codex, now safely secured in a high-security vault, became the cornerstone of the investigation. Its intricate diagrams, detailing the network of seismic triggers, needed deciphering. Each symbol, each cryptic phrase, spoke of locations, rituals, and a chillingly precise understanding of geophysics that far surpassed anything Ana had encountered. Teams of experts – seismologists, historians, linguists – pored over the manuscript, their faces etched with a mixture of awe and fear.

The Sentinel, however, hadn't vanished into thin air. Their

global network, though shattered, still possessed latent strength. Ana, working closely with a lead Carabinieri detective, Inspector Lorenzo Moretti, began piecing together the organization's fragmented remnants. Moretti, a seasoned investigator with a steely gaze and an unshakeable resolve, had initially been skeptical of Ana's claims. The sheer audacity of the conspiracy – a clandestine group manipulating global seismic activity – was almost unbelievable. But the evidence – the Codex, the physical proof of the mechanisms within the solar temple, and the testimonies of a handful of captured Sentinel members – slowly chipped away at his skepticism.

The surviving Sentinel members were a diverse group, ranging from disillusioned academics to hardened mercenaries, bound together by a shared belief in their cause, a twisted interpretation of an ancient prophecy, and the threat of brutal retribution. Their interrogations were arduous, fraught with contradictions and evasions. Many had been indoctrinated, believing they were acting for the greater good, purifying the earth from the supposed "impurity" of humanity's excesses. Others, however, showed a ruthless ambition, seeking power and control over the planet's fate. Ana found herself playing a crucial role, not just as a linguist, but as a translator of their twisted ideology, dissecting their belief system to uncover the cracks and exploit their internal divisions. She discovered that their leadership structure was far more complex than initially thought, a web of interconnected cells operating independently yet bound by a strict code of secrecy and brutal efficiency.

One of the key breakthroughs came from a low-ranking member, a former geologist named Elias Thorne, who had been part of the team responsible for activating the seismic triggers in the Carpathian Mountains. Thorne, disillusioned and terrified by what he had witnessed, revealed details of a secondary network, a smaller, more secretive cell operating within the Vatican itself. This cell, he revealed, served as a conduit, relaying information and instructions between the higher echelons of the organization and their field operatives. They were the organization's silent, unseen hand, manipulating events from within the very heart of the Catholic Church. This discovery shook Ana to her core. The betrayal was profound – the institution that housed the very documents that had saved the world was also harboring its would-be destroyers.

The investigation expanded, leading to a tense standoff within the Vatican walls. Moretti, with Ana's invaluable assistance, carefully navigated the delicate political and religious implications, collaborating with select members of the Vatican's internal security force. The operation was carried out under the cover of darkness, a silent infiltration of hidden chambers and secret passages, echoing the stealth and clandestine nature of The Sentinel itself. The apprehension of these members within the Vatican was a risky gamble, one that could easily destabilize the already fragile political landscape. The world teetered on the brink of chaos, and a single misstep could send it spiraling into anarchy.

The discovery of the secondary network, however, also revealed the existence of a hidden archive, a collection of documents even older and more perilous than the Black Sun Codex. This archive contained details of past awakenings, hinting at a cyclical pattern of destruction and rebirth woven into humanity's history. The documents suggested that The Sentinel was not a new organization, but a centuries-old society, its roots buried deep within the annals of time, its members possessing knowledge and power that spanned millennia. The implications were staggering.

With the arrests of several key figures, including the Vatican-based cell, the immediate threat was neutralized. Yet, the investigation was far from over. The deeper Ana and Moretti delved into The Sentinel's history, the more they realized the complexity of the conspiracy. They began to uncover a network of hidden societies, cryptic symbols etched into ancient structures across the globe, all pointing towards a common goal, a grand design beyond their immediate understanding. The fight for justice had evolved into a pursuit of truth, a quest to understand the ancient secrets that had fueled the ambitions of The Sentinel for centuries. The work would require years, perhaps decades, to unravel, but Ana, armed with Gábor's legacy and the haunting echo of his sacrifice, knew that she would dedicate her life to this task. The fight for humanity's future had only just begun. The sun might sleep, but the vigilance of those who sought to protect it would never cease.

Ana found a small, worn leather-bound notebook in Gábor's belongings, tucked away within a secret compartment of his satchel. It was filled with his meticulous notes, his own deductions about the Codex, and observations that went far beyond what had been deciphered thus far. It was a treasure trove of knowledge, a continuation of his research, a silent promise that he would still guide her, even in death. In one entry, a cryptic message caught her eye – a series of coordinates, a location, a tantalizing hint that hinted at a new mystery, a trail that might finally lead to the origins of The Sentinel. This, she realized, was his final gift to her. A testament to his unwavering belief in her, and a challenge to continue the fight, a new chapter in the unending battle against the forces of darkness. The shadow of Gábor's loss remained, a constant presence, a source of both profound grief and unwavering determination. But Ana knew, with absolute certainty, that his spirit lived on in the work she was now determined to complete. The awakening might have been delayed, but the war against the ancient shadows had only just truly begun. The hunt for the surviving members of The Sentinel was not merely an investigation; it was a pilgrimage, a quest to honor the sacrifice of a great man and protect the world from the darkness that lurked within its heart. And Ana, armed with knowledge, courage, and the unwavering support of those who had fought alongside her, was ready to face whatever challenges lay ahead.

Chapter 7

Hidden Message

Gbors Last Clue

The dust motes danced in the single shaft of sunlight slicing through the Vatican library's arched window, illuminating the worn leather binding of the Black Sun Codex. Ana Dragan traced the intricate, almost imperceptible carvings on its cover, the faint scent of old parchment and incense filling her senses. Gábor's death still felt raw, a gaping wound in her heart. The escape from the collapsing solar temple, the chaos, the sheer terror, now felt like a distant, surreal nightmare. Yet, the Codex remained, a testament to their shared struggle, a physical manifestation of Gábor's sacrifice.

She had spent the intervening weeks in a daze, a blur of official testimonies, interviews with bewildered authorities, and the unending press clamoring for details about the thwarted catastrophe. The world had, thankfully, averted a global seismic event, but the victory felt hollow. The exposure of The Sentinel, the shadowy organization dedicated to unleashing the ancient mechanisms, had sent shockwaves through global intelligence agencies, but their full scope, their origins, remained shrouded in mystery. And Gábor... he was gone.

It was in a moment of quiet reflection, while cataloging the Codex's contents – a painstaking process given the archaic language and the deliberately obfuscated script – that she found it. A barely perceptible indentation on the inner cover, a subtle imperfection easily overlooked. Her fingers, calloused from hours of painstaking work, brushed against the area, and a small, almost invisible flap sprung open.

Inside, a single sheet of extremely thin, almost translucent parchment lay folded. It was incredibly fragile, the edges brittle with age, yet seemingly untouched by the centuries. Gábor's handwriting, precise and elegant even in the hasty scribble, filled the tiny space. It wasn't a long message, but every word felt weighted with significance, imbued with the urgency of a final testament. It was written in a mix of Latin and a cipher that resembled the runes adorning Dr. Lupu's body, a language Ana had only begun to understand during her harrowing journey.

The Latin portion was straightforward enough: "The Sun does not set. The shadow lengthens. Seek the Serpent's Eye." The cryptic phrase sent a shiver down her spine. The Sun, a recurring motif throughout the Codex, was clearly not a literal celestial body. The Shadow, Ana suspected, referred to The Sentinel's influence, its ever-growing reach. But the Serpent's Eye...?

The remaining portion of the message was the encoded sequence. It wasn't a simple substitution cipher, the type they had frequently encountered in the Codex. This was more intricate, a layered puzzle of symbols, each one possibly representing multiple layers of meaning. She remembered Gábor's frustration, his countless hours spent poring over seemingly meaningless combinations, before a pattern would finally emerge. Now, she found herself facing his unfinished work. This final clue felt more personal, intimate, as if Gábor had entrusted her with a secret far beyond the cataclysmic threat they had just averted.

Ana spent the next several days immersed in the cipher, consulting every linguistic resource available, from ancient Sumerian texts to obscure Romanian dialects. She delved into her father's research – research that had unwittingly laid the groundwork for her own journey – seeking connections, cross-referencing symbols, searching for a key. The Serpent's Eye. The phrase echoed in her mind, becoming both an obsession and a guiding light.

The initial breakthroughs were frustratingly slow. The cipher was a multi-layered enigma, a series of interlocking codes within codes. Days melted into nights as she meticulously analyzed every symbol, every stroke of Gábor's pen. She consulted specialists in cryptography, experts in ancient languages, even reaching out to a few contacts from her time in Bucharest, contacts she had maintained despite the dangers and the betrayal she had suffered.

Slowly, painstakingly, the puzzle began to yield its secrets. The symbols, she discovered, were not merely representing letters; they denoted locations, coordinates, and specific historical events. The sequence wasn't random; it was a chronological narrative, a trail of breadcrumbs leading to a specific place and time. As the patterns emerged, the location revealed itself. It was not a place she had encountered in her previous research; it was a hidden location in the Caucasus mountains, an area known for its enigmatic caves and long-forgotten history. A place she had never even considered before.

And the time... It pointed to the summer solstice, the longest day of the year, a date that held significant symbolic meaning in many ancient cultures, often associated with the rebirth of the sun, a stark contrast to the "Black Sun" concept they had unravelled previously. This, Ana realized, was not a mere coincidence; the timing was crucial.

The final piece of the puzzle was the most chilling. Within the coded sequence, she discovered a new set of symbols, totally different from those in the Codex. These symbols, she recognized from her father's research, were associated with a secretive society known only as "The Obsidian Order," a group rumored to predate even the origins of The Sentinel. This was a far older, and seemingly even more dangerous threat, one that dwarfed The Sentinel in both antiquity and influence. The Obsidian Order, she surmised, represented the serpent, its eye being the single, unifying symbol at the heart of this new mystery.

Ana felt a surge of icy dread, yet a simultaneous fire of resolve ignited within her. Gábor's sacrifice had not been in vain. He had not only saved the world from imminent catastrophe; he had also opened a window to an even deeper, more profound mystery. A mystery that now inextricably bound her to a legacy far older, and potentially far more lethal, than anything she had previously encountered. The path ahead would be treacherous, fraught with unknown dangers, but Ana Dragan, armed with the Codex and Gábor's final message, was ready to face the challenge. The Serpent's Eye awaited.

The journey wouldn't be easy. She would need to tread carefully, to forge new alliances, and to trust those who deserved her trust and reject those who had betrayed her in the past. The trail of symbols would lead her through perilous mountain passes, into hidden archives, and potentially into the heart of a conspiracy that spanned centuries.

She knew the risks. She had already lost Gábor, her friend, her partner, her confidant. The thought of further loss haunted her, but she was no longer alone. She had the Codex, Gábor's legacy, and the burning desire to understand the truth, to honor his sacrifice, to prevent the catastrophe he had worked so hard to stop. She looked at the small piece of parchment, at Gábor's final message, and knew that his spirit was guiding her. His legacy was not just in the saved world but in the unanswered questions, the lingering mysteries, and the unending pursuit of knowledge.

The summer solstice was approaching, and Ana, armed with Gábor's last clue, embarked on a new chapter, a journey into the heart of the unknown. The Serpent's Eye, she vowed, would be found. And the Obsidian Order, the ancient enemy that lurked in the shadows, would be exposed. This was not merely an investigation; it was a quest for justice, a testament to a friendship forged in the fires of danger, and a race against time to unveil a truth hidden for millennia. The sun, for Ana, had not set. The shadow might lengthen, but she would follow it, until the ultimate truth was revealed. The pursuit had just begun. And she knew, with a chilling certainty, that this was only the beginning of a far larger and more perilous adventure.

Deciphering the Message

The Vatican library, with its hushed reverence and the scent of aged paper, felt like a sanctuary after the harrowing events in the solar temple. Yet, the peace was deceptive, a fragile veneer over the churning anxieties within Ana. Gábor's last words, a whispered promise etched onto the inside cover of the Codex, haunted her. It wasn't a simple message; it was a cryptic puzzle, a riddle wrapped in an enigma, a challenge posed from beyond the grave.

The inscription, barely visible under the fading ink, resembled a series of seemingly random symbols – a combination of Latin letters, ancient Romanian runes, and strange geometric shapes. Ana spent days, weeks even, poring over the Codex, comparing the symbols to her notes, to ancient texts gathered from Dr. Lupu's research, to the linguistic databases she had accessed during her time at the university. Each symbol felt like a piece of a colossal jigsaw, frustratingly out of place, yet undeniably connected.

She started with the Latin script. Several phrases were discernible, fragmented sentences that seemed to speak of a "Serpent's Eye," an "Obsidian Order," and a place called "Aethelred's Sanctuary." These words echoed the clues Gábor had left her before their perilous journey to the hidden temple. The cryptic messages were more than just places; they were names, organizations, and symbols connected by a shared history—a history as old as time. The phrases themselves were like pieces of a puzzle, the fragmented sentences hinting at a larger narrative—one that she had to piece together.

The Romanian runes proved more challenging. Ana's knowledge of Old Romanian was extensive, but these runes were unlike anything she had ever encountered. Their angular forms and esoteric glyphs hinted at a language far older, perhaps predating even the Dacian tribes. She spent countless hours in dusty archives, consulting with experts in runology and comparative linguistics, searching for any hint, any clue that might unlock their meaning. She discovered that the runes were not simply alphabetic characters but rather a system of ideograms – symbols that conveyed ideas and concepts rather than simply sounds. Each rune held a meaning that needed to be correctly interpreted to reveal the deeper meaning within the ancient script.

The geometric shapes were the most perplexing. They were reminiscent of astrological symbols, yet they didn't correspond to any known constellations or celestial bodies. Ana suspected they were a form of celestial cartography, perhaps indicating specific locations on Earth or even points in time. This suspicion led her to consult with experts in astronomy and archaeoastronomy who were able to provide some guidance.

The breakthrough came unexpectedly, during a late-night session in the library, while Ana was comparing the geometric symbols with a set of ancient Sumerian clay tablets she had managed to acquire through a contact in the British Museum. A peculiar alignment of symbols on one of the tablets mirrored a sequence of shapes in Gábor's message. The alignment of symbols revealed a hidden pattern: a sequence of coordinates. Not geographical coordinates, Ana realized, but temporal coordinates—a date.

The date coincided with the autumn equinox, a time when ancient civilizations had often associated with significant cosmological and ritual events. This was not a coincidence, she reasoned. The date pinpointed a precise moment in time, a time when something crucial was to happen, a specific event in the distant past, an event that held the key to understanding Gábor's cryptic message. But what was it?

With the temporal coordinate decoded, the linguistic elements of Gábor's message began to fall into place. The "Serpent's Eye," she now understood, wasn't a literal eye but a metaphor – a keyhole, a hidden entrance, a concealed passage leading to a forgotten place, perhaps Aethelred's Sanctuary. The Obsidian Order, she suspected, was a secretive society that guarded this location, protecting a truth so dangerous it threatened to shatter the world's understanding of history.

Armed with this newfound understanding, Ana began to unravel the larger narrative. Gábor's message wasn't just a collection of clues; it was a detailed itinerary, a roadmap guiding her to a hidden location, one that held the key to the true meaning of the prophecy, a place where the Obsidian Order's influence was strongest. A location that had been deliberately obscured throughout history.

The location pointed to a hidden monastery, not in the Carpathians, as she and Gábor had initially believed, but in a remote region of England, near the ancient city of York. A region shrouded in myth and legend, a location that held a place in history as one of the most active and important religious hubs in all of Western Europe—Aethelred's Sanctuary.

The monastery's existence was entirely undocumented. It had vanished from historical records centuries ago, swallowed by time and oblivion. Yet, Gábor's message provided a faint glimmer of hope. It offered a cryptic sequence of instructions, a series of clues hinting at the monastery's hidden location, providing a pathway through the maze of history and leading Ana to uncover a truth that had been buried for centuries. The monastery wasn't marked on any map. It didn't show up in any historical records or databases.

The Autumn Equinox approached, adding to the urgency. The time frame suggested that this secret location would only be accessible during that specific period. The Autumn Equinox represented a unique celestial alignment, a cosmological phenomenon connected to ancient rituals and myths. A date that was central to the beliefs and practices of the Obsidian Order.

A renewed sense of purpose fueled her. She was no longer merely a linguist deciphering ancient texts; she was a detective tracking a hidden organization, an archaeologist pursuing a forgotten history, a historian correcting the lies of centuries. She was the inheritor of Gábor's legacy, carrying his torch into the darkness.

The journey ahead was fraught with danger. The Obsidian Order was undoubtedly aware that Gábor's message had survived; they would be searching for Ana, anticipating her next move. She would need to be cautious. The pursuit was dangerous, but Ana, fueled by a mix of grief and determination, knew she would uncover the truth.

Ana meticulously prepared for her journey to England, carefully analyzing Gábor's message for any additional clues, cross-referencing the information with her research notes and Dr. Lupu's findings. The final part of the message revealed a symbol—a serpentine knot intricately interwoven, reminiscent of the Ouroboros, the ancient symbol of eternity and cyclical renewal. It was a symbol commonly associated with the Obsidian Order. But within this knot were smaller symbols, nearly imperceptible, requiring microscopic analysis.

This deeper analysis revealed a sequence of numbers, hidden within the very weave of the symbol. It was a code—a sequence of coordinates, this time geographically precise, pinpointing the exact location of Aethelred's Sanctuary, a location that had been deliberately hidden from history.

The quest to uncover the truth had only just begun. The mysteries deepened, and with each deciphered piece of the puzzle, the stakes grew even higher. Ana knew that uncovering the secrets of Aethelred's Sanctuary and confronting the Obsidian Order was not merely a quest for knowledge but a race against time to prevent another catastrophe, a catastrophe far greater than the one she had narrowly averted in the solar temple. The weight of the world, it seemed, now rested on her slender shoulders. The sun might have set on Gábor's life, but for Ana, the pursuit of justice, and the unraveling of the ancient mysteries surrounding Aethelred's Sanctuary, had just begun. The journey to England, and the confrontation with the Obsidian Order, awaited her. And she was ready.

A New Threat Emerges

The worn leather of the Codex felt cool against Ana's fingertips. Gábor's final message, etched in minuscule script on the inside cover, remained a frustrating enigma. It wasn't a simple farewell, nor a confession, but a carefully constructed cipher, a riddle layered with symbols she hadn't encountered before. The familiar runes of the Black Sun Codex were interspersed with strange, angular glyphs that resembled nothing she'd ever seen – not in her years of studying ancient languages, nor in Dr. Lupu's extensive research. The message seemed to reference a location, a name perhaps, but shrouded in ambiguity. The words themselves, even where she recognized the script, felt deliberately distorted, as if deliberately obfuscated to mislead any casual observer.

Days blurred into weeks as Ana poured over the message, consulting every linguistic resource she could access. She travelled to Oxford, to the Bodleian Library, its towering shelves packed with forgotten texts. She spent hours hunched over illuminated manuscripts, meticulously comparing the unfamiliar glyphs with the myriad of ancient alphabets and symbols. The pressure was immense – the knowledge that she carried a secret, a secret that could potentially unravel a conspiracy of global proportions. Every night, she replayed Gábor's sacrifice in her mind, the harrowing events in the subterranean temple, his fading breath, the haunted look in his eyes as he entrusted her with this final enigma.

Her breakthrough came unexpectedly, not in a dusty archive, but in a small, unassuming bookshop nestled within the cobbled streets of Prague. She stumbled upon a rare, out-of-print book on esoteric symbology, its pages filled with diagrams and descriptions of obscure societies and cults. Within its worn pages, she found it – a section dedicated to the "Order of the Obsidian Serpent," an organization whose symbols bore a striking resemblance to the glyphs in Gábor's message. The book offered little detail about the Order's history or purpose, but it hinted at a vast, shadowy network operating across centuries, connected to the same ancient power sources that had fueled the Sentinel. The organization's secrecy was profound; their existence barely acknowledged, even in the most obscure historical records.

The discovery sent a shiver down Ana's spine. The Sentinel, it seemed, were only one branch of a far more extensive, more sinister conspiracy. The Obsidian Serpent, if the book was to be believed, was an ancient order that predated even the Black Sun cult, its roots buried deep within the pre-Christian world. Its objectives, if they could be guessed, were as chilling as they were obscure. The book referenced rituals, sacrifices, and the manipulation of powerful geological forces – a chilling echo of what she'd witnessed in the hidden solar temple.

Armed with this new knowledge, Ana revisited Gábor's message. The location referenced by the glyphs, previously an indecipherable jumble, now held a frightening clarity. It wasn't a place on a map, but a historical event, a specific date marking a catastrophic geological incident: the eruption of Vesuvius in 79 AD. The message, Ana realized, wasn't simply a clue; it was a warning. The Obsidian Serpent was planning to trigger a similar event, a chain reaction of seismic upheavals, on a scale far greater than Pompeii. The Sentinel, she now understood, had been merely a pawn in their larger game.

Ana's investigation led her to Naples, to the shadowed alleys and ancient ruins surrounding Mount Vesuvius. She spent days scouring the local archives, studying ancient texts and local folklore. She learned about the forgotten cults and beliefs that thrived in the shadow of the volcano, about the ancient rites and prophecies that whispered of its power. She unearthed accounts of unusual geological activity preceding the eruption, accounts often dismissed as superstition or exaggeration, but now revealing themselves as potential clues. These accounts frequently mentioned a clandestine organization, whose symbols mirrored the Obsidian Serpent's markings, active in the region in the years leading up to the disaster.

Her research revealed that the Obsidian Serpent wasn't merely interested in causing cataclysmic events; they sought to harness the power released during these upheavals. They believed the earth held untapped energy, a mystical force that could be controlled and weaponized. The solar temple she'd discovered earlier, a mere satellite in their larger network, was only one of numerous sites across the globe, each designed to amplify and direct this earth-shattering energy. The location of these sites remained a mystery, but the pattern hinted at a global network, a terrifyingly well-organized scheme to plunge the world into chaos.

The weight of this revelation was almost unbearable. The threat was far greater than she had ever imagined, extending far beyond the power of the Sentinel. She was no longer merely deciphering an ancient text; she was fighting against a force that spanned millennia, a conspiracy that aimed to reshape the world in its own terrifying image. The seemingly simple message from Gábor was, in fact, a testament to the depth of the conspiracy, a desperate warning from the grave. His sacrifice had bought her time, given her the knowledge to identify this new, far more dangerous threat.

Ana's search led her to hidden passages beneath the ruins of Pompeii, passages sealed for centuries. Within these subterranean labyrinths, she discovered frescoes depicting the Obsidian Serpent's rituals, their symbols intricately interwoven with depictions of geological events. She found cryptic maps indicating the location of other "earth-energy amplifiers," hidden across the globe. The maps were incomplete, many sections destroyed by the eruption of Vesuvius itself. Yet, the fragments that remained provided enough information to confirm the global scale of the Serpent's operations. She needed to find the remaining fragments – fragments that might be scattered across the world, from ancient sites in the Americas to forgotten temples in the Far East.

Ana knew she couldn't face this new threat alone. She needed allies, experts in various fields – geologists, seismologists, historians who could help her identify and analyze the data, to locate the remaining sites. She sought out old contacts from her time with Dr. Lupu, reaching out to scholars across the globe, each a specialist in a specific area of expertise, building a team of dedicated and brave individuals to help her in this desperate fight against time. This time, she wouldn't be working in the shadows. She'd need to involve international authorities, possibly even the military, to prevent the world-altering catastrophe that the Obsidian Serpent was so diligently preparing. The journey ahead was fraught with peril, but Ana knew that the fate of the world rested on her ability to unravel the Serpent's plan and expose their nefarious plot before it was too late. Gábor's sacrifice, the message he had so painstakingly left for her, had given her the impetus to carry the fight forward, to finish the task he couldn't. The fight was far from over. The Obsidian Serpent represented a threat of unimaginable proportions – a challenge that would test her resilience, her intellect, and her courage to their absolute limits. The game had just begun.

The Location

The worn leather of the Codex felt cool beneath her fingertips, the scent of aged parchment and something faintly metallic clinging to the air. Ana traced the intricate script of Gábor's final message, the minuscule characters etched with a precision that belied the circumstances of its creation. The familiar runes of the Black Sun Codex, the symbols she'd spent months deciphering, were interwoven with a new set of glyphs, angular and sharp, utterly alien. These were not the elegant curves of ancient Dacian script, nor the stark linearity of Etruscan. They were something else entirely, something older, something... unsettling.

She had initially dismissed them as mere ornamentation, a decorative flourish added to the cryptic message, but the more she studied them, the more convinced she became that they were integral to the cipher. They weren't random; they followed a pattern, a rhythm, a logic she couldn't yet grasp. Some resembled constellations, others echoed the complex geometry of the Black Sun itself, but warped, distorted, as if viewed through a fractured lens.

Days blurred into a whirlwind of research. Ana consulted every linguistic database she could access, poring over obscure texts on forgotten languages, comparing Gábor's glyphs to everything from ancient Sumerian cuneiform to the enigmatic Voynich manuscript. The frustration was palpable, the weight of responsibility crushing. Each dead end chipped away at her resolve, each unanswered question gnawing at her sanity. She felt the ghost of Gábor's presence beside her, his silent encouragement a constant companion in her solitary struggle.

Then, a breakthrough. While examining a collection of pre-Roman artifacts from the Carpathian region – a collection Dr.

Lupu had been particularly interested in – she found it: a reference, a fleeting mention in a dusty academic paper, to a previously unknown tribe, the Alpsini , who inhabited the remote valleys of the eastern Carpathians. Their language, described as a "complex system of pictographs and symbolic representations," was largely lost to history, only fragmented examples surviving in scattered archeological finds.

The paper included a single, crudely drawn image of a seemingly insignificant artifact – a small, intricately carved stone amulet. The amulet's design, however, mirrored the strange, angular glyphs in Gábor's message. The realization hit Ana with the force of a physical blow. Gábor's message wasn't just a cipher; it was a map, a coded reference to the Alpsini and their lost language. The glyphs were not merely decorative; they represented locations, specific coordinates tied to significant sites associated with the Alpsini's unique culture.

The stone amulet in the paper showed a stylized representation of the Carpathian Mountains, their peaks marked by small, distinct symbols. Ana superimposed the amulet's image onto a modern map of the Carpathians, carefully comparing the positions of the symbols with the glyphs in Gábor's message. One by one, the locations started to emerge. The symbols weren't arbitrary; they corresponded to specific mountain passes, hidden valleys, and remote caves. Each location represented a point in a larger network, a pattern gradually revealing itself.

The message's final glyph, a complex, swirling symbol resembling a stylized sun, pointed to a specific location: a remote, almost inaccessible cave system nestled high in the Făgăraș Mountains, a region known for its dense forests and treacherous terrain. According to local folklore, the cave system was believed to be the ancient burial ground of the Alpsini, a place shrouded in mystery and steeped in local legends of hidden treasures and forbidden knowledge.

Armed with this newfound knowledge, Ana assembled her team. Her contacts from the academic world were quickly mobilized, their specialized expertise proving invaluable. Dr.

Elena Popescu, a leading expert in Dacian archaeology, joined the expedition, bringing with her years of experience and an encyclopedic knowledge of the region's history. Professor Ionel Stanescu, a renowned geologist, would analyze the geological formations of the cave system, searching for any evidence of the seismic triggers mentioned in the Black Sun Codex. And Marius Florescu, a skilled cartographer, meticulously mapped the cave system based on Ana's decoding of Gábor's message, using satellite imagery and historical maps to navigate the treacherous terrain.

Their journey to the Făgăraș Mountains was arduous. The winding mountain roads were barely passable, and the terrain was unforgiving. The team battled torrential rain, treacherous landslides, and the ever-present threat of encountering wild animals. But their determination remained unshaken. The weight of the world, quite literally, rested upon their shoulders.

The cave system itself was a labyrinth of narrow tunnels, vast chambers, and subterranean lakes. The air hung heavy with the scent of damp earth and something else, something ancient and faintly unsettling – a musty odor reminiscent of decaying organic matter. The walls were adorned with intricate carvings, the same angular glyphs that had appeared in Gábor's message, repeating endlessly, forming complex patterns and cryptic narratives.

The deeper they ventured into the heart of the cave system, the more Ana was convinced that they were dealing with something extraordinary. Professor Stanescu's preliminary geological surveys confirmed the existence of significant geological fault lines, the very kind of seismic triggers the Black Sun Codex had described. The cave system was not merely a natural formation; it was a meticulously engineered network, a subterranean complex built by the Alpsini thousands of years ago.

As they explored the deeper recesses of the cave system, they discovered a hidden chamber, its entrance concealed behind a cleverly designed stone wall. Inside, they found a collection of artifacts: intricately crafted tools, ceremonial objects, and numerous examples of the Alpsini's unique writing system. Among these artifacts, they found a large, stone tablet, its surface covered in elaborate carvings that were strikingly similar to the symbols in Gábor's message. The tablet's surface seemed to depict a complex system of levers and pulleys, a kind of intricate mechanism – a machine of some sort.

Ana, with the help of Dr. Popescu, began to decipher the carvings on the tablet. It wasn't a simple inscription; it was a schematic, a blueprint of a sophisticated mechanism capable of manipulating the geological fault lines in the region. The Alpsini had not simply built a cave system; they had built a device capable of triggering catastrophic earthquakes. The Obsidian Serpent, it seemed, were far from the only ones who held this kind of power.

The implications of their discovery were staggering. The Obsidian Serpent wasn't simply exploiting ancient technology; they had somehow discovered and learned to control the Alpsini's hidden mechanism. Ana knew she and her team had to act quickly, to shut down the device and prevent a catastrophic seismic event. The race was far from over, and the stakes had just risen dramatically. The whispers of ancient power, the shadows of forgotten history, had taken a new, terrifying form. The fight for the world's future had just begun in earnest. The Alpsini's hidden knowledge was the key, but unlocking its secrets would require more than just linguistic skill and archaeological expertise. It would require facing the darkest depths of humanity's past, confronting the echoes of long-forgotten civilizations, and ultimately, averting a future where the earth itself would be their enemy.

Anas Decision

The flickering candlelight cast long, dancing shadows across the worn map spread out on her desk, the parchment brittle with age. Ana traced the faded ink lines with a trembling finger, the chilling reality of Gábor's sacrifice settling heavily on her soul. He was gone, yet his unwavering dedication, his brilliant mind, his quiet courage, echoed in the silence of her Bucharest apartment. The weight of his loss threatened to crush her, but a fierce determination, born from grief and fueled by a renewed sense of purpose, began to stir within her. Gábor's death couldn't be in vain. His final cryptic message, a symphony of unfamiliar glyphs interwoven with the familiar runes of the Black Sun Codex, was a testament to his enduring spirit, a challenge she couldn't refuse.

She leaned back in her chair, the cold Bucharest night pressing against the windowpane. The city lights blurred into indistinct streaks, mirroring the chaotic thoughts swirling in her mind. The Obsidian Serpent, the shadowy organization that had orchestrated Dr. Lupu's murder and pursued them relentlessly, remained at large. Their sinister plan, the activation of the Alpsini's seismic trigger, was thwarted, but only temporarily. Ana knew, with a chilling certainty, that they wouldn't simply disappear. They would regroup, they would adapt, they would undoubtedly seek another way to unleash their catastrophic scheme.

Gábor's message, however, held the potential to unravel their future plans. Those unfamiliar glyphs – what language did they represent? What civilization, long vanished from the annals of history, held the key to their understanding? Ana picked up a worn volume on Etruscan linguistics, its pages dog-eared and annotated with her own hurried notes. It provided a starting point, a familiar framework to compare the strange script against. Yet, the more she examined the symbols, the more evident it became that this was something profoundly different, something that lay beyond the scope of her current expertise.

Days bled into weeks as Ana immersed herself in research, poring over obscure texts, seeking the counsel of forgotten languages. She delved into the archives of the Romanian Academy, her fingers tracing the delicate script of ancient manuscripts, her eyes straining to decipher the faded ink. The library's hushed atmosphere became her sanctuary, a refuge from the turmoil of her grief and the looming threat of the Obsidian Serpent. She contacted colleagues around the world, specialists in ancient languages and forgotten cultures, seeking their expertise and collaboration. The response was a mix of skepticism and reluctant intrigue, a testament to the unusual nature of the glyphs and the potential implications of their discovery.

One such contact, Dr. Elias Thorne, a renowned expert in pre-Roman cultures of the Carpathian region, expressed a cautious interest. His initial skepticism gradually eroded as Ana shared her findings. He recognized certain stylistic elements that hinted at a connection to a long-lost civilization, a culture shrouded in myth and legend, known only through fragmented accounts and scattered archaeological discoveries: the Getae. This ancient Thracian tribe, possessing a rich and complex culture, had vanished without a trace, leaving behind only whispers of their existence and a few enigmatic artifacts. Dr. Thorne believed that Gábor's message held the key to understanding their advanced knowledge, a technology potentially far beyond their time.

Fueled by this new lead, Ana embarked on a perilous journey through the rugged Carpathian Mountains, retracing Gábor's steps, seeking the remnants of a forgotten world. She followed cryptic clues from his field notes, her heart pounding with a mixture of fear and anticipation. She visited remote villages, seeking information from the locals, their tales interwoven with ancient folklore and whispered legends. She spent hours deciphering fragmented inscriptions on ancient stones, their weathered surfaces whispering secrets from a bygone era. The mountain air was sharp and cold, the wind howling through the ancient forests, yet Ana felt a strange sense of connection to the land, as though the spirits of the past were guiding her, urging her forward.

Each clue, each fragmented inscription, each whispered legend, brought her closer to unraveling the mystery of Gábor's final message. The Getae, it seemed, possessed a sophisticated understanding of seismology, far surpassing that of their contemporaries. They had mastered the ability to harness the earth's energy, using it to power their enigmatic technology, a technology that the Obsidian Serpent had apparently rediscovered and sought to weaponize. The seismic triggers weren't simply ancient mechanisms; they were sophisticated devices, capable of triggering earthquakes of unprecedented magnitude. Ana realized the true scale of the threat they faced. This wasn't just a regional catastrophe; it could potentially trigger a global seismic event, reshaping the face of the planet.

The research was painstaking, the journey perilous, but Ana persevered. Driven by a desire to honor Gábor's memory and avert a global catastrophe, she refused to yield to despair or fear. She visited the Vatican Secret Archives once more, hoping to find further evidence to corroborate Dr. Thorne's findings, and stumbled upon ancient maps detailing a hidden network of subterranean tunnels that spanned the Carpathians. These tunnels, according to the maps, connected a series of sacred sites associated with the Getae, including a hidden solar temple – the very place where the Alpsini device was activated.

The implications were staggering. The Obsidian Serpent hadn't merely stumbled upon the Alpsini device; they had systematically mapped out and explored this ancient network, seeking to control the earth's energy for their nefarious purposes. They sought to awaken something far more ancient and powerful than anyone could have imagined. And it was clear that they were closer to achieving their goal than anyone had initially suspected. The discovery of the ancient network was not simply a historical curiosity, but a grim warning: the Obsidian Serpent was on the cusp of achieving their ultimate objective.

Ana's determination hardened. The weight of Gábor's sacrifice, coupled with the enormity of the threat, galvanized her resolve. She would continue their work, unraveling the secrets of the Getae, exposing the Obsidian Serpent, and ensuring that the world would never have to face the consequences of their terrifying ambition. The journey ahead was fraught with danger, filled with uncertainty, but Ana knew that she couldn't stop. Gábor's spirit lived on, not only in the memories she cherished but in the unfinished work that lay before her. The fight for the planet's future had only just begun. The ancient whispers, once faint and distant, now echoed with a chilling clarity, urging her onward, toward a confrontation with a power far older and more terrifying than anything she could have imagined. The ancient secrets of the Carpathians had only begun to reveal their true depths, and Ana, armed with her knowledge and the memory of Gábor's sacrifice, was ready to face them head-on. The world's fate rested on her shoulders, and she would not fail.

Chapter 8

Father's Research

Revisiting Fathers Work

The worn leather-bound journals felt cool beneath Ana's fingertips, the scent of aged paper and decaying ink filling her small, cluttered study. Dust motes danced in the single shaft of afternoon sunlight slicing through the grimy windowpane, illuminating the intricate script within. These were her father's journals, a collection of meticulously documented research spanning decades, a legacy she had initially dismissed in the wake of Gábor's death and the harrowing events surrounding the Black Sun Codex. Now, faced with a cryptic message hinting at a far greater conspiracy, the journals represented her only hope.

Gábor's final message, scrawled in barely decipherable code across the last page of the Codex, had been a chilling echo of her father's life's work: a network far older and more sinister than The Sentinel. It spoke of a hidden order, predating even the earliest known civilizations, pulling strings from the shadows, its motives as opaque as its origins. The message included a series of symbols, strikingly similar to some she'd seen fleetingly in her father's annotations, symbols that seemed to predate even the oldest known languages.

The first few weeks were a blur of frantic searching, sifting through mountains of handwritten notes, sketches of ancient artifacts, and faded photographs. Her father, Professor Nicolae Dragan, had been a respected but eccentric linguist, his research focusing on the pre-Indo-European languages of the Carpathian region – a field considered by many to be bordering on fringe science. He had spent years meticulously tracing linguistic roots, believing that the keys to understanding humanity's past lay hidden within forgotten tongues and long-lost dialects. His obsession had bordered on the obsessive, fueling countless nights spent poring over dusty texts and exploring remote archaeological sites, leaving behind a vast, disorganized repository of knowledge.

Ana began with the most recent entries, hoping to find a logical starting point, a roadmap to follow through the labyrinthine world of her father's research. But the notes were fragmented, filled with cryptic references, tantalizing clues that seemed to lead nowhere. She found references to obscure texts, long-lost dialects, and rituals that seemed pulled from mythology. There were mentions of places she had never heard of, names whispered only in hushed tones by local villagers – remote mountain villages nestled deep within the Carpathians, places untouched by modern civilization.

One particular entry caught her eye – a detailed description of a specific type of runic inscription, similar but not identical to those found etched onto Dr. Lupu's body. Her father had labeled them "Proto-Runes," suggesting an even older origin than the commonly understood Norse runes. He hypothesized that these symbols were a form of proto-writing, predating even the earliest known forms of written language, a system of communication used by a lost civilization that had existed long before recorded history. He postulated this civilization had mastered technologies beyond human comprehension, technologies capable of manipulating the earth itself.

Days turned into weeks, and weeks into months. Ana immersed herself in her father's work, slowly piecing together the fragmented puzzle. She consulted with experts, contacted academics specializing in ancient languages and forgotten cultures, comparing her father's findings to other known inscriptions and archaeological discoveries. The deeper she delved, the more she realized the scope of her father's research, the incredible magnitude of the hidden knowledge he had unearthed.

She discovered hidden codes within his seemingly random notes, mathematical sequences woven into the margins of his pages, geometrical patterns suggestive of astronomical alignments, hinting at a deep understanding of celestial mechanics. Her father, the quiet, unassuming scholar, had been on the brink of a groundbreaking discovery, a discovery that had led to his, or possibly his associates', death.

She found sketches of artifacts, painstakingly drawn representations of tools and implements that defied categorization, objects that looked like they belonged to a science fiction film rather than a pre-historic culture. These images were accompanied by notes written in an archaic form of Latin, interwoven with elements of languages she couldn't identify. She discovered that he had translated some fragments into modern Romanian, but the full meaning eluded her.

One particularly chilling entry detailed her father's encounter with a secretive society, a clandestine organization dedicated to the preservation – or perhaps the manipulation – of these ancient secrets. He had described them as guardians of an ancient knowledge, protectors of a technology that had the power to reshape the world, a power that, in the wrong hands, could unleash unimaginable destruction. His description echoed eerily Gábor's last words, confirming the existence of a power far greater and more ancient than The Sentinel.

The journals contained detailed maps of remote locations in the Carpathians, marked with symbols that corresponded to those found in the Black Sun Codex and on Dr. Lupu's body. These were not just random markings; they were coordinates, pinpointing specific sites of historical significance. These sites were more than just ancient ruins; they were points of power, nodes within a network that seemed to link the earth's geological fault lines.

As Ana pieced together the fragmented clues, a horrifying truth began to dawn on her. Her father's research wasn't just about uncovering a lost civilization; it was about understanding a technology capable of triggering catastrophic geological events, a technology that had been guarded for millennia by a hidden organization, an organization that Gábor and Lupu had both stumbled upon, and paid the ultimate price.

The weight of the responsibility settled heavily upon her. She was no longer just a linguist; she was the inheritor of a dangerous legacy, the guardian of secrets that could either save the world or destroy it. Gábor's sacrifice, the horrifying events she had witnessed, all pointed to a single terrifying conclusion: the fight was far from over. The ancient order still existed, and now, it knew she was coming. The new mystery was not just a continuation of the old one – it was its escalation. The game had changed. And the stakes were far higher than she could have ever imagined. She was alone, but she had her father's work. And she would not fail him. She would find them. And she would stop them.

Uncovering Connections

The first journal, dated 1988, was a deceptively simple account of his fieldwork in the remote Carpathian villages. Ana skimmed through familiar descriptions of folk traditions, dialect variations, and architectural styles – all meticulously documented with photographs and hand-drawn sketches. Then, a subtle shift. A seemingly innocuous note, tucked away in the margin: "The old woman's tale of the 'Sunken City' – dismissed as folklore, but the detail of the 'three-pointed star'… warrants further investigation." The underlining was heavy, insistent. This was no casual observation; this was a flag planted in the landscape of her father's mind. The "Sunken City" – a phrase that echoed vaguely in her memory, a whisper from the margins of her own childhood.

Days bled into weeks. Ana painstakingly transcribed her father's notes, meticulously cross-referencing entries, comparing handwriting styles, analyzing the evolution of his thought processes over decades. She found inconsistencies, deliberate omissions, and a carefully cultivated trail of red herrings, a deliberate obfuscation of his true purpose. Was it self-preservation? A desire to protect someone, or something? Or was it simply a matter of professional caution, knowing the dangerous implications of the knowledge he was amassing?

One particular entry, from 1995, caught her attention. It described a visit to the Vatican Secret Archives, a pilgrimage fueled by a cryptic letter he'd received. The letter itself was not included in the journal, only a carefully worded description of its contents: "reference to the 'Black Sun'… a different context entirely… not celestial… the key lies in the linguistics… the forgotten tongue." The entry continued with frustrated scribbles, notes about linguistic dead-ends and the limitations of existing historical records. He'd mentioned a particular dialect, a pre-Romanian tongue with barely any surviving documentation, spoken only in isolated communities in the highest reaches of the Carpathians.

The frustration was palpable, a testament to his relentless pursuit of answers and his eventual defeat. But it wasn't a complete defeat. Hidden within a loose page, tucked between the brittle leaves of a dried flower, Ana discovered a rough map, sketched in haste, annotated with indecipherable symbols. It resembled a star chart, but the constellations were wrong, the relationships between the celestial bodies distorted, almost deliberately flawed. This was no ordinary astronomical map. It was something else. Something far more sinister.

Ana's knowledge of linguistics became her most powerful tool. She spent weeks immersed in obscure linguistic texts, dusty academic papers, and long-forgotten scholarly debates. She followed the threads of her father's research, piecing together fragments of information, chasing whispers from the past. She tracked down obscure linguistic scholars, experts in dead languages and forgotten dialects, seeking guidance, validation, and perhaps, answers. Some were helpful, offering insights into the linguistic intricacies of ancient Romanian and its various iterations. Others were dismissive, their skepticism fueled by the outlandish nature of her father's theories.

The map remained the biggest puzzle. Its cryptic symbols, a strange mix of astrological imagery and pre-Romanian script, defied easy interpretation. She consulted with several experts in ancient symbology, all of whom offered varying interpretations, none of which were truly satisfactory. The key, she realized, lay not in the symbols themselves, but in their arrangement, the subtle relationships between them, the patterns hidden beneath the surface. It was a riddle wrapped in an enigma, obscured by deliberate obfuscation.

Meanwhile, she uncovered further details from her father's

research. He had meticulously documented the existence of a hidden society, an ancient order that predated Christianity, its origins lost in the mists of time. The organization worshipped a deity they called the 'Black Sun', not a celestial body, but an abstract concept, a personification of humanity's darkest impulses, its inherent capacity for destruction and self-annihilation. He documented their rituals, their beliefs, and their seemingly limitless resources. They were the ones who had activated the seismic triggers detailed in the Black Sun Codex. This was no mere conspiracy; it was a centuries-old organization operating on a global scale.

Her father's research revealed that the organization had been manipulating global events for centuries, using subtly placed triggers that would cause massive earthquakes and tsunamis. He had found evidence of their involvement in numerous historical catastrophes, from the Lisbon earthquake of 1755 to the San Francisco earthquake of 1906. They were using ancient knowledge, manipulating the earth itself, to achieve their malevolent goals. And the earthquakes weren't random acts of nature; they were carefully orchestrated events designed to reshape the world in their image.

One chilling entry recounted her father's discovery of a network of ancient solar temples, hidden beneath the earth's surface, acting as nodes in a vast, interconnected system. These temples were not mere places of worship; they were sophisticated engineering marvels, ancient technology capable of manipulating tectonic plates and triggering seismic activity. The system resembled a gigantic, subterranean network, controlled by a central hub – a location her father was never able to identify.

As she delved deeper into her father's work, Ana understood the true scope of the threat. The organization wasn't simply interested in causing chaos; they were seeking to reshape the world, to usher in a new era of darkness, an era governed by their twisted vision of order. They believed themselves to be guardians of an ancient secret, a cosmic truth that justified their actions, a twisted justification for their genocidal ambitions.

The deeper Ana dug, the more she realized her father's research was incomplete, fragmentary. It was a jigsaw puzzle with many pieces missing, the picture obscured by deliberate omissions and cryptic references. He had been close, tantalizingly close, to uncovering the full truth, yet he had never fully understood the organization's ultimate goal. He had been close to exposing them, to bringing them to justice. But he had failed. Or had he? There was something more, a missing piece of the puzzle. A final entry, hidden at the back of the final journal, held a single, underlined sentence: "The key is not in the stars… but in the earth."

This cryptic message gave Ana a renewed purpose. The "Sunken City" – mentioned so casually in the 1988 entry – held the key. Her father had dismissed it as folklore, but now, Ana knew it was far more than that. It was a clue, a breadcrumb leading her to the final answer. It was a location, a hidden city lost beneath the waves, the ultimate repository of the organization's ancient secrets. And it was where she would have to go next. She packed a bag, the weight of her father's legacy heavy in her heart, and prepared for the journey. The fight, far from over, had only just begun. Her father's sacrifice would not be in vain.

Hidden Symbolism

The second journal, bound in cracked leather and smelling faintly of woodsmoke and old paper, was a stark contrast to the first. Gone were the neat, organized entries; this was a chaotic jumble of notes, sketches, and hastily scribbled equations. The handwriting, initially legible, deteriorated towards the end, becoming a frantic scrawl that mirrored the urgency of the discoveries within. Ana traced her finger along the margins, her eyes scanning the pages with a growing sense of unease. This wasn't just research; it was a desperate race against time.

Early entries detailed his further investigations into Carpathian folklore, focusing on the recurring motif of the "three-pointed star" – the symbol etched onto her father's body. He'd unearthed tales from numerous villages, each with slight variations but all pointing towards a common origin: a submerged city, a sacred place swallowed by the sea long ago. The consistency of the details was striking, especially the descriptions of a specific astronomical alignment – a conjunction of the sun, moon, and a particular star constellation – said to have occurred during the city's submergence. This wasn't just a legend, Ana realized; this was a precise historical record, encoded within folklore.

Then came the mathematical notations. At first, they appeared random, a bewildering array of numbers and symbols. But as Ana studied them, a pattern emerged – a complex system of coordinates, intricately linked to the astronomical alignments mentioned in the folklore accounts. Her father, a historian by training, had somehow deciphered the astronomical and mathematical language of the ancient texts, transforming legends into geographical data. The coordinates, she suspected, pointed to the location of the Sunken City. But what was the purpose? What secrets did this lost city hold?

Interspersed amongst the numbers and astronomical charts were drawings – remarkably detailed sketches of ancient artifacts, symbols, and architectural designs. One recurring image was a stylized sun, not the simple circle she had previously encountered, but a complex, geometric design resembling a multifaceted crystal. Ana remembered seeing similar designs etched onto the walls of the Transylvanian monastery, a subtle echo connecting the Sunken City to the Black Sun Codex. This wasn't just a coincidence; it was a deliberate link, carefully woven into the fabric of her father's research.

The symbolism became increasingly intricate. Ana identified recurring patterns – the three-pointed star, the multifaceted sun, and various geometric shapes, all intricately intertwined in a complex tapestry of meaning. Her knowledge of linguistics proved invaluable here, as she recognized some of the symbols as variations of ancient alphabets – Etruscan, Phoenician, even remnants of pre-Indo-European scripts. These were not simply decorative elements; they were part of a sophisticated system of encoding, a secret language designed to conceal the true nature of the Sunken City's secrets.

One entry stood out – a frantic, almost desperate scribble filled with a mixture of Romanian and Latin, along with a series of equations and symbols that defied immediate understanding. It seemed to be a desperate attempt to unravel the final piece of the puzzle – a warning, perhaps, or a last-ditch attempt to decode a crucial element before time ran out. Next to it, a small, almost imperceptible sketch of a mechanism – a complex device involving gears, levers, and a central crystal structure. It resembled the diagrams of ancient astronomical instruments, but with a sinister, almost threatening undertone.

As Ana delved deeper into her father's research, a terrifying realization dawned upon her. The Sunken City wasn't just a lost city; it was a powerful weapon – a nexus of immense energy, capable of triggering catastrophic events, as foretold in the Black Sun Codex. The mechanisms depicted in the final journal entry weren't just astronomical instruments; they were control systems, potentially capable of manipulating seismic activity. The ancient prophecy, previously dismissed as a fanciful legend, was now a terrifyingly plausible scenario. Her father had understood this, and in his desperate pursuit of knowledge, had inadvertently triggered the attention of a powerful, shadowy organization – the Sentinel.

The hidden symbolism wasn't just a random collection of symbols; it was a map, a roadmap to the Sunken City. The three-pointed star represented a specific geographical location, possibly a triangulation point. The multifaceted sun symbolized the city itself, its many facets representing different aspects of its function. The mathematical coordinates were not just random numbers, but a sophisticated encoding system, linking the city's location to the astronomical alignment that had occurred during its submergence. It was a sophisticated cryptographic puzzle, ingeniously hidden within the seemingly innocent folklore and astronomical data.

The closer Ana got to understanding her father's work, the

more she realized the depth of the threat. The Sentinel wasn't just some ancient order protecting ancient knowledge; they were actively seeking to weaponize it. They sought to awaken the Sunken City, unleashing a cataclysmic event that would reshape the world. And her father, in his pursuit of truth, had stumbled upon their plan, triggering the events that led to his murder.

The final pages of the journal contained a series of sketches of the city's supposed architecture. Intricate designs, reminiscent of both ancient Egyptian and Mesopotamian structures, hinted at a civilization far more advanced than previously imagined. The buildings were not simply temples or palaces; they appeared to be sophisticated machinery, carefully integrated into the city's structure. The descriptions of hidden chambers, elaborate mechanisms, and complex power sources pointed to a technologically advanced society that had mastered energy sources beyond anything currently known.

The weight of this discovery pressed down on Ana. She was not just unraveling an ancient mystery; she was facing a global threat that could extinguish humanity. She was walking in her father's footsteps, but now, the path was far more treacherous, the stakes far higher. The Sunken City was not merely a lost city, it was a dormant weapon of unimaginable power, ready to awaken at the hands of The Sentinel. The race against time was far from over; in fact, it was only just beginning. She had to find the city, understand its mechanism, and stop The Sentinel before they could unleash its devastating potential. The cryptic clues hidden within her father's research weren't just symbols; they were a lifeline, a path leading her to confront the greatest challenge of her life. The legacy her father left behind was not just a collection of notes and equations; it was a battle cry, a call to arms against a darkness older than time itself.

Her father's last entry, a fragmented sentence in a mixture of Romanian and Latin, hinted at a possible weakness in the Sentinel's plan, a flaw in the mechanism of the Sunken City. It was a glimmer of hope in the face of overwhelming despair. A cryptic phrase, almost indecipherable, suggested a countermeasure, a way to neutralize the power source of the city.

But to understand it, she needed to venture into unknown territory, to piece together the last fragments of her father's research before The Sentinel could act. The path ahead was dangerous, filled with uncertainties and unimaginable threats, but Ana, armed with her father's legacy and the knowledge she'd gleaned from his cryptic research, was ready to face it. The fight was far from over. The Sunken City awaited. And the world held its breath.

The Researchs Significance

The weight of her father's legacy pressed down on Ana. The chaotic scrawl of his final journal entries, a testament to his frantic race against time, was more than just a collection of notes; it was a roadmap to a future he hadn't lived to see. She traced the faded ink, her fingertip lingering on a particularly cryptic passage – a series of seemingly random symbols interspersed with Latin phrases she recognized as fragments of ancient Roman prayers to Sol Invictus, the unconquered sun. The connection to the "Black Sun" prophecy was undeniable. It wasn't merely a metaphorical representation of darkness; it was a literal key to unlocking a catastrophic event, an event her father had dedicated his life to preventing.

His research, she now understood, wasn't just about deciphering ancient languages or unearthing forgotten civilizations. It was about stopping a cataclysm. The Sunken City wasn't merely a legend; it was real, a nexus of immense power, potentially capable of triggering global seismic activity. Her father's work represented the single most significant body of knowledge on the subject, a culmination of decades of tireless investigation, painstaking research, and calculated risks. The implications were staggering.

Ana meticulously examined the pages, her mind piecing together the fragmented clues. She recognized certain symbols as variations of those etched onto her father's body – a macabre signature of his assassins. Others resembled archaic astronomical charts, seemingly charting the celestial movements of stars unknown to modern astronomy. She cross-referenced the symbols with his earlier, more organized journals, searching for patterns, for context. Each small detail, each seemingly insignificant stroke of the pen, held a potential key.

Days blurred into weeks as Ana immersed herself in her father's research. She consulted with experts – historians, linguists, even geophysicists – each contributing a piece to the larger puzzle. The Vatican archives, a place her father had often frequented, yielded further insights. She discovered that the prophecy, far from being a superstitious tale, was a highly detailed account of a technological marvel – a sophisticated network of seismic triggers hidden within the Sunken City, a network designed to manipulate the Earth's tectonic plates. The "awakening" her father had spoken of wasn't a mystical event; it was the deliberate activation of this ancient technology.

The implications were chilling. The Sentinel, the shadowy organization that had pursued her father and ultimately claimed his life, were not merely interested in ancient artifacts or obscure prophecies. They sought to control this technology, to unleash a global catastrophe. The reasons remained unclear, but the potential consequences were devastating: widespread earthquakes, tsunamis, volcanic eruptions – a planet-wide disaster of unimaginable proportions.

Ana's knowledge of linguistics proved invaluable. She uncovered a series of hidden codes embedded within the seemingly random scribbles of her father's final journal. One code, written in a dialect of ancient Dacian, revealed the location of a hidden chamber within the Sunken City. This chamber, according to her father's notes, contained the primary control mechanism for the seismic network – a device capable of both activating and deactivating the entire system. This was the countermeasure her father had alluded to in his final, fragmented entry.

Another code, written in a complex cipher that combined elements of Etruscan and Proto-Indo-European languages, revealed the Sentinel's plan. They intended to activate the seismic network in stages, triggering smaller earthquakes initially to mask their activities and gradually escalating the intensity until they achieved their ultimate objective – global chaos.

But there were still mysteries to unravel. Her father's notes contained numerous references to a "keystone" – a specific component within the control mechanism. Without it, the activation process would be incomplete, rendering the seismic network inert. However, the location and nature of this keystone remained elusive. Ana's research revealed that the keystone was not a physical object, but rather a specific sequence of astronomical events, a celestial alignment that only occurred once every several millennia.

The urgency mounted. The Sentinel, alerted to Ana's involvement, stepped up their pursuit. She faced constant threats, close calls, and betrayals, her every move shadowed by unseen eyes. She had to rely on her intellect and her father's cryptic notes to outwit them, to decode the remaining secrets before it was too late. Ana understood that the race wasn't just about finding the keystone or deactivating the seismic network. It was about understanding the larger motive, understanding the true goals of The Sentinel.

Her father's research revealed that The Sentinel was not a monolithic organization. It was a network of disparate factions, each with its own agenda, united only by their pursuit of power and the ultimate control over the Sunken City's mechanism. The conspiracy extended beyond national borders, beyond political ideologies – a tapestry of intrigue stretching back to the dawn of civilization.

As Ana delved deeper, she discovered that her father had uncovered a secret history, a hidden narrative that challenged everything she thought she knew about the ancient world. The Sunken City wasn't just a technological marvel; it was a testament to the power of ancient knowledge, a testament to forgotten civilizations, and to their capacity for both creation and destruction.

Ana found her father's detailed notes on the city's construction, a breathtaking feat of engineering involving advanced techniques lost to time. This wasn't merely a city swallowed by the sea; it was a deliberately submerged technological marvel, a feat of unimaginable ingenuity that rivaled any modern-day wonder. Her father's research painted a picture of a highly advanced civilization, capable of manipulating the Earth's natural processes with a level of precision that defied comprehension. This civilization, however, had vanished without a trace, leaving behind only fragments of its knowledge and a warning that could not be ignored.

The final pieces of the puzzle fell into place when Ana deciphered a section of her father's journal that seemed to be a personal reflection rather than scientific observation. In it, he spoke of a moral dilemma, a profound awareness of the potential consequences of tampering with such immense power. He hinted at a hidden ethical code embedded within the ancient texts, a safeguard against the misuse of the Sunken City's capabilities. Ana realized that her father's research wasn't just about preventing a catastrophe; it was about safeguarding humanity from its own potential for self-destruction.

The research was a testament to her father's intellectual prowess, his meticulous dedication, his relentless pursuit of knowledge, and his unwavering commitment to the truth, even in the face of overwhelming danger. His life's work wasn't just about deciphering an ancient code; it was about preventing a global catastrophe. It was a legacy she now bore, a responsibility she had to shoulder, regardless of the risks. The future of the world rested on her ability to fully comprehend and apply his findings. The fight was far from over, and the weight of her father's research, a weight both profound and terrifying, would guide her steps every step of the way. The Sunken City awaited, and the world held its breath.

New Allies

The chill Bucharest air bit at Ana's exposed skin as she hurried across the cobblestones, the worn leather of her father's journal clutched tightly in her gloved hand. Gábor's sacrifice echoed in her ears, a constant, painful reminder of the stakes. His cryptic final message, a barely legible scrawl hinting at a hidden network stretching far beyond the confines of the solar temple, fueled her resolve. She couldn't mourn him now; she had a world to save.

Her first stop wasn't a grand institution or a shadowy government agency; it was a small, unassuming bookshop tucked away in a quiet side street. Its owner, Professor Emil Popescu, a renowned expert in Dacian history and a man her father had often consulted, was her first hope for finding allies. The bell above the door jingled as she entered, the scent of aged paper and leather enveloping her. Professor Popescu, a wizened man with kind eyes and a shock of white hair, looked up from behind a towering stack of books. He recognized her instantly.

"Ana," he said, his voice raspy but warm, "I heard... I heard about your father." A shadow passed over his face, a mixture of grief and understanding.

Ana explained her situation, carefully revealing the fragments of her father's research she considered safe to share. She spoke of the Black Sun Codex, the prophecy, the Sentinel, and the impending catastrophe, withholding only the most sensitive details regarding the seismic triggers and their precise locations. Professor Popescu listened intently, his eyes widening with each revelation. When she finished, he leaned back, his gaze thoughtful.

"Your father was a visionary," he said, his voice hushed with awe. "He saw connections that others missed, threads woven through millennia. I knew he was working on something significant, but the scale... it's breathtaking." He paused, stroking his chin. "I may be able to help. I have contacts, resources... people who understand the hidden currents of history."

He spoke of a clandestine network of scholars, historians, and archaeologists, united by their shared passion for unraveling ancient mysteries. They weren't officially affiliated with any institution, operating in the shadows to protect their research from exploitation by those with less benevolent intentions. He called it the "Circle of Hermes," a name that sent a shiver down Ana's spine, connecting it to the ancient Greek god of knowledge, secrets, and alchemy.

He introduced her to two individuals: Dr. Iulia Costin, a specialist in ancient Roman religion and mythology, and Professor Alexandru Bălan, a geophysicist with a keen interest in seismic activity and tectonic plates. Dr. Costin, a sharp-witted woman with an intense gaze, proved invaluable in deciphering the remaining fragments of the Latin prayers from her father's journal. She identified them as invocations to Sol Invictus, but not just any invocations; they were linked to specific rituals, rituals associated with manipulating the earth's energies, a concept that seemed almost fantastical until Professor Bălan weighed in.

Professor Bălan, a man whose enthusiasm for his subject bordered on mania, explained that certain geological formations, particularly those aligned with specific celestial events, could indeed amplify seismic waves. He possessed a detailed map of fault lines throughout the region, pinpointing areas of heightened risk. Combining the information gleaned from her father's notes, Dr. Costin's linguistic analysis, and Professor Bălan's geological expertise, a disturbing picture began to emerge. The "seismic triggers," her father had referred to, weren't merely natural fault lines; they were ancient, man-made structures, strategically placed and engineered to amplify seismic energy, potentially triggering a devastating chain reaction across the globe.

Over the next few days, Ana, Dr. Costin, and Professor Bălan painstakingly pieced together the puzzle. They discovered that the locations mentioned in her father's notes corresponded to several obscure sites throughout the Carpathian Mountains – ancient Dacian temples, Roman military outposts, and even some locations shrouded in local legend. Each site was situated near a major fault line, a fact that chilled Ana to the bone. The

Sentinel, it seemed, were not just guardians of an ancient secret; they were the architects of a global catastrophe.

The Circle of Hermes provided logistical support, funding, and protection, a vital lifeline as they worked against time. Ana learned that the organization had been tracking The Sentinel for decades, quietly gathering information and thwarting their plans. Her father had been their most valuable asset, unbeknownst to her. His death had dealt a heavy blow, but his research was a legacy that would ensure their ultimate victory.

Their investigation led them to the forgotten city of Sarmizegetusa Regia, the ancient capital of Dacia. Amidst the ruins, using ground-penetrating radar and Professor Bălan's expertise, they discovered a vast network of tunnels and chambers, far more extensive than even the most ambitious archaeologists had imagined. Dr. Costin identified markings within the tunnels as a type of Dacian script, far older than any previously discovered. Ana recognized some of the symbols; they were strikingly similar to those etched onto her father's body.

Within the depths of this underground city, they uncovered a breathtaking discovery: a massive stone mechanism, complex and intricate beyond comprehension. It was a type of ancient seismometer, far more advanced than anything known to exist, capable of detecting and amplifying seismic activity across vast distances. The Sentinel, it became clear, planned to use this mechanism to trigger a global earthquake. The "Black Sun" wasn't just a symbol; it was the name given to this devastating machine, its ominous implications echoing in the silent chambers.

The race against time intensified. Ana, using the knowledge gained from her father's research and the expertise of her new allies, deciphered the final parts of the Black Sun Codex. It revealed the mechanism's operational principles and the methods for disabling it. But the Sentinel were close behind, their network vast and their resources seemingly limitless.

They faced countless challenges - treacherous terrain, booby traps, and the ever-present threat of The Sentinel's agents.

But fueled by the memory of Gábor and her father's unwavering commitment to truth, they pressed on, their combined skills forming a formidable alliance against the impending doom. The weight of the world rested on their shoulders, and the fate of humanity hung in the balance. The ancient city held its breath, waiting for the next move, as did the entire world, unaware of the cataclysm brewing beneath their feet. The final confrontation was inevitable, a clash between ancient knowledge and modern technology, between hope and annihilation. The old gods, it seemed, were about to make a return. The fight for the future had truly begun.

Chapter 9

The New Mystery

Following the Clues

The cryptic message Gábor had left, hidden within the seemingly impenetrable layers of the Black Sun Codex, was a puzzle wrapped in an enigma, shrouded in the bittersweet scent of his sacrifice. It wasn't a simple note, a straightforward direction; instead, it was a series of interwoven symbols, a linguistic labyrinth only he and Ana, with their combined knowledge of ancient languages and esoteric symbolism, could hope to unravel. The initial symbols, familiar from the Codex itself, pointed towards a location – a remote village nestled deep within the Carpathian Mountains, a place almost erased from modern maps, known only to a select few. The village, according to Gábor's coded message, was the key, a place where the whispers of a new, equally formidable threat echoed from the shadows.

Ana, still reeling from Gábor's death, found a strange sort of solace in the challenge. Grief threatened to consume her, to drown her in despair, but the urgent need to decipher Gábor's final message, to understand the threat it hinted at, became her anchor. She spent days immersed in the puzzle, pouring over ancient texts, consulting forgotten linguistic dictionaries, and painstakingly comparing Gábor's symbols with those found in Dr. Lupu's research and the Codex itself. The village's name, hidden within a complex cypher, revealed itself slowly, letter by painstaking letter, like a ghost emerging from the mist. It was called Săliștea, a name that resonated with a chilling familiarity, a forgotten echo in the recesses of her own memories.

The journey to Săliștea was fraught with peril. The mountain roads were treacherous, winding through dense forests and past sheer cliffs. Ana, though initially hesitant to venture out alone, understood that Gábor's message was not just a warning; it was a call to action, a baton passed in a relay race against time. She secured the help of an old colleague from her university days, Professor Lucian Ionescu, a specialist in Romanian folklore and mythology. Lucian, initially skeptical, was eventually convinced by the weight of the evidence Ana presented – the fragments of the Codex, the symbols, and the chilling prophecy.

Their journey was not without incident. They were followed – subtly at first, then more overtly – by individuals who moved with the same chilling efficiency as the members of The Sentinel. Ana recognized the same ruthlessness in their movements, the same cold calculation in their eyes. Were these remnants of The Sentinel, a splinter group determined to continue the organization's dark work? Or was this a new threat entirely, equally menacing and far-reaching?

Săliştea, when they finally reached it, was a picture of stark desolation. Nestled in a valley shrouded by imposing peaks, it seemed untouched by time, frozen in a state of forgotten antiquity. The houses, built of dark wood and stone, leaned precariously, their roofs sagging under the weight of years. A thick silence hung in the air, broken only by the distant whisper of wind through the trees. The villagers, wary and reticent, spoke in hushed tones, their eyes darting nervously. Ana and Lucian sensed a palpable fear emanating from them, a fear that transcended the simple apprehension of outsiders.

Ana's investigation began cautiously. She spoke to the elderly villagers, weaving her questions into the fabric of everyday conversation, seeking clues hidden beneath the veneer of their cautious politeness. She learned of local legends, of hidden tunnels and forgotten shrines, of an ancient cult that had once worshipped a "dark star," a celestial body that mirrored the "Black Sun" mentioned in the Codex. The villagers' stories, though veiled in superstition and myth, contained fragments of truth, echoes of a darker reality.

Through a network of clandestine whispers and furtive glances, Ana discovered a hidden cave system beneath Săliştea, a system that had been sealed for centuries. The villagers spoke of it in hushed tones, associating it with the ancient cult and its forbidden practices. The cave, according to local lore, was the final resting place of a powerful artifact, an artifact that might hold the key to understanding the new threat.

Entering the cave with Lucian, they were met by an oppressive darkness and the chilling dampness of centuries-old stone. The air hung heavy with the scent of earth and decay. As they ventured deeper, the claustrophobic tunnels opened into cavernous chambers, the walls adorned with ancient carvings that bore a striking resemblance to the symbols from the Codex. The carvings depicted a complex astronomical chart, hinting at a celestial event, a convergence of stars and planets that resonated with the prophecy Dr. Lupu had deciphered.

In the deepest chamber, they found it – a massive obsidian obelisk, its surface covered in intricate glyphs that pulsed with an eerie inner light. The obelisk was the artifact, a powerful focus of energy, a conduit for a force that seemed both ancient and terrifyingly modern. The glyphs, when examined closely, revealed themselves to be a sophisticated form of coding, a language far older than any known to Ana or Lucian. As they began to decipher the glyphs, a tremor shook the cavern, sending dust and debris raining down from the ceiling. The ground trembled beneath their feet, a silent warning of the power they had awakened.

Suddenly, they were attacked. Emerging from the shadows were figures clad in dark robes, their faces obscured by hooded masks. They were not the same as The Sentinel, though they shared the same chilling ruthlessness and precision. These figures were faster, more agile, their movements imbued with an almost supernatural grace. They were clearly trained, their fighting style incorporating elements both ancient and modern, a deadly blend of martial arts and ruthless efficiency.

Lucian, though a scholar, proved to be a surprisingly resourceful and effective fighter. He used his knowledge of the cave's layout to their advantage, leading the attackers through a maze of tunnels, buying Ana precious time to study the glyphs and decipher their meaning. The fight was brutal, a desperate struggle for survival in the heart of a subterranean labyrinth. But as the fight raged, Ana discovered something terrifying: the attackers were not merely trying to kill them; they were attempting to capture the obelisk, to harness its power.

Their escape was a harrowing flight through the twisting tunnels, a chaotic scramble for freedom in the heart of the mountain. They barely managed to reach the surface, the obsidian obelisk clutched tightly in Ana's hands. As they emerged into the light, they realized the true extent of the danger. The tremor they had felt in the cave was only a prelude to a much larger, far more devastating event. A catastrophic earthquake was looming, and the obelisk was the key to it. Ana understood that the new threat was not merely a group of assassins; it was a force far more ancient and powerful, a force that sought to unleash the earth's fury upon the world. This was only the beginning. The true mystery, the ultimate challenge, lay ahead. And Ana, armed with the obelisk and the chilling knowledge of what it represented, was ready to face it. The weight of the world, literally and figuratively, rested on her shoulders. The fight for humanity's survival was far from over. The shadows were lengthening, and a new dawn of peril was fast approaching.

Unexpected Allies

The village of Săpânța, nestled deep within the Carpathian Mountains, was a relic of a forgotten time. Its weathered wooden houses clung precariously to the slopes, their painted shutters a riot of faded colours against the backdrop of the eternally green hills. The air hummed with a strange, almost palpable energy, a blend of the ancient and the present that prickled Ana's skin. Gábor's cryptic message had led her here, to this seemingly insignificant village, yet the weight of its significance pressed down on her like the looming Carpathian peaks.

Her first unexpected ally emerged in the form of an elderly woman named Mama Elena. Her wrinkled face, etched with the stories of a lifetime spent in the mountains, held a wisdom that transcended the years. She spoke little Romanian, preferring instead a dialect so archaic Ana initially struggled to comprehend. It was a language closer to the ancient Dacian tongue than anything she had encountered in her research – a language Gábor had mentioned in his notes, a language he believed held a key to unlocking the mysteries surrounding the Black Sun Codex. Mama Elena's initial reluctance to speak melted away when Ana presented the obelisk. The sight of the obsidian artifact seemed to awaken something deep within the old woman, an ancient recognition that sparked a flicker of understanding in her eyes.

Through a painstaking process of gestures, fragmented phrases, and the occasional helpful word from a young village boy named Mihai who'd picked up some Romanian from the tourists who rarely ventured this far into the mountains, Ana began to understand. Mama Elena wasn't just a resident of Săpânța; she was the keeper of its secrets, a custodian of a hidden history. The village, she revealed, was more than just a collection of houses; it was built upon the ruins of a much older settlement, a pre-Roman Dacian sanctuary, a place where the earth itself whispered ancient stories. And within those ruins, according to Mama Elena, lay the key to the new mystery, a mystery even more perilous than the one Ana had so recently escaped.

Mihai, a surprisingly astute young boy with an uncanny ability to navigate the labyrinthine pathways hidden beneath the village, became Ana's guide into the subterranean world beneath Săpânța. He spoke of his grandfather's tales, whispers of hidden tunnels, of subterranean chambers echoing with the voices of forgotten gods. He knew the village like the back of his hand, able to identify the subtle shifts in the earth, the subtle tremors that hinted at the hidden passages. He wasn't just a guide; he was a key, a link between Ana and the hidden world beneath the village. His knowledge, passed down through generations, became an invaluable asset in Ana's quest.

Their descent into the darkness was as perilous as any dungeon delve of old. The air was thick with the scent of damp earth and something else, something ancient and unsettling – a faint metallic tang that hinted at the proximity of the old Dacian metalwork. Mihai led them through a network of narrow tunnels, their walls adorned with carvings that echoed the symbols from the Black Sun Codex but with a darker, more sinister twist. The air grew colder, the silence deeper, broken only by the rhythmic drip of water and the echo of their footsteps. As they ventured deeper, the passage widened, revealing a vast subterranean chamber, its ceiling lost in the shadows.

In the center of the chamber stood a massive stone altar, its surface covered in intricate carvings that depicted a scene of cosmic conflict, stars clashing, planets colliding. It was a visual representation of the prophecy, a tangible manifestation of the global seismic network that Gábor had uncovered. But this altar was different; it was not just a warning; it was a control mechanism, a device capable of amplifying the earth's natural energies, a tool capable of triggering earthquakes of unimaginable magnitude. This was the source of the new threat, a power far more ancient and devastating than The Sentinel.

As Ana stood there, contemplating the scale of the danger, a figure emerged from the shadows, silhouetted against the flickering light of their torches. He was a tall, imposing man, his features sharp and his gaze intense. He introduced himself as Professor Lucian Ionescu, a geophysicist who'd been researching the unusual seismic activity in the Carpathian region for years, his work largely ignored and dismissed by the scientific community. He'd tracked the anomalies, sensed the unnatural disturbances, and finally stumbled upon the legends of Săpânța, leading him to the very chamber where Ana now stood.

Professor Ionescu wasn't just a scientist; he was a historian, deeply knowledgeable in the ancient Dacian culture and their understanding of the earth's energies. His expertise complemented Ana's linguistic skills and Mihai's intimate knowledge of the village's hidden passages. He understood the mechanics of the altar, the way it interacted with the earth's tectonic plates, and he possessed the knowledge needed to deactivate it – to prevent the catastrophic awakening that loomed. He had been searching for a way to stop it, but he lacked the key, the ancient knowledge that only the obelisk and the deciphered writings could provide. He was another unexpected ally, a man of science brought together with a linguist and a young village boy by a common enemy – an enemy that transcended human ambition and threatened the very survival of the planet.

Their alliance, however, was fragile. The shadows that had pursued Ana and Gábor still loomed, their presence felt in the chilling silence of the subterranean chamber. They knew that their discovery wouldn't remain secret for long. The Sentinel, or whatever power remained from them, might be defeated, but other players, other forces, were awakening, drawn by the very power they sought to control. Ana now understood that the fight to save the world was not a singular battle but a continuous war against forces ancient and unknown. Their alliance wasn't just about survival; it was about preserving the very fabric of existence.

The collaboration between Ana, Mihai, and Professor Ionescu was a masterclass in interdisciplinary cooperation. Professor Ionescu, with his scientific expertise, explained the intricacies of the altar's mechanism, detailing the specific pressure points and energy conduits that needed to be manipulated. Ana, with her knowledge of the ancient Dacian language and the symbols on the obelisk, deciphered further inscriptions on the altar, revealing instructions for its safe deactivation – a procedure as delicate as brain surgery. Mihai, with his intimate knowledge of the subterranean pathways, ensured their safe navigation, constantly monitoring for any signs of intrusion. He even identified small, concealed passages which turned out to be ventilation shafts that allowed for an efficient supply of fresh air to the chamber, preventing a total oxygen depletion.

Their work was painstaking, requiring meticulous precision and unwavering patience. Each symbol deciphered by Ana was a step closer to understanding the altar's function, each pressure point identified by Professor Ionescu was a step closer to deactivating it safely. Mihai's vigilance kept them ahead of any potential intrusion, providing warnings of approaching danger. They worked for days, fueled by adrenaline and a shared sense of urgency, the looming threat constantly hanging over them. The very air seemed to crackle with tension, a tangible reminder of the immense power they were attempting to control. The ancient stones whispered secrets only they could now comprehend, their combined knowledge revealing a tapestry of human history intertwined with the planet's ancient geological heart.

As they worked, Ana discovered a hidden compartment within the altar, containing a collection of ancient scrolls written in a language older even than Dacian. The scrolls, she realized, were a record of the ancient civilization that had built the altar, a civilization with a profound understanding of the earth's energies, a civilization that had seemingly vanished without a trace. Their knowledge, passed down through the generations in whispered legends and fragmented traditions, was now becoming tangible. The scrolls detailed the altar's creation, its purpose, and the catastrophic consequences of its misuse, providing them with a clearer and much more detailed understanding of the system than they could've possibly imagined.

With the combined efforts of the unlikely trio, the final stage of deactivation was successfully achieved. The earth trembled slightly, as if exhaling a sigh of relief. The immediate danger was averted. But even as they stood, exhausted but triumphant, Ana knew this was not the end. The scrolls spoke of other such altars, scattered across the globe, remnants of a long-lost civilization. The threat was not vanquished, merely contained. The quest to locate and deactivate the other altars was a task that would demand a continued effort. This newfound peace was temporary; the battle for the earth was only beginning, and the world's fate rested on their ability to continue their pursuit, to uncover the secrets of this hidden, ancient, and ever-powerful enemy. The weight of the world, once again, rested on Ana's shoulders, but this time, she was not alone. The seeds of a new alliance, forged in the heart of the Carpathian Mountains, held the promise of a brighter future, a future that depended on the collaboration of knowledge, courage, and an unwavering resolve to safeguard the planet. The journey had only just begun.

Dangerous Encounters

The biting Carpathian wind whipped at Ana's face as she stared at the crumbling stone marker, half-buried in the earth.

Gábor's final message, a barely legible inscription etched onto a shard of obsidian, had led her here – to a forgotten Dacian burial ground, hidden amongst the dense forests surrounding Săpânța. The inscription, a series of runic symbols and a single, chillingly familiar phrase in ancient Latin: "Sol Niger resurget." The Black Sun will rise again. The same phrase etched onto Dr. Lupu's body. The weight of the unsolved mysteries pressed down on her.

The discovery unsettled her. The seemingly dormant threat, contained in the depths of the Carpathian Mountains, had already shown its power. The mere thought of other similar locations, other dormant mechanisms waiting to be triggered, sent shivers down her spine. Gábor's sacrifice had bought them time, a reprieve, but the fight was far from over. His cryptic message suggested that the Black Sun wasn't just a metaphor; it was a network, a complex system of ancient devices designed to unleash some catastrophic event. And the location of these devices was the missing piece of the puzzle.

Days bled into weeks as Ana meticulously documented her findings, poring over ancient Dacian texts and forgotten maps, her small team – a handful of trusted scholars and archaeologists – working tirelessly to unravel the mysteries encoded in the runes and symbols. The burial ground itself was a treasure trove of artifacts, revealing a sophisticated understanding of astronomy and engineering far exceeding anything previously known about the Dacians. Ornate gold torques, intricately carved wooden tablets, and tools of an unknown metal lay scattered among the skeletal remains. Each discovery fueled her determination, yet each also deepened the sense of foreboding.

One particularly frigid evening, while excavating a newly discovered chamber, they unearthed a massive stone disc, covered in intricate carvings. It resembled a celestial map, depicting constellations unknown to modern astronomy, and a series of symbols echoing those found on the obsidian shard. As they carefully cleaned the disc, a hidden mechanism clicked into place. A low hum emanated from within the stone, and a beam of faint, pulsating light projected onto the chamber ceiling, revealing another set of symbols, this time radiating an eerie red glow.

Ana felt a surge of adrenaline. This wasn't just a map; it was a key. A key to unlocking the next location in this global network. The red symbols formed a pattern, a sequence of coordinates, but not in the familiar geographical sense. They seemed to be encoded in a system of celestial alignments, using specific star constellations as reference points. It was a sophisticated method of hiding information, requiring an advanced understanding of both ancient astronomy and advanced cryptography.

The team spent weeks deciphering the celestial coordinates, cross-referencing their findings with ancient astronomical charts and texts. The task was arduous, requiring an intricate understanding of precession, the slow wobble of the Earth's axis, and the changes in the night sky over millennia. The task proved to be frustratingly complex, as some of the constellation references were now obscured by the natural drifting of stars over time. The team painstakingly compared various star maps from various epochs, trying to piece together the movements of stars to determine the precise point of reference. After days of relentless work, exhaustion threatening to overwhelm them, they hit a breakthrough.

The coordinates pointed to a specific location – the ruins of a pre-Columbian city deep within the Amazon rainforest. A place shrouded in legend, a place where the whispers of ancient magic mingled with the relentless humidity of the jungle. The journey there was fraught with peril. Navigating the treacherous terrain was a test of endurance, and the constant threat of unseen dangers – venomous snakes, jaguars, and the ever-present humidity – pushed them to their limits. The dense jungle canopy blotted out the sun, casting the team into an oppressive darkness, a world teeming with unseen creatures and echoing with the haunting sounds of the wild.

Despite the challenges, they pressed on, driven by the weight of their discovery and the knowledge that time was running out. The ancient Amazonian city, half-buried beneath the jungle foliage, was a breathtaking sight – a testament to a forgotten civilization and a chilling reminder of the potential destruction looming. Pyramidal structures, overgrown with vines and trees, stood sentinel, their stones eroded by centuries of rain and decay. They found evidence of an advanced culture, skilled in mathematics, astronomy, and engineering, their artistry expressed in intricate carvings and symbolic representations that hinted at a sophisticated spiritual understanding. This city, Ana realised, was not merely a ruin; it was another piece of the Black Sun's intricate mechanism, and it held the potential for catastrophic consequences if activated.

Their investigation into the city's ruins revealed another chamber, hidden beneath a central plaza. The chamber contained a similar stone disc, but this one emitted a far more powerful hum, its surface pulsing with a red light that seemed to penetrate their very being. The team discovered that the discs didn't simply indicate locations; they were interconnected, part of a global network capable of amplifying seismic activity, using a process they struggled to comprehend. The discs were not just maps; they were amplifiers. Ana felt the weight of history and the potential of destruction.

As they delved deeper into the Amazonian city's mysteries, they encountered unexpected resistance. A shadowy group, resembling the Sentinel, but bearing different insignia and wielding different weaponry, confronted them. These individuals, seemingly guardians of the ancient city, were fiercely protective of their secrets. They were armed not with conventional weapons, but with advanced energy-based devices, and their knowledge of the jungle's hidden paths and dangerous creatures seemed uncanny. A fierce confrontation ensued, testing their skills and determination. The team's expertise in ancient languages and symbology became their greatest weapons, but they were outnumbered and outgunned.

Escaping with their lives, but not without casualties, Ana and her team were forced to flee the Amazonian city, carrying with them the knowledge of yet another critical link in the Black Sun network. The discovery reinforced their belief in the global scope of the ancient conspiracy, and the horrifying potential of the network of powerful devices scattered across the globe. The fight was far from over. The Black Sun was not merely a myth or metaphor, it was a real and imminent threat, a terrifying reality waiting to be unleashed. Ana's quest, far from concluded, was only beginning. The whispers of the ancient past continued, beckoning her forward, into a future that was uncertain, but one that she was determined to shape. The world's fate hung in the balance. And Ana knew, with chilling certainty, that the next encounter would be even more perilous. The shadow of the Black Sun loomed large.

Betrayal

The biting wind seemed to mock Ana's solitude. The Dacian burial ground, shrouded in the perpetual twilight of the Carpathian forest, felt less like a place of rest and more like a tomb waiting to claim another victim. The obsidian shard, cold against her palm, pulsed with a sinister energy, a tangible link to the ancient conspiracy that had claimed Gábor's life. Sol Niger resurget . The Black Sun will rise again. The words echoed in her mind, a chilling refrain.

Days blurred into weeks as Ana immersed herself in Gábor's research notes, a chaotic jumble of sketches, linguistic analyses, and fragmented historical accounts. He had meticulously documented the locations of several other potential seismic triggers, sites that mirrored the Amazonian temple in their intricate design and ancient origins. The network stretched across the globe, a terrifying web woven by hands long turned to dust. The scale of the conspiracy dwarfed even her wildest imaginings. She felt the weight of the world on her shoulders, the fate of billions resting upon her ability to decipher the remaining clues.

Her initial investigation focused on a previously unknown passage in the Vatican Secret Archives, a section sealed off for centuries, its existence only hinted at in Gábor's cryptic annotations. Gaining access proved difficult, but Ana, leveraging her growing reputation as a leading expert in ancient languages, finally secured permission under the guise of a scholarly research project. She spent weeks in the hushed silence of the archive, sifting through dust-covered scrolls and brittle parchments. The air itself seemed thick with the weight of forgotten secrets.

Amongst the dusty tomes, she found a heavily redacted document, its pages stained and fragile. It detailed a clandestine organization, older than any known nation, dedicated to the preservation—or perhaps the activation—of the Black Sun network. The Sentinel, the organization that had hunted her and Gábor relentlessly, was not merely a modern-day cabal; it was a millennia-old shadow organization, its roots buried deep in the prehistory of humanity. The document offered tantalizing glimpses into their methods, their rituals, and their ultimate goal: a global cataclysm that would reshape the world in their image.

A name, recurring throughout the document, sent a chill down Ana's spine: Professor Lucian Ionescu. A respected colleague, a man Ana had considered a friend. He had been assisting her and Gábor in their research, providing access to academic resources and historical data. His knowledge of ancient Dacian culture had been invaluable, his insights sharp and perceptive. But now, staring at the carefully disguised references to Ionescu within the Vatican document, a sickening realization dawned upon her.

He had been feeding them disinformation, subtly guiding their research towards dead ends, deliberately obscuring critical details. His seemingly altruistic assistance was nothing more than a carefully crafted web of deceit. The betrayal cut deep, not just for the intellectual dishonesty, but for the profound breach of trust. Ionescu was not simply a misguided academic; he was a high-ranking member of The Sentinel, a wolf in sheep's clothing. His actions had jeopardized their mission, potentially costing them precious time and lives.

The immediate implications were devastating. Ana's network of contacts, meticulously built over years of research, had been compromised. She needed a new strategy, a way to circumvent Ionescu's influence and expose The Sentinel's plans. But her resources were limited. Gábor's death had left a void, not just in her personal life, but also in her investigative capabilities. She was alone, vulnerable, and hunted by an organization with seemingly limitless resources and a history stretching back to the dawn of civilization.

The weight of her responsibility bore down on her, crushing her spirit. The enormity of the task threatened to overwhelm her. She retreated to her Bucharest apartment, the walls closing in on her as the full weight of her predicament crashed over her. The city, once a vibrant hub of intellectual pursuits and personal connections, now felt like a cage, every shadow a potential threat, every familiar face a potential enemy.

Sleep evaded her. The ghosts of Gábor and Dr. Lupu haunted her dreams, their faces etched with a mixture of fear and determination. The cryptic symbols from Dr. Lupu's body replayed in her mind, a terrifying visual puzzle that she still hadn't completely solved. She knew she had to push forward. The lives of billions rested on her shoulders, and she was not one to surrender easily.

Drawing strength from the memory of Gábor's unwavering dedication, Ana began to systematically rebuild her network, meticulously verifying every source and double-checking every fact. She utilized her extensive linguistic expertise, deciphering cryptic messages hidden in seemingly innocuous historical texts. The ancient languages, once arcane and obscure, now whispered secrets to her, revealing a deeper layer of the conspiracy.

Ana discovered that Ionescu's betrayal was not random. He had been pursuing a specific objective: preventing Ana and Gábor from accessing the final piece of the puzzle, a hidden temple located deep within the Amazon rainforest, a place described only in fragmented legends and obscure maps. It was a place that was supposedly the central hub of the Black Sun network, the origin point of the catastrophic event predicted in the ancient prophecies.

The Vatican documents held a hint about the location of this temple, an almost imperceptible clue hidden within a seemingly unrelated manuscript about early Christian missionaries in the Amazon basin. Ana realized that the missionaries weren't spreading the gospel, but trying to stop the construction of the temple centuries ago. Their attempts had failed.

Fueled by a newfound resolve, Ana devised a plan. She needed to reach the temple before Ionescu and The Sentinel could activate the seismic network. She would have to forge alliances with unlikely partners, navigate treacherous political landscapes, and outwit an enemy whose cunning was legendary. Her journey would take her to the furthest reaches of the globe, across continents and oceans, into the heart of the Amazonian jungle, a place where ancient mysteries intertwined with modern-day dangers.

The fight was far from over. The Black Sun loomed, its shadow stretching across the world. The betrayal, the loss, the burden of responsibility - all coalesced into a fierce determination. She would expose Ionescu, dismantle The Sentinel, and prevent the impending cataclysm. The fate of the world rested upon the shoulders of one woman, armed with knowledge, courage, and the ghost of a promise whispered in the biting Carpathian wind. The whispers of the ancient past continued, beckoning her forward, promising a confrontation that could save or destroy the world. And she would answer their call. She had no choice. The survival of humanity depended on it.

The Stakes

The obsidian shard, still cold against her palm, felt heavier now, burdened with the weight of Gábor's sacrifice and the chilling prophecy he'd helped her decipher. The Carpathian wind, a mournful symphony through the skeletal branches of the ancient trees, seemed to whisper his name, a constant, haunting reminder. Sol Niger resurget . The Black Sun will rise again. But now, the words held a new meaning, a new urgency. It wasn't just about preventing a global catastrophe; it was about honoring Gábor's memory, about fulfilling the promise she'd made to him, a promise whispered amidst the chaos of the collapsing solar temple.

The coded message Gábor had left, hidden within the seemingly innocuous annotations of the Black Sun Codex, was a cryptic puzzle in itself, a trail of bread crumbs leading to another layer of the conspiracy. It referenced his father's research, research Ana had dismissed as eccentric ramblings of an obsessed academic – a research project centered on the enigmatic Dacian King Burebista and a network of underground tunnels rumored to connect various significant Dacian sites across the Carpathians. Gábor had always maintained his father's work was not mere conjecture, but that he'd been close to something truly groundbreaking, something dangerous. Now, Ana understood. Gábor hadn't been talking about ancient treasures or forgotten languages. He was talking about something that could rewrite history, something that could change the very fate of the world.

The weight of responsibility pressed down on her. She had faced down Ionescu and The Sentinel, exposed their machinations, and narrowly escaped with her life. But the victory felt hollow, tainted by the loss of her partner, her friend. The world, she realised, wasn't simply threatened by the seismic triggers; it was threatened by a deeper, more insidious force, a force that had manipulated history for centuries, pulling the strings from the shadows, guiding events toward a predetermined outcome. And Gábor's final message suggested she was only scratching the surface.

Ana's apartment in Bucharest felt strangely empty. Gábor's presence, usually vibrant and chaotic, was absent. The silence was deafening, punctuated only by the rhythmic ticking of the grandfather clock inherited from her grandmother, a relic of a bygone era, somehow reflecting the weight of the centuries-old conspiracy she now found herself battling. The Black Sun Codex lay open on her desk, its ancient script a tangible testament to the vast, dangerous web she was entangled in. The decoded message, transcribed in Gábor's neat handwriting on a loose piece of parchment, was a starting point, nothing more. It detailed a series of coordinates, a pathway winding through the Transylvanian mountains, marked by barely discernible symbols matching those found etched on the body of Dr. Lupu, symbols hinting at a language far older than Latin or even Greek, a language whispered by the wind through ancient stones.

She traced the coordinates on a weathered map of the Carpathian Mountains, her fingertip following the trail Gábor had laid out for her. The route led to several Dacian fortresses, sites already familiar to her from her own research, but these were not the main settlements, the grand cities of Sarmizegetusa Regia and Piatra Craiului. Instead, they were smaller, less explored sites, overlooked by history, yet clearly significant to this new mystery. Each location was connected by a system of subterranean passages and hidden chambers, a network that potentially stretched across the entire region – the network that Gábor's father had dedicated his life to uncovering. And at the center of this network lay the key to understanding the true nature of the Black Sun.

Before embarking on her journey, Ana had to retrace her steps, revisit some of the key information and evidence gathered during her previous investigation. She spent days poring over Dr. Lupu's research notes, searching for any clues, any fragments of information that Gábor might have missed. Lupu's obsessive attention to detail had proven invaluable, but his obsession had also ultimately cost him his life. Ana found several references to Burebista's unconventional methods of governance, his deep understanding of astronomy, and his rumored mastery of what Lupu described as "earth-shaping technologies." These technologies, according to Lupu's notes, weren't just about building structures; they involved harnessing the Earth's energy, manipulating its tectonic plates, controlling the very foundations of the world. A terrifying thought, especially considering the global network of seismic triggers revealed by the Black Sun Codex.

The first location on Gábor's list was a small, almost forgotten Dacian settlement nestled deep within the Apuseni Mountains, a region known for its dense forests and labyrinthine cave systems. It was a remote place, difficult to reach even in the modern era, a place where the past still clung to the present. The settlement, barely visible from the air, was a testament to the advanced engineering skills of the Dacians. The carefully constructed walls and terraces were evidence of a sophisticated civilization, far more advanced than previously thought. This civilization, Ana suspected, possessed a profound understanding of the Earth and its energies, knowledge that could potentially unleash unimaginable power – a power that The Sentinel had obviously discovered and attempted to exploit for their own sinister purposes.

The descent into the cave system beneath the settlement was a perilous undertaking. Armed with only a headlamp, a compass, and a battered copy of Gábor's field notes, Ana navigated the claustrophobic tunnels, her heart pounding in her chest. The air was thick with the smell of damp earth and something else, a metallic tang that sent a shiver down her spine. The ancient passages were surprisingly well-preserved, the walls adorned with intricate carvings that bore a striking resemblance to the symbols on Dr. Lupu's body and the Black Sun Codex. Ana understood now. This wasn't just about decoding a hidden language; it was about deciphering a forgotten technology, a technology that could change the very future of the world.

As she delved deeper into the subterranean labyrinth, Ana discovered hidden chambers, concealed passages, and ancient machinery of unknown purpose. The chambers were filled with elaborate carvings depicting celestial events, astronomical charts, and symbols that seemed to represent a complex system of interconnected energy points. This wasn't just a burial site; it was a functioning control center, a mechanism designed to interact with the Earth itself. The thought was terrifying in its implications. The Sentinel hadn't just stumbled upon a prophecy; they had uncovered a technological marvel capable of causing global devastation. Gábor had been right, and now Ana had to pick up where he left off.

Days turned into weeks as Ana meticulously documented her findings. She mapped the cave system, photographed the carvings, and analyzed the strange metallic residue coating the ancient machinery. The material appeared to be a type of ancient alloy, possessing properties that defied modern scientific understanding. It seemed to resonate with the earth's magnetic field, absorbing and radiating energy in ways that were both astonishing and alarming. Ana realized that Gábor's death had been no accident. He had stumbled upon something crucial, something that had to be prevented from falling into the wrong hands, a secret so powerful that even The Sentinel wasn't the ultimate threat. A much larger, more ancient force was at play.

Her discovery led her to a chilling realization: Burebista hadn't just been a powerful king; he had been a custodian of an ancient technology, a technology capable of both creation and destruction. The prophecy about the Black Sun wasn't just a metaphor; it was a warning, a testament to the devastating power of this forgotten technology, and a challenge to prevent its rediscovery and misuse. The stakes were far higher than she'd ever imagined. The survival of humanity rested not just on her shoulders but on the secrets buried deep within the Earth, secrets that Gábor had given his life to uncover. And now, the torch had been passed to her. The weight of the world, indeed, the weight of centuries, rested upon her shoulders. But unlike Gábor, Ana wouldn't face this challenge alone. His memory, his sacrifice, and his coded message would guide her, fueling her resolve and giving her the strength to face whatever lay ahead. The quest was far from over, but the new mystery, the one Gábor had uncovered, offered a pathway, a chance to not just prevent catastrophe but also unveil the secrets of a forgotten civilization, a civilization whose wisdom might hold the key to a different future – a future she was determined to build.

Chapter 10

A New Beginning

Confrontation

The biting Carpathian wind whipped Ana's hair across her face as she stood on the precipice, the wind a physical manifestation of the turmoil churning within her. Below, nestled in the valley, lay the village of Săliște, a picture of idyllic tranquility that starkly contrasted with the storm raging in her soul. Gábor's death, though expected in the face of the Sentinel's ruthlessness, still clawed at her, a raw, gaping wound. His sacrifice, his final, cryptic message hidden within the Black Sun Codex – it fueled her, propelled her forward, even as it threatened to consume her in grief.

The message, a series of seemingly random symbols interwoven within the already complex script of the Codex, had taken weeks to decipher. It wasn't a simple location, not a straightforward address. Instead, it was a riddle, a complex linguistic puzzle built upon layers of ancient Romanian, Latin, and a cryptic dialect Ana suspected was a precursor to Proto-Indo-European. Gábor, with his deep understanding of ancient languages and his almost preternatural intuition, had undoubtedly known what he was doing. He had left her a trail, a winding path leading to the heart of a mystery far grander than the one they had just narrowly averted.

The riddle spoke of a hidden library, a repository of knowledge dating back to the Dacian civilization, concealed within a seemingly unremarkable cave system in the Apuseni Mountains. The key to its location wasn't geographical, but temporal – a specific astronomical alignment, only occurring once every hundred years, during the winter solstice. The alignment, according to Gábor's coded message, would unlock a mechanism within the cave system, revealing the entrance to the library. It was a breathtaking gamble, a desperate hope hanging on a celestial clockwork.

Ana had spent the intervening weeks preparing. She had sought out allies – not powerful institutions or government agencies, but individuals who operated in the shadows, people with a keen understanding of the clandestine world she now inhabited. Among them was Marius, a former intelligence officer with a network spanning the globe, his skills in surveillance and information gathering invaluable. Then there was Elena, a renowned expert in Dacian history and archaeology, whose knowledge of the region and its hidden history proved crucial. Even Father Lucian, the aged monk from the monastery where Dr. Lupu had met his end, offered his cryptic support, his silence as revealing as any spoken word.

The journey to the Apuseni Mountains was fraught with peril. Marius's network had helped them evade the lingering grasp of the Sentinel – or at least, the remnants of the organization that hadn't been completely decimated in the collapse of the solar temple. The whispers of the Sentinel's survival sent shivers down Ana's spine, fueling her sense of urgency. The stakes were impossibly high; failure meant not only the exposure of the library's secrets but the potential unleashing of something far more sinister.

The cave system itself was a labyrinth of echoing chambers and narrow passages. Elena, navigating with the confidence born from years of exploration, led the way, her headlamp cutting through the oppressive darkness. The air hung heavy with the scent of damp earth and something else, something ancient, something primal. Ana could feel the weight of history pressing down on her, the echoes of centuries whispering in the cavernous silence.

As they delved deeper, the air grew colder, the silence more profound. The only sounds were the rhythmic drip of water and the occasional scraping of their boots on the rough stone floor. Finally, they reached the chamber described in Gábor's message – a vast cavern dominated by a colossal stone monolith carved with intricate symbols, a mirror image of those on the Black Sun Codex.

The monolith, it turned out, wasn't just a decoration; it was a complex astronomical clock. The celestial alignment Gábor had foreseen was taking place, the positions of the stars and planets aligning perfectly with the carvings on the stone. As the alignment completed, a low hum resonated through the cavern, and a section of the wall, seemingly solid stone, began to shift. A hidden doorway, perfectly concealed within the rock face, slowly slid open, revealing a passage leading into the darkness beyond.

The hidden library was beyond anything Ana could have imagined. Rows upon rows of ancient scrolls and tablets lined the walls, illuminated by strategically placed sconces casting a soft glow upon the priceless collection. The air was dry, the scent of aged parchment filling the space. The sheer volume of knowledge contained within this hidden repository was staggering, spanning millennia and encompassing a vast array of subjects, from ancient astronomy and linguistics to lost technologies and forgotten religions.

But the library wasn't just a collection of historical documents; it was a living archive, a repository of secrets that had been carefully guarded for centuries. As Ana and her team began to explore the collection, they discovered evidence of a far more extensive network than they had ever suspected, a conspiracy stretching back to the dawn of civilization, a hidden war between those who sought to control humanity's destiny and those who strived to protect its freedom.

Within the library, nestled amongst the ancient scrolls, Ana found a hidden compartment containing a final message from Gábor. This message, even more cryptic than the first, hinted at a larger conspiracy, one involving a global network of hidden societies and a struggle for control of an artifact even more powerful than the Black Sun Codex – a relic known only as the 'Serpent's Eye'. The final line of Gábor's message was simple yet chilling: "The awakening is not over. It has only just begun."

The confrontation wasn't a dramatic showdown with a shadowy organization. It was a silent battle against time, a race against the unraveling of ancient secrets, a struggle to understand the true nature of the threat and how to confront it. Ana knew the fight was far from over; this was a new beginning, a terrifying and exhilarating step into a world far more intricate and dangerous than she could have ever predicted. The weight of history, the burden of these ancient secrets, now rested squarely on her shoulders, a daunting legacy she embraced, spurred onward by Gábor's sacrifice and the knowledge that the fight for humanity's future had only just begun. The Serpent's Eye awaited, and with it, a new chapter in the ongoing saga of the Black Sun. The world held its breath, unaware of the storm brewing in the quiet corners of history, a storm Ana was now uniquely positioned to face. The darkness was deep, but Ana, armed with knowledge, courage, and the memory of her fallen comrade, stepped confidently into the unknown, ready to unveil the truth, no matter the cost.

Resolution

The adrenaline that had propelled her through the harrowing events of the past few days began to ebb, leaving a chilling emptiness in its wake. The solar temple, a silent testament to a forgotten civilization, stood behind her, a mausoleum to Gábor's sacrifice. The mechanisms, deactivated thanks to her understanding of the Codex and a frantic, desperate improvisation, lay still. The immediate danger, the impending seismic catastrophe, was averted, at least for now. But the sense of accomplishment was overshadowed by a profound loneliness, a vast, echoing silence that filled the void left by Gábor.

She clutched the Black Sun Codex to her chest, its leather cover worn and cracked, a tangible link to the man who had given his life to protect it. The cryptic symbols, once a source of terror and confusion, now held a different significance – a map, not just to the past, but to the future. Gábor's final message, a barely visible inscription hidden beneath a layer of aged parchment, shimmered in her mind. It wasn't a simple clue; it was an invitation, a challenge, a continuation of the story they had only just begun to unravel. It spoke of the Serpent's Eye, a term she hadn't encountered before in his research, but a phrase that resonated with a chilling familiarity, evoking images of hidden knowledge and obscured truths.

The escape from the temple had been a desperate scramble, a blur of shadows and near misses. The Sentinel, though momentarily stunned by the sudden cessation of the ritual, would undoubtedly be pursuing her relentlessly. The feeling of being hunted, a constant companion since Dr. Lupu's death, was amplified tenfold. She knew she couldn't stay in Romania, not anymore. The network of informants that Gábor had cultivated – a clandestine brotherhood of scholars and archaeologists dedicated to protecting these ancient secrets – would be her only hope. One name immediately surfaced in her thoughts: Professor Emilia Popescu, an esteemed historian at the University of Bucharest, whom Gábor had mentioned as a potential ally. Emilia was known for her independent research, her unwavering dedication to uncovering the truth, even when facing opposition from powerful, and potentially dangerous, factions.

Her journey began under the cover of darkness, a harrowing trek across the treacherous Carpathian Mountains, the wind howling like a banshee, mirroring the turmoil in her soul. She carried with her not only the Codex, but also a heavy burden of grief and responsibility. The weight of the world, it seemed, rested on her slender shoulders. She moved with a newfound stealth and determination, her mind racing, strategizing, planning her next move. Every rustle of leaves, every snap of a twig, sent a jolt of adrenaline through her, reminding her of the ever-present danger.

Reaching Bucharest was a triumph in itself. The city, usually bustling with life, felt desolate and menacing, the shadows stretching long and ominous, reflecting the hidden dangers lurking within. She sought refuge in the quiet anonymity of a small, almost forgotten pension, its walls whispering stories of a bygone era. Days bled into nights as she painstakingly deciphered Gábor's final message, poring over historical texts, researching ancient languages, and piecing together the fragments of information he had left behind. The Serpent's Eye, she discovered, wasn't merely a location; it was a metaphor, a symbol pointing towards a network of hidden knowledge, a secret society dedicated to preserving – and perhaps manipulating –

ancient prophecies.

Professor Popescu, initially hesitant, eventually agreed to meet. The meeting took place in a secluded room within the National Library of Romania, bathed in the soft glow of ancient manuscripts and forgotten texts. Emilia, a woman of sharp intellect and unwavering resolve, listened intently as Ana recounted her experiences, the perilous journey, Gábor's sacrifice, and the lingering threat of the Sentinel. Emilia didn't express surprise; instead, she nodded grimly, her eyes revealing a depth of knowledge that suggested she had been aware of the Black Sun Codex and its implications for a much longer time.

"The Sentinel," Emilia said, her voice a low murmur, "they are older than any nation, more powerful than any government. They operate in the shadows, manipulating events, controlling history. They are the guardians of the old ways, and they will stop at nothing to protect their secrets."

Emilia's knowledge extended beyond Ana's current understanding of the Black Sun prophecy. She revealed the existence of other similar prophecies, hidden within ancient texts scattered across the globe, prophecies detailing a chain of events leading to the awakening of something far more sinister than just seismic triggers. It was a larger conspiracy, a plot spanning millennia, a clandestine struggle between those who sought to control the world's fate and those who dared to challenge their dominion. The Serpent's Eye, Emilia explained, wasn't a physical location but a metaphorical one – a hidden network of influence, a clandestine society that stretched from the Vatican archives to the forgotten temples of the Andes, a hidden order that controlled information, power, and the very narrative of history.

Ana, armed with this newfound knowledge, felt a surge of determination. The fight wasn't over; it had only just begun. Gábor's sacrifice wasn't in vain; it had illuminated a path towards a larger, more complex mystery. The Codex, she now realised, was not just a key to preventing a global catastrophe; it was a roadmap to a hidden world, a world where the lines between history, mythology, and reality blurred into a terrifyingly intricate tapestry. She had a new mission, a new purpose. She would follow Gábor's trail, unraveling the secrets of the Serpent's Eye, exposing the Sentinel, and safeguarding humanity from a threat that dwarfed the immediate danger they had narrowly avoided.

The journey ahead was perilous and uncertain. The Sentinel would undoubtedly be hunting her, their resources far greater than hers. Yet, Ana, strengthened by Gábor's memory and fueled by the weight of responsibility, felt a growing confidence. She was no longer merely a linguist; she was a guardian, a protector, a warrior in a silent war that spanned centuries. She was armed with knowledge, with courage, and with the unwavering determination to honor Gábor's sacrifice and expose the truth, no matter the cost.

The information from Emilia led Ana to a series of obscure archives, tucked away in libraries and forgotten monasteries across Europe. She discovered that the Serpent's Eye wasn't a singular entity, but a network of individuals, scholars, and historians who had, for centuries, protected and misinterpreted the ancient prophecies, twisting them to serve their own agenda. Some were noble, others were corrupt, some were unaware of the full implications of their actions. She found evidence of forged documents, altered translations, and deliberate misinterpretations of ancient texts, all designed to obscure the true nature of the threat and maintain the Sentinel's control.

Her investigation took her to the Vatican Secret Archives, where she faced resistance at every turn. Yet, through meticulous research and her exceptional linguistic skills, she managed to uncover fragments of information corroborating Emilia's revelations, piecing together a timeline of events spanning millennia, a history of manipulation and deceit, a clandestine war fought in the shadows of power. She found references to the Serpent's Eye in ancient Sumerian tablets, Egyptian hieroglyphs, and even in the cryptic writings of the Knights Templar, confirming the existence of a long-standing, intricate conspiracy.

Ana understood now. The Sentinel wasn't merely a shadowy organization; it was a global network, a hidden order that controlled the flow of information, manipulated historical narratives, and shaped the destiny of nations. The seismic triggers were merely one part of a larger plan, a method of exerting control and ensuring the continuation of their power. The true nature of the threat was far more insidious – the manipulation of history itself.

With each piece of the puzzle that fell into place, the weight of the responsibility pressed down on her. But the grief that had threatened to consume her began to transform into a fierce determination. Gábor's sacrifice was not a tragic end, but a necessary beginning. She would carry his legacy forward, continuing his work, unraveling the mystery of the Serpent's Eye, and exposing the insidious network that had held humanity captive for centuries.

Her final confrontation with the Sentinel wouldn't be a physical one, but an intellectual battle, a struggle to control the narrative, to expose their lies and reveal the truth to the world. It would be a fight waged in the corridors of power, in the halls of academia, and in the silent archives where history itself was rewritten. The world, unaware of the impending danger, was poised on the precipice of an era defined by the manipulation of truth. Ana, however, was ready. She carried the weight of history, the burden of ancient secrets, and the burning memory of Gábor's sacrifice. The fight for the future had just begun. And she would not rest until the truth was revealed.

The Remaining Mystery

The chill mountain air bit at Ana's exposed skin, a stark contrast to the stifling heat she had endured within the hidden solar temple. The escape had been a blur of adrenaline and desperate action, a chaotic ballet of shadows and near-misses. She still felt the phantom weight of Gábor's hand in hers, the silent strength he had conveyed even in death. His sacrifice, the ultimate act of selflessness, resonated within her, a constant, throbbing ache that overshadowed even the relief of survival.

The Codex, clutched tightly to her chest, felt heavier now, imbued with a new significance. It was more than just a collection of ancient symbols; it was a testament to Gábor's life, his unwavering dedication to uncovering the truth, a legacy she vowed to uphold. The cryptic symbols, once a daunting enigma, now felt like a roadmap, a pathway leading to a future she couldn't yet fully comprehend. Each glyph whispered of a hidden narrative, a story waiting to be told. She glanced at the worn leather cover, its surface scarred by time and the harsh conditions of its hidden location. She traced a finger over the intricate carvings, a silent prayer for her fallen companion.

The journey back to Bucharest was a silent one, the car a metal cocoon shielding her from the harsh realities of the world outside. The memory of the temple, its intricate mechanisms and the chilling prophecy it held, haunted her every waking moment. Sleep offered no solace, only fragmented visions of collapsing structures and the echoing laughter of the Sentinel. She replayed the final moments with Gábor, his selfless act a beacon of courage amidst the darkness. His last words, barely audible above the grinding of gears within the temple, still resonated. "The Black Sun... it's not what you think... look deeper..."

Back in her Bucharest apartment, the silence was almost deafening. The familiar surroundings offered little comfort. The apartment, once a haven, now felt like a mausoleum, each object a painful reminder of her loss. Yet, amidst the grief, a steely resolve began to harden within her. Gábor's words echoed in her mind: "look deeper". He had hinted at a larger mystery, a secret buried beneath the layers of the already-uncovered truth.

The Codex, laid out on her worktable, beckoned her. Its pages, filled with arcane symbols and cryptic drawings, seemed to throb with untold stories. She spent days immersed in its labyrinthine complexities, meticulously deciphering its intricate code. She employed her linguistic expertise, drawing parallels between the ancient symbols and various extinct languages, from Getic to Proto-Indo-European. Each clue unearthed, each deciphered sentence, only deepened the mystery.

The Codex spoke not only of the seismic triggers but of a deeper, more insidious threat – a network of ancient organizations, linked by bloodlines and shared secrets, spanning millennia. The Sentinel, she realised, was only one branch of this far-reaching conspiracy. Its origins predated even the Roman Empire, weaving its way through history, manipulating events from the shadows. The "Black Sun" was not merely a metaphor; it was a symbol of this hidden network, a symbol of power, control, and manipulation.

The more she learned, the more she understood the profound implications of Gábor's sacrifice. He hadn't just stopped a seismic catastrophe; he had bought her time, giving her the opportunity to unravel the vast conspiracy that had haunted her father's research for so long. His death wasn't the end; it was the beginning of a new, more perilous phase in her quest for the truth. He had left her a legacy – not just the Codex, but a responsibility.

One particular section of the Codex caught her attention, a series of seemingly disconnected passages written in a dialect she initially failed to recognize. It was only after painstaking research, comparing it to fragmented texts from the Vatican archives and obscure scholarly articles her father had collected that the truth dawned upon her. It was a dialect spoken by a small, isolated community in the remote regions of the Carpathian Mountains – a community known for its ancient traditions and esoteric knowledge.

The passages alluded to a forgotten ritual, a ceremony meant to appease the "Black Sun", a ceremony that held the key to unlocking the network's ultimate goal – a ritual that seemed to be inextricably linked to a specific location hidden somewhere amidst the sprawling wilderness of the Carpathians. She realised with a growing sense of dread that the conspiracy reached beyond the seismic triggers. It involved a much grander, more terrifying plan.

A chilling realization settled upon her. The Sentinel had only been a piece of the puzzle. The actual threat was far greater, far more insidious, than she could ever have imagined. The prophecy, she had initially believed to be about a seismic catastrophe, spoke of a spiritual awakening, a summoning of some ancient, malevolent entity. The Codex was not just a warning; it was a manual – an instruction book for unleashing a catastrophic event that dwarfed any natural disaster.

The weight of this discovery pressed upon her, a crushing burden of responsibility. She was no longer just a linguist, deciphering ancient texts. She was a warrior, armed with knowledge and courage, fighting against an enemy that was both ancient and impossibly powerful. The journey wouldn't be easy, but Gábor's sacrifice had fuelled a fire within her, a burning resolve that would not be extinguished.

Days turned into weeks, and weeks into months. Ana's investigation took her to remote villages nestled deep in the Carpathian Mountains, her only companions the whispering pines and the haunting calls of the night birds. She interviewed elders who spoke of ancient legends and whispered tales, their knowledge gleaned from generations past, hinting at a forgotten power, a hidden truth, lying dormant within the earth.

She discovered a hidden monastery tucked away in a secluded valley, a sanctuary of weathered stone and hushed secrets. This monastery, she learned, was the heart of the community she had discovered within the Codex, the keepers of the ritual and the final piece of the puzzle. The monks, initially resistant to outsiders, reluctantly revealed fragmented pieces of the ritual, guarded with religious zeal, their words imbued with both fear and fascination.

They spoke of a powerful entity trapped within the earth, an ancient being of immense power, waiting to be unleashed. The ritual, they explained, was a method of containing this entity, a delicate balancing act that had been maintained for centuries. However, The Sentinel's actions had disrupted the balance, causing a crack in their protective barriers. Now, the entity was stirring, awakening from its ancient slumber. And only Ana, armed with the knowledge gleaned from the Codex and the secrets whispered by the monks, could prevent its release.

The final pieces of the puzzle started to fit together. The seismic triggers were not intended to destroy the world as she had initially thought; they were a preparatory ritual, designed to weaken the barriers, to prepare the way for the awakening. This was a war waged on a spiritual plane, a struggle against forces beyond human comprehension. The fight had just begun, and this time, Ana would be facing an enemy that was far more terrifying than any human organization.

Hidden within a secret chamber beneath the monastery, Ana discovered a final cryptic message from Gábor, tucked away within a hollowed-out section of a centuries-old wooden box. It was a simple sketch, a map, pointing towards a location far removed from the monastery, a place unknown, a place seemingly devoid of any historical significance. But in Gábor's final message, there was a hint of excitement, of a new challenge, a new mystery waiting to be unearthed. He had left her a final task, a final testament to their partnership, a promise of a future investigation that would unravel even greater secrets. The fight for the future continued, and Ana, armed with the Codex, the memories of Gábor, and a renewed sense of purpose, knew that she would face the coming darkness head-on. The Black Sun had yet to fully reveal its secrets.

Anas New Journey

The crumpled map, a faded sketch on worn parchment, felt strangely warm in Ana's hands. Gábor's final gift. It depicted a seemingly unremarkable stretch of coastline, a sliver of land nestled between the unforgiving cliffs and the restless Adriatic Sea. There were no prominent landmarks, no easily identifiable features, just a series of subtle curves and indentations that hinted at a hidden cove, a secret place known only to a select few – or perhaps, only to Gábor. The accompanying note, penned in his hurried, almost frantic scrawl, simply read: "The Sun's Shadow hides its truth. Find the echo."

Ana traced the lines of the map, her fingertip lingering on

a small, almost imperceptible symbol etched near the supposed cove. It wasn't a symbol she recognized from the Black Sun Codex or any of Dr. Lupu's research. It was different, more primal, yet strangely familiar, resonating with a forgotten part of her own ancestral memory. It evoked images of sun-drenched shores and weathered stones, of ancient rituals and whispered prophecies. The symbol itself was a spiral, a vortex swirling inwards towards a central point, a miniature representation of a galaxy, or perhaps something far older, far more profound.

Days bled into weeks. Ana, still reeling from the loss of Gábor, found herself driven by a relentless need to understand, to decipher, to continue the fight that had cost her friend his life. She immersed herself in research, poring over forgotten texts, obscure historical maps, and antiquated nautical charts, hoping to find a clue, a reference, anything that might pinpoint the location on Gábor's cryptic map. The Vatican archives, once a haven of discovery, now felt like a mausoleum, a testament to the secrets the Church had carefully guarded for centuries. She knew, however, that the answers lay elsewhere, buried beneath layers of time and deception.

Her initial searches led her to the dusty corners of the Croatian National Archives in Dubrovnik. She spent weeks sifting through faded documents, brittle manuscripts, and centuries-old sea logs, hoping to find a mention of the coastline depicted on Gábor's map. The Archivist, a kindly old woman with a sharp mind and an even sharper wit, was initially skeptical, but Ana's persistence, combined with the tantalizing fragment of the symbol, gradually chipped away at her reserve. The Archivist, whose family had been keepers of historical records for generations, recognized a glimmer of familiarity in the spiral symbol. She revealed that it was a variant of a symbol found on ancient Illyrian artifacts, a pre-Roman civilization that had once thrived along the Adriatic coast.

"The Illyrians," the Archivist whispered, her voice raspy with age, "they were masters of secrets. They believed in the power of the sun, the moon, and the stars. They built their cities along the coast, harnessing the power of the sea, but also hiding their most precious secrets within the very earth itself."

The Archivist's words sparked a new line of inquiry. Ana shifted her focus to Illyrian history, their mythology, their beliefs. She learned of their intricate network of coastal caves and hidden tunnels, their sophisticated knowledge of astronomy and navigation. She discovered stories of legendary underwater cities, of lost temples dedicated to forgotten deities, and of a prophecy that spoke of a time when the "sun's shadow" would reveal a truth hidden for millennia.

Ana's journey took her to the coastal towns of Split and Zadar, where she meticulously examined ancient ruins, crumbling fortresses, and forgotten cemeteries. She scoured local museums, poring over weathered artifacts and fragmented pottery, searching for any trace of the spiral symbol. Each find, however small, fueled her determination, leading her closer to the truth Gábor had hinted at. She began to suspect that the "Sun's Shadow" was not a literal celestial event, but rather a metaphor – a reference to a specific geographical location, possibly a place where the sun's rays cast a unique shadow at a certain time of year, revealing a hidden entrance, a secret passage, or a previously undiscovered structure.

The local fishermen, weathered men with sun-kissed skin and eyes that mirrored the deep blue of the Adriatic, proved to be a surprising source of information. They spoke of legends, of stories passed down through generations, of a hidden cove known as "Uvala Tajna" – the Secret Cove. It was said to be a place where the ancient Illyrians had performed their most sacred rituals, a place where the veil between worlds was thin. The fishermen claimed the cove was inaccessible, guarded by treacherous currents and unpredictable weather, but Ana suspected there was more to it than mere folklore.

Using a combination of the map, the fishermen's accounts, and the detailed coastal surveys she had meticulously examined, Ana finally pinpointed the location of the Secret Cove. It was tucked away in a remote stretch of coastline, hidden behind a towering cliff face, its entrance obscured by dense vegetation.

Reaching it required a perilous journey by sea, navigating treacherous rocks and hidden currents. She chartered a small fishing boat, hiring a seasoned captain who had navigated these waters for decades. The captain, initially reluctant, became intrigued by Ana's determination and the cryptic details of her quest.

The journey to the Secret Cove was fraught with danger. The sea churned and roared, waves crashing against the boat, threatening to capsize them at any moment. The cliff face loomed before them, a forbidding wall of stone, seemingly impenetrable. Yet, as they approached the spot indicated on the map, a narrow opening appeared, a small fissure in the cliff face, barely visible amidst the swirling waves.

Ana, with the help of the captain, managed to navigate their way through the narrow passage, entering a hidden cove shielded from the fury of the sea. The cove was surprisingly sheltered, a small, secluded bay with crystal-clear water. As the sun began to set, casting long shadows across the water, Ana noticed something peculiar. The sun's rays, at this specific angle and time, fell upon a particular rock formation, creating a shadow that mirrored the spiral symbol from Gábor's map. This was the echo – the revealment of the sun's shadow.

Upon closer inspection of the rock formation, Ana discovered a hidden mechanism, a series of intricately carved grooves and levers. With careful manipulation, she managed to activate the mechanism, revealing a concealed entrance, a doorway leading into the darkness beyond. She knew, with a mixture of fear and excitement, that she was on the verge of uncovering another profound ancient mystery. Gábor's legacy continued. The Black Sun's secrets were far from exhausted. The journey was far from over. Her next journey – the exploration of the hidden chamber behind the newly opened entrance – promised to reveal even more profound and potentially dangerous secrets. The true meaning of "the Sun's Shadow" was waiting to be discovered, hidden behind the entrance and waiting for her courageous exploration.

Looking Ahead

The air hung heavy with the scent of brine and seaweed as Ana descended into the hidden chamber. The entrance, a narrow fissure barely wide enough for a single person, led down a steep, uneven slope. Her headlamp cut a wavering swathe through the oppressive darkness, revealing damp, moss-covered walls that seemed to breathe with the rhythmic pulse of the sea. The air grew colder the deeper she went, a chill that settled deep in her bones, distinct from the dampness of the coastal cave. The passage twisted and turned, a labyrinthine path that tested her resolve and agility at every turn. Each echoing footstep amplified her solitude, the silence broken only by the occasional drip of water from the unseen heights above.

After what felt like an eternity, the passage opened into a larger cavern. The contrast was stark; the claustrophobia of the narrow tunnel replaced by an expansive, cathedral-like space. Her headlamp beam swept across the vast chamber, revealing a breathtaking sight. Before her stood a circular structure, a monolithic construction of dark, polished stone that seemed to absorb the light, leaving it cloaked in an almost unnatural shadow. Intricate carvings, weathered but still remarkably preserved, adorned its surface, depicting swirling patterns and enigmatic symbols that resonated strangely with the markings she had seen etched onto Dr. Lupu's body.

These were not the crude, hastily-applied symbols of a desperate ritual; these were meticulously crafted, their precision hinting at a mastery lost to time. Ana recognized some of the glyphs – variations on the Black Sun motif, but far more complex, hinting at a deeper, more nuanced understanding of the ancient cosmology that Gábor had only begun to unravel. The stone itself seemed to pulse faintly with a low, almost imperceptible hum, a vibration that resonated not just in her ears, but deep within her chest, a subtle tremor against her ribs.

As she cautiously approached the structure, she noticed a series of depressions circling its base, perfectly formed receptacles that seemed to await something. One of them contained a small, intricately carved wooden box, its surface worn smooth with age, yet somehow strangely intact. Inside, nestled on a bed of faded velvet, lay a single, obsidian black stone, perfectly spherical and impossibly smooth, radiating a subtle warmth that seemed to contradict the damp chill of the cavern. It pulsed with the same faint hum she had felt in the structure, a rhythmic heartbeat that mirrored the ocean's ebb and flow.

Ana carefully picked up the stone, its weight surprisingly substantial for its size. It felt strangely alive in her hand, a conduit of energy that thrummed with barely contained power. As she held it, the carvings on the central structure seemed to shift and rearrange before her eyes, the patterns subtly altering, revealing new sequences and combinations of symbols. It was as if the stone itself was unlocking the secrets of the chamber, revealing its hidden layers of meaning.

The glyphs spoke of a forgotten civilization, a technologically advanced people who possessed a profound understanding of the earth's energy systems, its geological fault lines and tectonic plates. They had harnessed these forces, channeling them for their own purposes, creating a network of subterranean conduits and mechanisms capable of triggering seismic events on a global scale – a network hinted at in the Black Sun Codex but only partially understood. This was not merely a prophecy of destruction; it was a blueprint, a plan meticulously laid out in stone and symbol.

The stone in her hand was a key, a control mechanism, capable of activating or deactivating this global network. The carvings revealed a series of pressure points and control mechanisms, an intricate system of levers and valves that could unleash unimaginable devastation, or, perhaps, just as easily, be used to prevent it. The 'Sun's Shadow' was not a place, but a metaphor – the shadow cast by the sun's energy, the latent power hidden beneath the surface of the earth, a power that could be harnessed or unleashed.

The discovery weighed heavily upon Ana. She understood now the true nature of Gábor's final message. The "Sun's

Shadow" was not merely a geographical location, but a cryptic allusion to the concealed energy network, a hidden force that could reshape the world. He had entrusted her with the knowledge, a perilous burden that demanded unwavering courage, meticulous precision and a deep understanding of history, linguistics, and the Earth's hidden mechanisms.

The research he left behind was not merely a collection of scholarly texts and archaeological findings; it was a testament to a lifetime dedicated to unraveling the truth, to warning the world of impending doom, a warning that now fell upon her shoulders. She was no longer just a linguist, deciphering ancient texts; she was the guardian of a dangerous secret, a key to a power that could reshape the fate of humanity.

Days blurred into weeks as Ana immersed herself in Gábor's notes, cross-referencing his findings with the information gleaned from the chamber. She had translated the majority of the glyphs, piecing together a fragmented narrative of a civilization capable of manipulating the very fabric of the planet, a people who had used their power for both creation and destruction, leaving behind a network of dormant mechanisms that still held the potential for both.

Among Gábor's belongings, she discovered a series of meticulously drawn diagrams, sketches of intricate mechanical devices, blueprints of a hidden technology that defied modern understanding. He had delved far beyond the scope of the Black Sun Codex, uncovering a civilization that stretched back far beyond recorded history, a civilization whose technology mirrored the very processes of the earth itself.

This understanding of geophysics was beyond Ana's initial comprehension. She sought out the help of several leading geophysicists, specialists in seismic activity and plate tectonics. The diagrams, once incomprehensible, began to take on a new level of significance under their informed scrutiny. They confirmed Gábor's suspicions; the ancient civilization had not only understood the Earth's power, but had built systems to interact with it, to manipulate it to an astounding degree.

The network was dormant, but it could be activated. And the method of activation was chillingly simple, relying on a combination of precise geographical locations and the precise manipulation of the obsidian stone she had discovered in the hidden chamber. It was a terrifying realization: a single person, wielding the right knowledge, could trigger a catastrophic chain reaction, causing widespread devastation.

Ana knew she had to find a way to neutralize the network, to disarm this ancient technology before it fell into the wrong hands. She couldn't trust anyone completely, even her colleagues, especially given The Sentinel's continued, shadowy presence. Their pursuit had intensified after Gábor's death, their methods becoming more aggressive. She knew they were still searching for the Codex, but now their focus had expanded, their efforts shifting towards the acquisition of the obsidian stone and the knowledge it unlocked. The race against time was on, a deadly game of cat and mouse where the stakes were global devastation.

Ana knew that she couldn't face this alone. The scope of the threat demanded a coordinated effort, a collaboration between historians, archaeologists, geophysicists, and intelligence agencies. The weight of the world rested on her shoulders, a heavy burden that came with the knowledge that a civilization's long-hidden secrets were now hers to protect or, ultimately, to destroy. The next chapter in her life was now not just a continuation of Gábor's research, it was a fight for the survival of humanity. The echo of the Sun's Shadow reverberated in her heart, a constant reminder of the immense responsibility that lay before her. The fight had begun. The world's fate hung precariously in the balance.

Acknowledgments

My deepest gratitude goes to my research assistants, Ioana Popescu and Mihai Constantinescu, whose tireless efforts in navigating the archives of Bucharest and the Vatican, and deciphering obscure Romanian and Latin texts, were invaluable. Their expertise in historical linguistics and archaeology proved indispensable to the accuracy and depth of this novel. I am also indebted to Professor Alexandru Ionescu of the University of Bucharest, whose insightful comments on early drafts significantly enhanced the historical authenticity of the narrative. Finally, a heartfelt thank you to my family and friends for their unwavering support and patience throughout the writing process. Their belief in this project kept me going during the long nights spent in pursuit of the perfect sentence.

Glossary

Black Sun Codex: An ancient manuscript containing a prophecy and cryptic symbols relating to a network of seismic triggers.

The Sentinel: A shadowy organization dedicated to controlling the power described in the Black Sun Codex.

Carpathian Mountains: A mountain range in Central and Eastern Europe, forming a significant part of the novel's setting.

Dr. Petru Lupu: A renowned historian whose murder initiates the novel's plot.

Ana Dragan: A linguist who plays a central role in deciphering the Black Sun Codex.

Gábor Varga: A disgraced archaeologist who partners with Ana in the investigation.

Made in the USA
Las Vegas, NV
10 February 2025

17833152R00114